The Lady and the Lord

PAUL BREER

Table of Contents

Chapter 1

A Silver Necklace

The television is on as Jessica moves about the kitchen preparing lunch in her El Paso home. It is the first day of spring and the unseasonably hot weather calls for a salad. Once she's assembled all the ingredients on the counter, she launches a familiar sequence of steps. First comes the chicken, then the mayonnaise, some chopped scallions and yellow peppers, a few grapes, and finally a bed of red leaf lettuce. While she works, she sings to herself, oblivious to the drama unfolding on the TV screen just a few feet away in the living room.

It is the sound that alerts her. At first barely audible, it suddenly explodes as teachers and students shriek in horror. She immediately drops her knife and goes to look. According to the announcer, the scene was shot earlier by a man who was making a video of his daughter on her 10th birthday. Displayed in the footage are the headless bodies of three policemen dumped onto the schoolyard playground by a group of masked men.

Jessica covers her eyes. Unable to watch anymore, she turns off the TV and slumps into a chair. The scene is frightening enough in its own right, but knowing that it happened across the border in Juárez, Mexico makes it more terrifying. She even knows the school where it took place, having visited there once as part of an inter-city education project. She shakes her head violently in an attempt to wipe the image from her mind. It doesn't work; the scene lingers, amplified now by thoughts of the policemen's wives and what they must have felt if they were watching the program. Even if they weren't, they will soon be notified and asked to come to the morgue to identify their husbands. In her imagination sees a woman trying to identify her mate as she looks down at his headless body. Unable to process the image, she suddenly rises and heads to the bathroom, clutching her stomach.

Jessica Branson is a tall, blonde, statuesque beauty who just turned 37 but is typically thought to be at least five years younger. When she was in her 20's, she briefly considered a career in social work, but got married instead. Her husband, Lloyd, is slightly older, tall and lean with receding hair and a thin mustache. Like many of his colleagues at the University of Texas at El Paso (UTEP) where he teaches, he wears steel rimmed glasses. His department, philosophy, is generally thought to house the brightest people on campus…and Lloyd is considered to be the brightest of the bright. Over the years, few people have been willing to stand up to his acerbic wit in a debate, a lesson Jessica was quick to learn right after the wedding.

When Lloyd returns from work in the late afternoon, she rushes to tell him about what she saw on television. While agreeing that the incident indicates a worsening of violence in Mexico, he avoids any display of emotion and offers instead a rational explanation of why it happened. "You can't really blame the perpetrators for acting that way," he argues, "when they've been trained to perceive honest policemen as traitors to their cause."

"Traitors?" asks Jessica, wincing.

"Well yes. Like the drug people, the police come from poor families and to the assassin's way of thinking, they should welcome the chance to better themselves financially."

"You mean with payouts from the cartels."

"Exactly. So, when they refuse to be bribed, they are seen as thumbing their noses at their brethren in the drug business."

Jessica sighs. "And so, they have to be eliminated."

"Yes. But they really didn't have to be so cruel about it; they apparently did it to send a message to the other men on the force."

"You mean other police officers who might refuse to take a bribe."

"Yes."

"What a message...you either work for us or we'll cut off your head."

Lloyd bites his lip. "As I said, they really didn't have to go that far. That kind of behavior is going to upset the whole community and will come back to hurt them."

When Lloyd rises to leave, Jessica remains seated, stunned by what her husband just said. Head in her hands, she searches for answers. *We are so different. Why in the world were we ever attracted to each other?* She rubs her chin. *Okay, I was desperate to get out of the blue-collar world I grew up in. Lloyd represented a ticket into the upper-middle class...more money, more things, a chance to be around people with more education and more sophisticated tastes. And with that came a higher status in the community. Let's face it, I enjoy the look in people's eyes when I am introduced as the wife of a university professor. Of course, I had to learn how to act the part, but I think I'm pretty good at it now. But maybe it's simpler than that. Maybe it's just a case of opposites attracting each other. I respect him for his brain; he loves me because he thinks I'm beautiful. It all makes sense...even though it's a little hard to accept sometimes.*

Later in the day, as they prepare for dinner with their good friends, Ned and Dolores Kinsman, Jessica complains that she can't find the silver necklace Lloyd gave her years ago. It is in fact her favorite piece of jewelry, one that goes particularly well with the light blue summer dress she plans to wear this evening. Once Lloyd is dressed, she asks his help in finding it. Not surprisingly, Lloyd insists that the search be done in a systematic fashion. For him that means dividing up each room in turn…with Jessica going around the room clockwise while he does same counterclockwise. That way, he argues, every part of each room will get covered twice…until the whole house has been searched from top to bottom. Jessica agrees. They start in the guest room upstairs and proceed all the way to the laundry room in the basement. After more than an hour of searching, there is still no necklace.

After trying on several alternatives, Jessica decides to go without any jewelry. At 6:00 they head to the Kinsmans for what is rumored to be a dinner of barbecued chicken, baked potatoes, salad from the garden, and a round of bridge. Although the two couples enjoyed dinner together just two weeks ago at a Chinese restaurant in town, both Jessica and Lloyd are looking forward to the evening. It is, infact, not unusual for the two couples to get together twice a month…either at one of the two homes or out at a restaurant.

Ned Kinsman teaches psychology at UTEP where he specializes in the clinical side of the discipline. Newly 38, he is tall, with curly brown hair bordered by a few grays at the temples, hinting of his entry into middle age. Although he and Lloyd both teach at the university, it is obvious that he shares more with Lloyd's wife, among other things an interest in why people behave the way they do. Like her, he is open about his own feelings and curious, sometimes to the point of offense, about the way others feel.

When he and Dolores first met as undergraduates at Cornell University, he came on passionately. He found her submissive demeanor exactly what he wanted in a woman. From the very beginning, she allowed him to make all their decisions... including what part of town to live in, what kind of music to play, which couples to befriend, and where to go for vacations. He was aroused by her petite good looks, her wavy black hair, sensuous lips and small perky breasts (which he had to insist over and over that he liked). Early on in the relationship, Dolores discovered that the way to win Ned over was to shower him with praise...which he devoured in limitless quantities.

At that time he was extremely ambitious, although he is less so now as he approaches 40. The problem with Dolores's strategy is that Ned gradually came to take her love for granted; he no longer had to earn it. Because she submitted to his wishes even when she would have preferred to do something else, he gradually came to take her acquiescence as a given. In short, he stopped caring how she felt. She responded to his growing inattention by becoming depressed and withdrawn. In time, sustained periods of depression took a toll on her body. Her skin lost its youthful color...becoming lifeless and gray. In turn, her hair lost its natural waviness. To friends, she appeared wan and pallid...so much so that people often asked her if she were ill. Five years into the marriage, Ned brought up the possibility of divorce but recoiled when she said she would kill herself if he ever left her. In response he buried himself in his work, publishing article after article...and two books, one on shamanism among the Iroquois Indians and a more recent one on extra-sensory perception (ESP).

The Bransons are greeted at the door like friends unseen for years when in fact the two couples had dinner together at the Taipei-Tokyo restaurant just two weeks ago. In the living room, as drinks are served, the conversation quickly turns to the police killings in Juárez. Ned is outspoken about the "barbarism" of the act. "It was bad enough," he shouts, "that they beheaded these men, but to dump the mutilated bodies in a playground where teachers and children are present is unconscionable."

Lloyd is more soft-spoken. He begins by setting the event in an historical context. "There has been no significant change in human behavior over the centuries; we are as cruel now as we were in the Middle Ages when heretics were burned at the stake or in the 1930's when Stalin butchered all those kulaks or soon afterwards when the Nazis gassed millions of "undesirables." Still holding the floor, he cites William Golding's novel, Lord of the Flies, to support the case that civilization is no more then a thin crust of rules and laws covering a cauldron of animal impulses….impulses which are capable of exploding into barbaric behavior whenever the veneer of civilization is threatened. He concludes, "The drug wars in Mexico are now threatening that veneer."

For his part, Ned argues that unlike Golding's book in which a group of teenage boys were marooned on an island where they regressed to a state of 'might makes right', the drug cartels in Mexico are not isolated from the rest of society and all its legal institutions. "Because they are still a part of a civilized society," he continues, "they are subject to its control. Maybe the smugglers have the upper hand right now, but it is only a matter of time before they are stopped."

Jessica is less interested in history and more concerned with the pain endured by the policemen and their families. Privately, she wonders why anyone would ever want to become a policeman. Throughout the discussion Dolores says nothing.

As the two couples proceed to the terrace, Dolores leads the way, followed by Jessica, Ned and Lloyd in that order. From his position behind her, Ned is quick to notice that Jessica is wearing no jewelry, a first for her. When he comments, she explains that she couldn't find her favorite necklace and was so upset she refused to wear any jewelry at all. To prove her point, she reaches behind her head and fluffs her hair. "See… nothing," she coos. When Ned sees the back of her neck, so tantalizingly close now, he reaches out and touches it gently.

She turns, surprised by his boldness…and responds with a shy smile. Even though the two couples have known each other for several years, this is the first time that anyone of the four has ever made an overt sexual gesture. It is not the first time that they've been aroused, but the only time anyone has acted upon those feelings. In the weeks ahead, Jessica's tiny smile provides material for endless daydreams on Ned's part.

Chapter 2

The Search

The following day, Jessica calls the Kinsmans to ask if anyone found the earring she left behind last night. It is Ned who answers the phone. He already has the lost earring on his dresser and says he'll be happy to drop it off later in the afternoon on his way back from the university. Still reminiscing over Jessica's neck, Ned rushes through a lecture on Jungian archetypes and skips lunch so he can get to the Branson's house earlier. Once they are together in her living room, Ned hands over the missing earring. Jessica thanks him by squeezing his hand. Only slightly disappointed at the response, Ned asks about the necklace. "Any luck finding it?"

She shakes her head, then proceeds to tell him something unusual that happened this morning. "I was so concerned about the necklace that I fell into a kind of trance where my mind went blank except for the jewelry. The 'trance' lasted for several minutes…maybe even five." She goes on to say that she has never before been so completely concentrated on any one thing. Ned, who has studied ESP for years, is curious and asks if there were any visual images associated with the trance. Jessica nods. "I saw the necklace surrounded by other pieces of jewelry…diamond rings, bracelets, etcetera."

Ned, intrigued by the possibility of a clairvoyant experience, asks, "Anything else? For example, anything to indicate the context…you know, the setting."

"Not sure what you mean," she says.

"Well, did your image include things beyond the jewelry itself…something to suggest where the different pieces might be located? For example, were they in someone's house?"

"Well, if anything, I'd say they were in something like a glass display case."

"You mean the kind you would see in a jewelry store?"

"Perhaps…although nothing was very clear."

Ned gets excited and suggests that she might have had a clairvoyant experience in which she actually saw the missing necklace. Jessica laughs but dismisses the idea as a bit of wishful thinking on his part. In response, he cites several recent articles in psychological journals that confirm the reality of what is now called 'remote-viewing' experiences. "At the Stanford Laboratory for Paranormal Research," he says, "they repeatedly demonstrated that with no more than a few minutes training, an average person can identify objects hidden behind a thick wall. The researchers were equally successful having someone draw pictures of where an associate was hiding…you know, places like the waterfront or a church." He pauses. "Jess, this stuff is no longer based on anecdotes; it's been proven scientifically." Jessica listens carefully but reserves judgment.

Back home, Ned reviews what Jessica has told him, then decides to go looking for the missing necklace on his own. His first step is to look for jewelry stores in the Yellow Pages. There are three in downtown El Paso. Without bothering to tell Dolores where he's going, he heads for the first address given. A quick search of the 'Golden Calf' store on Almeida St. reveals nothing. The next two are no better. As he is about to give up and return to his car, he spots a pawn shop around the corner. "Why not?" he mutters as he walks in. There on his left is a glass display case with more than a dozen rings, necklaces, bracelets and earrings. When he stops to look more closely, the proprietor comes out from behind the counter and asks if he can help.

"There," Ned shouts. "That silver necklace. Can I see it up close?"

"Of course," answers the man as he opens the case and picks up the necklace.

"This certainly looks like Jessica's," Ned murmurs. "Do you remember who brought it in?"

"I do", the owner replies. "It was a little Hispanic lady…said she needed money for her grandson's operation."

"Do you remember her name?"

"I have it written down…but I don't usually give out information like that. It might even be illegal."

Ned looks at the necklace carefully. On the back is an inscription…recently filed down to obscure the writing. When he is convinced that it is Jessica's, he asks, "How much do you want for it?"

The owner returns to his counter and pulls out a thick notebook. Running his hand down to the entry he wants, he announces, "Three hundred dollars."

Ned pulls out his checkbook, writes a check for that amount and waits for the necklace to be wrapped. On his way back to his car, he begins whistling…a sure sign for him that things are going his way. Over and over he rehearses what to say as he hands the package to Jessica. With each iteration, he imagines her response…ranging from a clasping of his hands to an ardent hug and kiss. Hoping for the latter, he jumps into his car and races for the Branson's house.

Jessica is elated as she confirms that the necklace is indeed hers, but bemoans the fact that the writing on the back has been filed down. Caught between conflicting emotions, she offers a lukewarm hug. When Ned asks who could have stolen the necklace, she shakes her head. "The only one with access to my bedroom is Maria, the woman who's been cleaning the house for years. I trust her completely. In the beginning I went so far as to leave ten and twenty dollar bills around the house just to see if I could trust her. She never took a single one."

Ned answers by revealing what the pawn shop owner said…"a little Hispanic lady who needed money for her grandson's operation." Jessica cries out, "Oh no. Maria told me about her grandson. That does sound like her. Maybe I've been wrong to trust her all these years."

When Ned reaches out to take her hand, she doesn't resist. "Are you going to fire her?"

"I don't want to…but I must confront her. If it really was for her grandson, maybe I can help."

The generosity of Jessica's response touches something deep in Ned's psyche. This is the way he would like to react to disappointments…with charity rather than hostility… something he's definitely not good at. Subdued by what he sees, he withdraws his hand and rises to leave. Before closing the door, he stops to summarize what just happened. "This proves it," he says, smiling. "You can see things with something other than normal vision. You're clairvoyant,"

She greets his enthusiasm with a smile of her own, but says nothing. Once Ned has left, she retreats to the office upstairs and Googles 'clairvoyance.' For the next hour she reads everything she can about paranormal phenomena, in particular the ability some people have to identify objects hidden behind walls or wrapped in opaque containers. It's just as Ned argued at dinner last Saturday; there is scientific evidence that it can be done... even at great distances. Knowing how Lloyd would react to such 'silliness,' she decides to tell him about the necklace but leave it at that.

Later in the day she confronts Maria who breaks down, begging forgiveness. "You've never stolen from me all these years, Maria. You must have had good reason to do it now." Maria trembles...then relates story of her new grandson who was born with two webbed fingers on his right hand and needs an operation. "Do you want I go?"

"No, you can stay but if you ever steal from me again, I will have to fire you...(*pause*)...By the way, which hospital is your grandson staying at? I want to pay him a visit."

Chapter 3

Mata

On the following night, Lloyd and Jessica are in the living room watching television when a news flash reports yet another terrorist attack, this time the burning of a casino in Monterrey in which 50 people were killed when the building went up in flames. An interview with Carlos Medina, the owner who managed to escape the fire, suggests that it was the work of men from Los Zapas, a notoriously violent drug cartel that also runs a protection racket. The owner claims that he was approached by three men a week ago demanding $500 U.S. a week to protect the casino from rival gangs, in particular that of El Gordo who is eager to expand his Sinaloa operations into the Juárez area. Medina refused to go along and paid the price for his recalcitrance.

When the reporter adds that many of the 50 victims were women who worked at the casino, Jessica breaks into tears. Lloyd rises to comfort her, then changes his mind. He has tried giving emotional support in the past but has never felt comfortable doing so. The words seem artificial, the gestures contrived. Worst of all, Jessica never takes his concern seriously. Resorting instead to an approach that feels more natural, he offers an explanation of why and how the tragedy happened. "From what I have read, the Los Zapas started out in the Special Forces; they were a bunch of rebels who hoped to play the part of Robin Hood and fashioned their nick-name after that of the great Mexican hero, Emiliano Zapata. Most of them followed their leader Pancho Mata when he left the Forces to join a drug cartel for better pay." He leans forward as if addressing a group of students. "Once the soldiers entered the drug business, lessons learned in the military were quickly applied to relations with competing cartels and the police. Enemies were hunted down, tortured and killed when necessary. More recently they've branched out into the protection racket. We think of their methods as grotesque but they're really just doing what they were trained to do."

Jessica squints. "So, we really shouldn't blame them? Is that what you're saying?"

"I'm saying merely that their behavior is explainable. It's not a mystery why they do what they do."

Back in the privacy of her bedroom, she sits and lets the newspaper image of the Los Zapas leader, Mata, come to mind. She is reminded of the fierceness of his eyes, the high cheekbones, the thinness of his lips. She holds the image in her mind…then waits until all thinking ceases and her breathing slows down. First nothing appears…then suddenly she sees a grainy image of a table with several people around it, eating a meal. As the trance deepens, the image becomes clearer, revealing aspects of the surrounding area. It is a restaurant; emblazoned on the walls are pictures of cowboys on horses chasing mustangs across the plains. Outside, just next to the entrance, is a life-size horse…probably a mustang. She wakes, shaking her head. *I know that restaurant. It's just over the border in Juárez. I can't remember what it's called, but I've walked past it several times.* She is tempted to call Ned but is afraid of being seen as foolish. Just minutes later, she changes her mind and dials his number. When Dolores answers, she is about to put down the phone when she hears the TV news in the background. That means Ned is probably watching the news. She clears her throat: "Hi, Dolores, it's Jessica. Are you and Ned watching what happened in Monterrey?"

"Yes…it's horrible," comes the response. Then, "Do you want to talk to Ned?" The resignation in her voice, while innocent in itself, resonates like an accusation. For a moment Jessica considers lying, then changes her mind. "Yes please…I need to tell him about something I just saw."

"Okay. I'll get him."

Ned answers immediately. "Jessica? What's up?" "

"I hope I'm not intruding but I just had a strange experience…a daydream I guess you could call it…and I thought you might be able to make sense of it."

"Sounds exciting…what happened?"

Jessica relates the "daydream", being sure to include every detail she can remember. Ned doesn't disappoint her. "Sure sounds like another clairvoyant experience…like the one about the necklace in the pawn shop. If it's for real, Jessica, it means that Mata was probably at that restaurant at the time you went into your trance. As you know, the police are desperate to find this guy and lock him up…so maybe you can help."

"Doing what?"

"Well, calling the police and telling them where this guy is… assuming he's still there."

"But what if he isn't? What if it's nothing more than a normal daydream? Won't they be angry that I wasted their time?"

"Well, let them decide that for themselves. You can call and tell them everything you know…and let them take it from there."

"But I can't even remember the name of the restaurant."

"From what you've told me, I'm pretty sure it's the 'Mustang'.

She sighs. "Yes, of course. I should have known. But who should I call? I don't know anything about the police."

"The best place to try is the D.E.A....you know, the U.S. Drug Enforcement Agency. They have offices everywhere... both here in the U.S. and all over Mexico. They work with their Mexican counterparts...conducting raids, stings, stuff like that. In Mexico I think the agency is called the PGR...a subdivision of the Attorney General's Office. But the place to call is the D.E.A. office here in El Paso and let them notify the Mexicans; maybe they could work together on this. If you want, I can call the El Paso D.E.A. office and find out who you should contact. There's got to be somebody there who would give his right arm to know where Mata is at the moment."

Jessica agrees to Ned's plan and thanks him for his help.

"I'll call the D.E.A. right away," Ned responds, "and let you know what they say. Don't stray too far from the phone."

"But it's after 5:00 P.M. Maybe everybody's gone home."

"Not likely," he answers. "They'll be somebody there 24 hours a day; in their business, they can't afford to close shop."

"Maybe you better not give them my name...or my phone number. I don't want to find myself in the middle of a crossfire."

"I understand...you've got a good head on your shoulders... best to leave it where it is."

Jessica shudders. "Thanks Ned...your words are really reassuring."

"Sorry...couldn't resist. I'll call you tomorrow and tell you what I've found."

In bed that night the image of Pancho Mata returns, making it impossible for her to fall asleep. Frustrated, she tries massaging herself; it works. She waits until she hears Lloyd getting into bed in the adjoining room…then quietly opens his door and slides into bed next to him. This is the way their love-making usually starts…with Jessica taking the initiative while Lloyd submits…quite the opposite of how things appear outside the bedroom. For his part, the desire is there but it lies buried beneath a layer of words and logic…until, that is, she does something to arouse it. For Jessica, the arrangement is unnatural; what comes more naturally to her is playing the feminine role… receptive, compliant, comforting. It takes an unusually strong desire on her part before she can bring herself to play the part of the dominatrix her husband needs her to be. That, of course, is the reason they have sex so seldom…and why each feels more comfortable in a separate bedroom.

In the morning, Ned calls during a break between classes. "Hi Jessica, I talked to a Robert Dunwoody at the El Paso D.E.A. office yesterday. He said he would pass the information on to Commandant Mendoza at the PGR office in Juárez. Dunwoody said he gets reports like this all the time but they rarely turn out to be true."

"I thought he might say something like that."

"Well, yeah, he was pretty skeptical, especially when I refused to tell him who you were."

"So, what exactly did you say to him? I'm concerned"

"Just that a friend of mine had a clairvoyant experience in which she saw Pancho Mata eating at the Mustang restaurant. When he asked for your name, I told him you didn't want to be identified… and that I was calling on your behalf."

"Did you give him your name?"

"Nope...to be on the safe side, I even called from a public phone. I figured that once they learned my number, they could easily get my name from the phone company...and then get to you through me."

"Exactly. So, did he say they were going to do anything about your call?"

"He said he would call Mendoza and leave the decision up to him. I think Dunwoody took it seriously enough to suggest that Mendoza send someone over to the Mustang to check things out...maybe not a whole squad. For that to happen, Mendoza would need approval from his boss, a guy named Contréras. That makes sense. To send a whole squad would mean taking agents away from their other duties and wasting their time on what could turn out to be a wild goose chase. Not to mention the cost. What's more likely to happen, Dunwoody said, is that Mendoza will send out a plain-clothes agent to take a look inside the restaurant...you know, just to see if Mata is still there. If he is, he will probably have a whole bunch of fellow hoods with him... all armed to the teeth."

"But by the time the agent relays back to headquarters that Mata is there and Mendóza sends a squad out to capture him, it will be too late. Mata is not going to remain in the restaurant forever, is he?"

"I think what it really means is that before committing himself to an all-out assault, Mendoza wants to know if your information is reliable. If it is, he'll be more likely to trust you if you have a similar experience in the future."

"I understand. Don't worry...my feelings aren't hurt" "

(*Laughing*) Glad to see you're not upset...(*pause*)...By the way, I don't see why you can't call Dunwoody yourself if this happens again. Just don't call from home…or from somewhere near your house."

"So where should I go…Houston, Dallas, Phoenix?"

"No…just go to a town outside of El Paso…and use a public phone. That way, if they trace it, it will be impossible to connect the call to you."

"Well, if I really want to be careful, I should probably use a different phone in a different town each time I call…assuming this happens again."

"Why not…inconvenient yes, but much safer."

The following day, Ned goes to a public phone outside El Paso and calls Dunwoody. "Well, did you find out about Mata and the Mustang?", he asks, hoping the sound of his voice would be identification enough.

"Your friend was absolutely right," comes the answer. "Mata was there at the restaurant, getting ready to leave when Mendóza's agent appeared…just like your friend said…(*pause*)… So, tell me, how the hell did he do it?"

"Well, first of all, it's not a he; it's a woman. Like I told you… she's psychic. She focuses on a picture of a target person and then goes into a trance. Details about where he is come to her as she concentrates. That's all I can tell you."

"Well, be sure to call me if it happens again."

"There's no reason she can't call you herself…as long as you don't do something to scare her…like trying to find out who she is. She wants to help but prefers to remain anonymous. If you want her help in catching this guy, you'd better let her stay that way, comprendé?"

"Yeah, sure. No probléma."

Chapter 4

The Tunnel

A week passes before Jessica has another clairvoyant experience, this time after reading a magazine featuring photos of the five major Mexican cartel bosses. Responding to threats from the smugglers, most magazines and newspapers in Northern Mexico have muted their criticism while some have stopped publishing articles about the "drug war" altogether. Reforma, the one Jessica subscribes to, is one of the few still brave enough to say what it thinks. After reading about the atrocities, she thumbs back to the section with photos. Again, she focuses on Pancho Mata, the Los Zapas leader. The picture is enough to bring her mind to a focus. She closes her eyes. As she slips into a trance, she sees bars…like those on a prison cell. As more details emerge, she recognizes the gray walls, barbed wire and tall observation towers of the prison just outside Juárez, a prison famous as the place where El Gordo, the Sinaloan drug lord whose real name is Francisco León, escaped several years ago. She reaches for the phone and dials Ned's number at work. On hearing the news Ned gets excited, ventures the opinion that Mata is probably at the prison visiting a convicted member of his gang. "Get in your car and find a public phone just outside of town… then call Dunwoody."

"Won't Mata be gone by then?" she asks.

"Perhaps, but that's a chance we have to take." His use of the word "we" helps to reduce her anxiety.

"You make it seem like we're in this together. I don't think I'm ready to do it alone."

For Ned, her words hint at something more than friendship …something bordering on the romantic. When the conversation ends, he puts the phone down, drops his head back and slips into fantasy…one that ends with the two exchanging declarations of unending love. He wakes up when he hears a student pounding on his office door, wanting his grade changed.

When Jessica calls Dunwoody, she is told that he is at a meeting and does not want to be disturbed. Rather than speak to someone else, she hangs up. At Ned's suggestion, she calls again the next day when he's likely to be free. Once they are connected, she tells him what she saw in her recent trance. "Of course, it's too late to do anything about it now," she says, "but I was wondering if you could check to see if Mata was really at the prison yesterday. If so, you could relay that on to your Mexican counterpart. It might convince him that this is for real."

"And if he wasn't at the prison yesterday…what then?, he asks Dunwoody.

"Well, I guess there'd be no point in calling him. And probably no point in my bothering you again."

"O.K. I'll check. But how do I let you know what I find?"

"I'll call you again tomorrow…okay?"

"Still don't trust me enough to give me your number?"

"It's not you in particular. Everybody knows that the cartels have spies in the military and police. I'm not saying I can't trust you, but I don't want my personal information passed on to others. For example, you might jot my number down on a piece of paper where it could be picked up by your secretary.

Who knows what could happen then? I just don't want to take the chance."

When Jessica calls Dunwoody the following day, she hears what she hoped to hear.

"He was there alright…just like you said. I passed the info on to Mendóza. To tell you the truth, he didn't seem all that excited. I was surprised, given how long we've been looking for this guy."

"Did he think it was just luck on my part?"

"Maybe a coincidence. He said Mata goes there often to visit friends. And there's another thing. I think he was put off when I told him my informant was a woman."

"Is that what I am…an informant. It sounds a bit unsavory."

"What do you prefer…my psychic?"

"Psychic is more acceptable but I don't think I qualify for that title yet. This is all new for me; it may never happen again."

"Well, call me if it does. If it matters to you, I'm convinced you're for real. So, tell me right away if you have another one of your 'visions'; maybe I can persuade Mendóza to send in some troops this time."

"Yes. I will."

In the days that follow, television screens are filled with more bad news, some of it more barbaric than anything seen before. Worst of all are newsreels showing human faces attached to soccer balls tossed onto the dance floor at a popular night club. All of the faces belong to local policemen, individuals who presumably refused to work with the drug dealers. Some of the balls have Z's painted on them, leaving no doubt that the Zapas are responsible for this latest act of horror. According to the announcer, the whole city is talking about it. People are afraid to venture out at night; policemen are resigning from the force left and right. Even those citizens who have no interest in politics are appalled at the savagery of the acts. People throughout Northern Mexico are demanding action from Pres. Calderón. The president, long committed to eradicating the violence, promises to send in thousands of soldiers. News comes out later that the dead policemen were not working for the Zapas but for a rival gang. The Z's apparently used the murders to send a message: 'Work for somebody else and you'll lose your face.'

Jessica can't get the image of bloody, face-covered soccer balls out of her mind. On two separate occasions, she races to the toilet, clutching her stomach. Lloyd is of no help. Instead, she calls Ned to see if he is having a similar reaction. He agrees and encourages her to look for Mata again, using her remote-viewing abilities. "I don't think you need to have his picture in front of you. Just quiet your mind, ask yourself where he is, and slip into a trance. You know how to do it. Twice now you've been able to locate him remotely; next time it happens, insist that they go in after him…(*pause*)…Jessica, Mexico is falling into an abyss; we've got to stop this insanity before it goes any further. If we don't stop it here, it's going to spill over into the U.S."

"Okay. I'll try."

"Call me if something comes up. But call Dunwoody first. That should be your top priority. Remember to call from a public phone… and don't use the same one each time."

"Okay. I will…I mean I won't. Thanks."

Jessica spends the next few days attending an amateur art class and working on some sketches at home. While she has no illusions about future fame, she has been told by several knowledgeable friends that she has real talent. Up to now flowers and landscapes have been her favorite subjects. At the last class, however, the instructor suggests that she try her hand at a portrait...perhaps one of a family member or close friend...someone she sees often. Eager to try something new, she sits in front of a blank canvas and lets her imagination go where it wants to. With pencil in hand, she begins drawing the first thing that comes to mind. When an outline of Pancho Mata's face appears, she blinks, then shudders. This is not what she had in mind, but she's willing to follow the instructor's suggestion that she give 'free reign' to her imagination. All thinking ceases now as she becomes totally absorbed in the drug lord's emerging face.

The question 'Where are you?' echoes inside her head as she closes her eyes. First to appear is something resembling an animal's burrow...a large, dirt-lined enclosure with a single light overhead. The enclosure goes on for many feet, even yards. While she can't see Mata himself, she senses that he's there. *But what can that be?* she asks...*the Los Zapas leader in a rabbit hole? It doesn't make any sense.* When she can't come up with an explanation, she waits until the class is over and calls Ned.

"Tell me more about what you actually saw in the trance," he says. "Any other objects in the 'hole'?"

"Nothing that I can remember."

"Okay. Let's try a different approach. What were you feeling as you looked at the 'hole'?"

"Well, I was trying to find Pancho Mata, so my feelings were mainly about him."

"Feelings such as...?"

"I don't know...maybe anxiety...the whole thing seemed kinda scary."

"Let's take it a little further. How about pretending that you are in the 'hole'...place yourself there right now and tell me what you're experiencing."

"Okay....it feels dark and clammy...as if I were underground ...like a mole making its way through a tunnel."

"A tunnel? Holy cow! That's it! It all makes sense now."

"What makes sense?"

"Well, you're looking for Mata...and you end up getting an image of something underground...a tunnel. Now...what's the relationship between Mata and a tunnel?"

"Oh God...I did read something last week about how the Zapas were building tunnels under the border so they can transport drugs to the U.S. without being seen."

"Right...one's been discovered and blocked up, but there are many others that are rumored to exist...some possibly right in Ciudad Juárez."

"So, you think he might be in one right now?"

"Yes...get to a phone right away and call Dunwoody."

"But what can he do?"

"Well, for one thing he can send up a helicopter to look for dirt tailings at the mouth of a tunnel. If they've built one near Juárez, it's probably somewhere out beyond the suburbs. They might be able to see the entrance from the air even though it's hidden from our view down here. If it's at all like the one they dug in Nogales, it could be up to 50 yards long and strung with electric lights...a huge investment ...perhaps a million dollars or more."

"So, that means the tunnel, assuming it starts in Juárez and goes under the border, will come up somewhere here in El Paso."

"Yes. But it will be harder to spot on the U.S. side since the tailings are likely to be taken out on the Mexican side where the entrance can be camouflaged."

"I suppose by the time they find it…assuming it's there… and send in some agents, Mata will be long gone."

"True…but if he's overseeing the construction or even the maintenance of the tunnel, he's bound to show up often. Once we locate the tunnel, we…that is Mendoza…can wait to pounce on him."

"I'll call as soon as I can find a public phone. Okay?"

"Great. I really enjoy working with you, Jessica."

"Me too…bye for now."

Chapter 5

Mendoza

"Hi, Bob Dunwoody here. Can I talk to Commandant Mendoza? It's urgent."

"Yes sir…right away."

A minute later. "Mendoza here…whatcha got for me, Bob?"

"Are you in a private place?"

"Now, si." (*closes the door*).

"Okay. My informant, you know the woman I told you about earlier, tells me Mata's inside a tunnel…right now. We don't know where the tunnel is but we can take a look around. The best way to do that is to send up a 'copter, you know, one of those we gave you last year, to see if you can locate any tunnel entrances in the vicinity of Juárez."

"How do you know they make tunnel near Juárez? Maybe is 100 miles from here?"

"Yes…that's why I think it's a long shot. But look, if our info turns out to be wrong, no big deal and if…

(*Interrupting*) "No big deal? Hey amigo. I gonna get hell from Contréras if this is wild goose chase."

"True enough…but if the info is good, it means you can lie

in wait until Mata returns and then nab him. You should get some kind of ribbon for that. You'd like that, wouldn't you?"

"Ribbon no pay for rent; pay raise better."

"I'll see what I can arrange."

"You have big clout, yes?"

"I'm workin' on it."

Luis Mendoza comes from a wealthy family in the Mexican state of Jalisco. His family once owned a hacienda with over 2,000 acres of farm land. Unfortunately, the land lost much of its value in the 1990's when NAFTA was born, driving down the market value of most fruits and vegetables grown in Mexico. When both parents died, the farm was sold and the proceeds divided among the three children, Luis being the youngest. Forced to find a job in the city, he moved to Juárez and with the help of old family friends, wangled a job in the Attorney General's Office. He's been there for eight years now, rising from research assistant all the way to Commandant of the Drug Enforcement Division. Initially the switch from wealthy land owner in charge of nearly 100 workers to a city bureaucrat with a 9-5 desk job was traumatic. Almost overnight, he was forced to undergo a change in lifestyle …from playboy aristocrat to a lowly clerk chained to his desk and barely able to pay his monthly rent. While things improved with his most recent promotion to Commandant, he remains bitter at the loss of his family's status and wealth. Although he tries hard to hide his disappointment, signs of it can be seen in his impatience with people he considers his inferiors, most noticeably his subordinates. He is particularly disliked by those who work directly beneath him; some would go so far as to admit hating him. On the other hand, the people he considers his equals or better, like Robert Dunwoody over at the American D.E.A., have a more positive impression. At dinner parties with his U.S. counterparts, his behavior is quite predictable; he goes out of his way to fawn over anyone of superior rank and quickly agrees with anyone heard complaining about the 'bureaucrats in Washington'.

While irritating to some, colleagues of a similar rank put up with him because of his keen intelligence and good manners.

Mendoza doesn't know it, but his Operations Assistant, Eduardo Garcia, is good friends with Robert Dunwoody. Garcia and Dunwoody are about the same age, 30; they met originally on a basketball court in El Paso, the same court where both now play in a weekend non-professional league. Garcia is in some ways the opposite of his boss…friendly, relaxed and easy to be with. When faced with Mendoza's impatience, he typically shrugs it off…chalks it up to what he has learned over the years about his boss's history. It also helps to share any frustration with his friend Sebastián who works next to him in the department. After work they often go to a local bar and poke fun at their prickly superior over a beer or two.

Dunwoody's helicopter idea proves to a good one. According to initial reports, a large swath of different colored dirt in a field just outside Juárez is clearly visible from the air, highly suggestive of a tunnel entrance. While the local police are obviously aware of it, they have chosen not to intervene…presumably because the officers in charge have been bought off by one of the cartels. Given the time that has elapsed since Dunwoody's call, Mendoza decides to postpone an attack until he gets word that Mata has returned. When he calls to inform Dunwoody, his D.E.A. counterpart agrees with the strategy. "I'll let my informant know that we're waiting on her signal. If she can do her trance thing again soon, we might be able to catch him while they're still working on the tunnel."

"Tell her call right away if she see something."

"Yeah…but look Luis, there's something else we should talk about…like security."

"Whatcha mean?"

"Well, your department could have leaks."

"Hey, we all got leaks these days."

"Yeah, sure...but I think you've got more than your share over there on the Mexican side, yes?"

"Okay, so what?"

"Well, it's up to you of course, but I have a suggestion."

"Like what?"

"Since catching Mata is top priority, we should probably be extra cautious."

"What your point, Bob?"

"Here's my idea. To make sure none of your agents leak info about the raid, get them all in your briefing room and lock the door before you tell them where you're sendin' them."

"Well okay...but if we have mole, he could use cell phone to warn Mata, yes?"

"Right...so make 'em hand over their phones as they enter the briefing room."

"Sounds paranoid, but maybe you right. Not okay to take chances."

"Yeah. Just don't tell anyone until the last minute."

"I no dummy, Bob."

"Sorry...just being careful."

Chapter 6

The Raid

Three days later Dunwoody gets a call from Jessica at 10:30 A.M. "He's there right now…you know, Mata. The same place as before…what you say is a tunnel."

"How sure are you?"

"Very sure."

"Okay. I'll call Mendoza right away, thanks."

A minute later he's on the phone. "Luis…Mata's there…at the tunnel…right now. Do you have enough agents on alert… you know, that you can send in right away?"

"Of course…I have squad of 30 men all ready to go. This time we catch him, yes?"

"I sure hope so. The bastard has wreaked enough havoc already. Take him prisoner if you can; if that proves difficult, don't be afraid to shoot him."

"That my decision, right? I will do what I think right thing."

"Of course. I'm just throwing out ideas."

•••◦•▬▬▬▬▬▬•◦•▬▬▬▬▬▬•◦•••

That night Dunwoody gets an unexpected call. "Hey Bob, it's me, Eduardo. "I need see you, right away."

"Can't it wait until Saturday; we have a game then, in case you forgot."

"No, it's serious…we need talk tonight."

"Oh boy…does it have something to do with the fiasco this morning?"

"Yeah."

"Okay. C'mon over. You know where I live."

"Thanks. I be there in 30 minutes."

At Dunwoody's house, Eduardo waits until Bob's wife retires to the TV room before beginning his story. "You know Mata not there by time our agents get to tunnel.

"Yeah…Mendoza told me…said the info I gave him was wrong. When I mentioned another possibility…that someone leaked the info to Mata, he said it was impossible since all agents were locked in the briefing room and searched for cell phones before they were informed about the raid. He said that even goes for drivers.

That's true, but he not tell you something else. Like you say, everyone in briefing room…30 agents plus Mendoza and Administrative Assistant, Juan Carrasco…and me. He not tell you there is bathroom in back of briefing room."

"No, he didn't tell me that. Is it important?"

"Well, as soon as all agents leave for raid, I go to bathroom to take shit. Two minutes later someone comes in and goes into stall at far end. Then I hear his voice…whispering. I listen carefully. In Spanish he say 'Someone coming for dinner.' Then silence as other person speak. Then, one word 'yellow.' Finally, he say '20 minutes.' That's all. When he leave bathroom, I go to stall where he was sitting. Behind roll of toilet paper I see cell phone hidden. I check last number called…maybe you want it."

"Of course."

"Okay. It's 952-304-5718."

Dunwoody writes it down. "So, you think he was calling Mata?"

"Or someone who work with Mata."

"What does 'yellow' mean?"

"Probly code…maybe 'yellow' says location…tunnel. But Bob, next part scary. As man get ready to leave toilet, I bend over inside stall so I see his shoes. All agents wear black boots. This man have brown shoes."

"So., whose could they be?"

"Only two men in department have brown shoes…the men who stay behind to coordinate attack."

"Wait a minute Eduardo…you're not saying Mendoza was…"

(*Interrupting*) "Si…two men who stay behind and not wear black boots are Carrasco the Administrative Assistant and Commandant Mendoza. Nobody else possible."

"Holy shit…so one of them is working for Mata. No wonder the raid failed. One of them went into the bathroom and called Mata to warn him that a raiding party was on its way."

"Yeah."

"But can we be sure? Perhaps there was no leak; maybe Mata never got to the tunnel. That was Mendoza's explanation. He said my informant's info was incorrect…you know, that Mata simply wasn't there in the morning."

"I no buy that, Bob. In afternoon, I make like I go to supply house and go instead to tunnel. I wear civvies so nobody know me. I ask people who own café across street if they notice anything different in morning around 11:00…like lots of cars driving away fast. One say no…not notice anything, but other say yes…several men run from tunnel and jump into black cars and go fast from street."

"You didn't tell Mendoza, did you?"

"Oh no. Maybe he call from bathroom."

"So, which one do you think it was…Mendoza or Carrasco?"

"Not know."

"But in your gut, what's your guess?"

Eduardo hesitates. "If Mendoza worried about leak, he do what I did; he ask people in neighborhood if Mata and gang leave in hurry. But he not do that. So my gut say Mendoza call from bathroom."

"I lean that way too. A coupla of things he said to me have gotten me thinking. When he finished telling me that Mata had escaped or was never there, I asked him about the tunnel itself. 'Are you going to shut it down', I said, 'you know, block it up.' His answer surprised me. He said that it would be better to leave it open in hopes that Mata would return and get caught."

Eduardo nods. "That strange since other tunnels…like one in Nogales…they close right away."

"Well, yes...and another thing he said bothers me. He wanted to know more about my informant, that he had doubts about her information...where she was getting it, where she was calling from...things like that. He even said he wanted me to make a recording of her voice next time she called so he could judge for himself whether she was for real or not."

"You gonna do it? "

"Maybe. It could be a way of stringing him along until we figure out whether he's the one leaking the info...(*pause*)... What does it sound like to you?"

"Him askin' you to record her voice sounds...how you say... like he fishing...like he wants to know who she is...maybe get rid of her."

"Jesus...if you're right, we can't trust him with anymore info...with anything for that matter...(*pause*)...What do you think about calling Mendoza's boss, Contréras, and sharing our concerns with him?"

"I no like. If Contréras work for cartel, I am dead meat; maybe wife and daughters too."

"You're right. We can't afford to take that chance...(*pause*)... So, how we goin' to capture Mata and his gang without Mendoza's help?"

"I think about it, Bob. We talk after game on Saturday, okay?"

"I'll give it some thought too."

As Eduardo leaves the house, he looks around to see if anyone is watching. All is clear. Back in his car, he reviews what he and Dunwoody talked about, then ponders the wisdom of sending his wife and children to live with his parents for a while.

Chapter 7

A Bold Idea

After the basketball game on Saturday, Eduardo and Bob head for a favorite luncheonette out on the north side of town. Bob is the first to speak. "I've wracked my brains on this one, but so far I haven't come up with any brilliant ideas. How about you?"

"Maybe not brilliant, but I have idea. If we no trust Mendoza to go after Mata, we do it ourselves."

"What d'ya mean?"

"We make a small group of good men…men we trust…and use woman's information to go after capos on our own…people like Mata. No need Mendoza; only need weapons. But we have to find men who do only honest thing."

"Wow…that's a pretty bold idea, Eduardo. How many men would you need?"

"I think five or six enough."

"But capos like Mata, El Gordo and the Castellano brothers have 30, 40 or even 50 thugs working for them. How can a group of five men, even heavily armed, take down one of the top dogs?"

"We wait until they have few bodyguards…like when they go to restaurant or stay in safe house. Surprise very important…

and right information from informant. We work at night when it hard to see us."

"Well, we do have the informant…at least for now. Who knows how long she'll be willing or able to help us. And I can get whatever weapons you need…(*pause*)…That leaves finding the right men…not an easy task when so many cops and military people are on the cartel's payroll."

"If you think it good idea, I start looking. I know one already…my friend at work, Sebastián. Need maybe three or four more."

"Where can you find them?"

"Not know. Maybe they find us."

"Well, let me know when you're ready. I can get you whatever you need. If my informant calls, I'll tell her we're working on a new strategy." "You gonna tell her about the leak at PGR?"

"Yeah, why not. She deserves to know."

Chapter 8

Jesús

Jesús Bautista, a 17 year-old school drop-out who lives on a farm high in the hills of Sinaloa, Mexico, is hailed by two men in a car parked at the edge of the field where he is weeding. Fernando, a tall man with a big mustache, introduces himself as a 'representative' from the local cartel, the one presided over by Mexico's most-wanted man, Francisco León, more popularly known as El Gordo. From the driver's seat, Fernando reaches out to shake hands. When Jesús is slow to reciprocate, the visitor smiles and pulls out a wallet bulging with 100 peso notes. "How you like to make some real money, amigo? We give you 500 pesos a week (U.S. $40) to be our 'hawk'. You know what that means?

Jesús nods. "Yeah, I've heard about it…you follow people around."

"That's it…real easy. All you gotta do is tail somebody and report to me where he goes, what he does…stuff like that. If you do a good job, we give you more work…and more pay. You work hard, pretty soon you be El Gordo's right-hand man (*laughing*)."

Jesús squints. "Lemme think about it. Come back tomorrow and I give you an answer."

Fernando shakes his head. "No, you decide now…or we give job to somebody else. "You want it or no?"

Jesús stares at the ground. When he finally looks up, Fernando's wallet is open; he's already counting out five 100 peso notes.

"Okay, I do it," the boy says, reaching for the money.

"I come back tomorrow to give you assignment," says Fernando, his mustache twisting as he flashes a victory smile.

"Okay," replies Jesús, his voice barely audible. Once the two men are out of sight, he sits down in the field and counts the money again. As he strokes the bills, a smile forms. "I can give some to Mama and Papa, and spend the rest on Lili. She loves to go to restaurants but we never have enough money. With 500 persos comin' in every week, we can eat out a lot. I can buy her new clothes too." Satisfied with his decision, he rushes home to tell his parents.

Lili's aunt and uncle live down in the village where they run a small grocery store. Jesús is very familiar with the shop, having been there often to see Lili who works behind the counter. Early the next morning he rushes to the village to tell her the news.

"But will you get into trouble?", she asks, when he tells her about his new job.

"It ain't no worse than sellin' poppies and marijuana," he replies. "Everybody's doin' it. The capos take care of us. They pay police to look the other way. So don't worry."

"But what about other gangs," she counters, "like the one from Juárez? Aren't they tryin' to get in here?"

"Yeah, but El Gordo ain't goin' to let 'em."

Lili clutches his arm. "But you might get caught in the middle. I don't want to lose you, Jesús. Someday soon we get married and have family. You promised, remember?"

"I remember. I gonna make it happen. You'll see."

After two months of 'hawking', Jesús is approached again by Fernando and his partner. They praise him for his good work and offer him a chance to make even more money. "We got some folks in town who owes us some money," says Fernando, "and they ain't payin'. We need you to go in there and collect. That's all. We pay you $1,000 pesos (U.S. $80) a week to be our collector."

"But you say they not want to pay, so, why they pay me?", asks Jesús, clearly confused by the offer. Fernando's partner, Jaime, a short man who relishes the chance to awe his audience, smiles and pulls out a Colt-Python revolver. Reaching across Fernando's lap, he puts it in the boy's hand, saying, "This is why they goin' to pay you."

Jesús runs his fingers along the barrel, stroking it like a pet animal. Already familiar with a deer rifle, he knows the feeling of power that comes with having a gun. "So, what do I do?"

Jaime leans forward. "You go into the shop where the guy owes us money and tell 'im you're here to collect. If he say no, you point pistol at him." He smiles. "Then he pay. You bring money to us in car."

"But if he still say no, what do I do?" asks Jesús.

"You shoot 'im and collect money from the register. That way we send message to other fuckups who no pay what they owe."

Jesús strokes the pistol again, shocked by what he has just heard. "You're sayin' I gotta kill the guy?"

"You heard me."

Jesús rubs his chin. "I don't know about that. I never killed anybody before."

Jaime reaches for the revolver. "Gimme the gun. If you wanta be chicken, that's your business. But El Gordo don't want you."

Jesús pulls the gun back. "Is it okay if I think about it?", he asks.

"No," comes the immediate answer from the mustachioed partner. "You say yes now or we find someone else who not afraid to do job."

Jesús bites his lip, then nods his head.

"Good," says Fernando, handing the boy a box of bullets. "Here are names of three owners who owe us money (*hands list to Jesús*). You know these shops?"

"Yeah…they're right in the middle of town."

"Okay. We come by your house tomorrow and pick you up. Then we drive into town and you go into shops."

Jesús looks baffled. "If you're goin' to come with me, why can't you collect the money yourselves?" "Is your training. The boss wants you to join our organization. This is way for you to learn how we operate."

"You told El Gordo about me?"

The two men nod.

Now it's Jesús's turn to smile. "He is big man…everybody afraid of him."

"You got it right…so don't fuck up. He not like fuckups."

When Jesús tells his parents about the new job, he gets an approving slap on the back from his father. "Jesus Christ," Papa shouts, "a thousand pesos a week. That's more than we can make in a month, selling marijuana and poppies." The mother says nothing, her disapproval apparent as she bites her lips.

Jesús spends the rest of the day honing his shooting skills in a field behind the house. By the time he finishes practicing, the revolver feels comfortable…almost like an extension of his hand. The next morning he rises early, gulps down a quick breakfast of beans and rice and heads out to the road to be picked up by Fernando and Jaime.

Fernando takes the list of shops from his pocket and reads the first name…a beauty parlor. It's only ten minutes to the village and the address on the list. Just outside the parlor, he parks the car and nods to Jesús to get out. Butterflies are churning in the boy's stomach as he opens the shop door and walks in. The owner, a woman, is there alone, doing paperwork behind the counter. Jesús checks the revolver to make sure it can't be seen, then approaches the counter. "I'm here to collect what you owe," he says, using a louder voice than necesssary.

"Ain't you the Bautista boy?", the owner says, clearly surprised by what she sees. Jesús says nothing but moves closer.

Frightened by his silence, she opens the cash register. "Well, okay, I pay you, but you guys promised to take care of me… so I'm gonnna hold you to it." Again, Jesús says nothing… but extends his open hand. Still wordless, he counts the bills. Satisfied that all 800 pesos are there, he turns and leaves. Back at the car, Fernando takes the money and nods his approval.

The second shop, an appliance sales and repair store, proves to be equally easy when the manager hands the money to Jesús without a word. Jesús gives the money to Fernando and prepares to walk across the street to the third shop on the list when Fernando grabs him by the arm and pulls him back. "Not so fast. There's been a change. That guy over there (*pointing*) paid up last night…so you don't need to go there." He pulls out his list. "We got a new name instead… 112 Avenida…I think it's a small grocery store…about a block from here. Get in."

The third shop on the list turns out to be the grocery store belonging to Lili's aunt and uncle. Jesús hesitates outside the door, then turns to look back at the car. Fernando is thrusting his arm forward. Unaware that Jesús's girlfriend works there, he shouts, "Get the fuck in there before somebody comes."

Inside the store, Jesús steps up to Octavio, Lili's uncle, and whispers, "I'm here to collect."

It takes a moment before Octavio realizes what Jesús said. His face suddenly darkens. "What the hell are you doin', Jesús?", he shouts. "You workin' for the gang now?" Jesús steps back, saying nothing. Hearing the noise, Lili enters the shop from the office in back. She looks first at her uncle, then at Jesús. "What's going on?", she cries.

Jesús pulls his jacket pocket tighter to hide the gun, then turns and runs back to car. "I can't do it," he cries. "Lili's in there."

"Who the fuck is Lili?", Fernando asks.

"She's my girlfriend. We gonna get married some day." Fernando jumps out of the car and slaps the boy's face. "Get back in the car," he screams, then heads for the shop, pistol in hand.

Jesús cringes in the back seat...head buried in his hands. He sits up when he hears a shot ring out...then a second shot. Through the window, he sees Fernando leaving the shop, tucking the pistol back in his belt.

"Dya get the money?", asks Jaime.

"Yeah, over the old guys' body."

"You get 'im twice?"

"No, the second one was for the girl. She grabbed my arm, tried to stop me."

In the back seat, Jesús gasps. "You shot Lili?" he cries.

Fernando nods.

"Maybe she still alive," Jesús yells.

"Forget her…she's dead," comes the reply.

When Jesús attempts to get out of the car, Fernando grabs him by the arm and pulls him back in. "You in enough trouble already, asshole. When El Gordo hear you fuck up, you gonna get whacked." When Jesús begins sobbing, he adds, "If you be smart, you get out of town tomorrow…before the boss send somebody to get you."

"Go where?", the boy asks visibly trembling. "I dunno… jis' far from here…someplace where nobody find you. You understand…you stay here, you die. El Gordo no like fuckups… they make him look bad…comprendes?" When Jesús continues sobbing uncontrollably, Fernando turns around and screams, "Stop whining. I can't stand it. Yir a man now; you took the job…so shut the fuck up."

Once home, Jesús immediately heads for bed, pointing to his stomach. When he doesn't come out for supper, his mother looks in but sees nothing. Throughout the night, he tosses and turns, tormented alternately by Fernando's warning and what happened at the grocery store. By morning, his mind is made up. *I've gotta go. If I don't get outta here, they gonna kill me.* While both parents are still sleeping, he packs a sweater and shirt in his knapsack and slips out onto the road. At the intersection down the hill, he turns for a last look. "Will I ever come back," he murmurs. "Do I even want to come back?"

Chapter 9

The Untouchables

At work, Eduardo avoids looking his boss in the face… tries to act like nothing has changed when in fact everything is different now at PRG. He spends much of his free time working on his new problem…how to find three or four men to join his team of "untouchables". Sebastián assures him that he will join, but that still leaves him two or three men short. When stymied, he decides to call his brother Manuel, the priest, for advice. To be on the safe side, he goes to a public phone to make the call.

"Hey Manny (*in Spanish*)…how goes it? Save any souls lately?"

"Hey Duardo…good to hear from you. Hadn't heard so long I thought you mighta taken vows and vanished into a monastery.

"No way. My feet are stayin' right here in this world. But how you doin'? Seen Mama and Papa lately?"

"Saw them last week…they're both doin' fine…although they worry about you…you know, involved in all that drug business. I worry about you too and your wife and daughter as well."

"Yeah, well I'm careful. And that's why I'm calling. I could use some help with a new project."

"So, tell me."

"It's best if we don't talk about it over the phone. Maybe I can come down to Oaxaca and see you this weekend. I'll tell you everything then."

"Sure, but I hope you're not going to do something foolish… like getting mixed up with one of these drug gangs. I've been reading about the atrocities up north; it's unbelievable the depths they have sunken to. I get asked about it all the time by my parishioners."

"And what d'ya tell 'em…that God works in strange ways… that He shows us how much He loves us by arrangin' to have our heads cut off and rolled onto the nearest dance floor?"

Manuel pauses. "Still the skeptic, I see. I try to be a little more convincing than that. After all, you're forgetting that God gives us free will; if we choose to torture and kill our fellow humans, we have to suffer the consequences."

"Yeah, and the consequences are what…that we get sent to a Hell that is nothin' more than a figment of our imagination?"

"Hell needn't be a place that you go to; it can be right there in your own mind."

"You mean guilt, remorse…that kinda thing."

"Of course."

"Well, those aren't the only consequences…and that brings me to my project. Are you free this comin' weekend?"

"On Saturday, sure. On Sunday I have a few duties to perform (*laughing*)."

"Still fleecin' the innocent?"

"My assistants are actually the ones who take up the collection. I pretend to preach."

"O.K.…I'll get a mornin' flight…probably see you around 11:00. You be at the church…or should we make it Alfonso's Bar and Grill?"

"Church will be fine. Come around back. I'll be in my study."

"Great. See you there. Oh, and don't tell anyone I'm comin'."

"I don't like the sound of this, Duardo."

"Relax. You know what they say: Let Thy not my will be done."

As promised, Eduardo enters the church at 11:00. Once the study doors have been shut, he leans forward and begins his story. "You know where I work Manny…the PRG…we're the guys who go after the drug dealers…the capos who order the atrocities you been readin' about."

Manny shrugs his shoulders.

"Well, we got reason to believe that our boss, a guy named Luis Mendoza, is workin' for the cartels."

"What! Your own boss, the man who's supposed to lead the fight against all this terrorism, is actually on their payroll. That's hard to believe."

"Yeah."

"In confession I've heard some pretty depraved things but that's absolutely unconscionable. So, are you still working there?"

"Yeah, but things have changed."

"Does he know that you know? That could put you in real danger."

"No…and that brings me to our new project."

"You say 'our' project. Who else is involved?"

"So far, just me and my buddy, Sebastián. We're tryin' to recruit a few other guys…honest men we can trust…and go after the capos on our own."

"On your own…you mean without your boss knowing about it?"

"Exactly. I keep my job in the department and do our huntin' at night."

"But without all the intelligence that the PRG has access to, how are you going to locate these capos? You can't do it on your own, can you?"

"Good question. We have an informant, a woman nobody's ever seen, who's…I dunno what to call her…maybe like a psychic. I got no idea how she does it, but she knows how to find these guys without actually seein' 'em."

"That's amazing."

"She reports her guesses to a man in the D.E.A. over in El Paso, a guy named Bob Dunwoody. He's a good friend of mine; we play basketball together every week. So now, instead of passing this woman's info to Mendoza, he's gonna pass it to me. Once our team is ready, we'll use the info to go after Mata and other guys like him."

"So, where do I come in? You said on the phone you wanted some advice. Did I get that right?"

"Well maybe not so much advice as ideas. Do you know anyone around here who would fit into our plans?"

"You mean, someone who would be willing to join your new outfit?"

"Well yeah, somebody who's tough enough to risk his neck in a firefight."

"I assume you don't want a mercenary…someone who's willing to do it if you pay him."

"He's gotta be motivated by somethin' more than money. Maybe he's been hurt or seen people close to him gunned down by one of the gangs. Somebody with a chip on his shoulder."

"How old does he have to be?"

"I dunno…old enough to care about his country…maybe 18 or so. He can't be afraid to use a pistol either. This ain't gonna be no stroll in the park."

"You know how I feel about violence, Duardo."

"Yeah, I do, but sometimes the only way to stop violence is with violence, right? I don't see any other way outta this mess we're in."

"I don't either, but it still doesn't feel right to me."

"So, can you think of anybody?"

"Maybe…(*pause*)…There's this kid who I've gotten to know pretty well the last few weeks. I think he's from somewhere in Sinaloa. I saw him sitting in the back of the church after Sunday Mass. He was just sitting there, looking lonely and depressed, so I invited him to come back to my study where we could talk in private. I guess it's okay to tell you this since it wasn't given to me in confession; he just needed somebody to talk to. Apparently, he had run away from home and was living hand to mouth, you know, begging in the streets, sleeping on the ground. It took him a while to let it all out, but he finally told me that back home he agreed to work for one of the cartels, probably El Gordo's since it was in Sinaloa, and was ordered by his handlers to go into this shop and collect some money owed to the gang."

"Sounds like the old protection racket; several of the cartels are expandin' into that area."

"Precisely. Anyway, they gave him a pistol and told him to use it if the shop owner refused to pay up. To make things worse, the boy's girlfriend, a niece of the owner, came into the shop just as the boy was threatening the old guy. When the kid saw his girlfriend, he panicked and ran back to the car where the two handlers were waiting for him. The driver shouted at him, called him a chicken, then took his own pistol, went into the shop and promptly shot both the owner and the girl. When he got back to the car, he told the kid that El Gordo was going to kill him when he found out that he botched the job. That's when the boy took off…and after days of hitching rides and walking, ended up here at my church. I fed him and listened to his story. Now he's a regular member of our parish."

"So, you think he might be the kinda person I'm lookin' for?"

"I'm not sure, but he certainly has the motivation…girlfriend killed and a death threat from El Gordo hanging over him. At first what I saw was fear and loneliness. Now that we've gotten to know each other better, I'm beginning to see signs of something deeper and more powerful."

"Let me guess…anger."

"Yes, of course."

"So, what kind of plans does he have for the future?"

"He's itching to get on with his life but doesn't know where to go next. He can't go back to Sinaloa; they'll kill him if he does. He misses his parents but doesn't dare communicate with them. And he never did finish high school, so there aren't many opportunities for him here. In a word, he's stuck."

"Can I talk to him?"

"I think that would be alright. Why don't you come back here tomorrow morning; he usually drops by around 9:00."

"Okay. What's his name?"

"Jesús Bautista…*(pause)*…I assume you're going to spend the night at my place, yes?"

"Don't know if I can afford it (*grinning*)."

"We take Master Card or Visa (*smiling*)."

"Hmm…I may be maxed out."

"I'll take that chance."

When they meet the next day, Jesús proves to be more slender, even fragile, than Eduardo had imagined. "Are you getting' enough to eat?", he asks.

"I get by," the boy answers.

"You wanna talk over breakfast."

"Why not?"

Together they leave the church and head for the Primavera Restaurante across the way. Jesús orders jugo naranja, huevos Mexicana, pan dulce and café; Eduardo settles for café. Once the food is served, talking ceases while Jesús gulps down his food; Eduardo is content to sit and watch. Finally, when the waitress has taken away the last dish, Eduardo ventures a question, "Father Garcia, my brother, says you pretty angry about what happened in Sinaloa…any truth to that?"

"Maybe."

"Wanna tell me what happened?"

"Not really."

"Okay, maybe I'm askin' too many questions, but I wanna know how you feel about drug dealers, you know, like El Gordo and his gang."

"Why?"

"Cuz I'm lookin' for people who itch to get back at 'im. Thought you might be one."

Jesús looks around the restaurant, as if checking his safety. "What are ya goin' to do about it?"

"About El Gordo?"

"Well, yeah, him and other guys."

"I'm not gonna give you details until I'm sure you want in."

Jesús squints. "Want into what?"

"Let's call it a program; we're goin' after the drug lords on our own…this ain't no government agency…we ain't the police or military…just a bunch of guys who are tired of seein' people get murdered by the narcos and are willin' to risk their necks to stop it."

"You mean like the casino that got burnt down in Monterrey?"

"Yeah. Everybody screamin' about it, but so far they ain't arrested anybody."

Jesús sits up straight. "And they never will. The Zapa's are too smart. They got people inside the police to tip 'em off, so they never get caught."

"I agree. That's why we started this program; we're gonna bypass the police...get the job done on our own."

"But how you gonna do that? The capos have hundreds of guys workin' for 'em, all armed with AK-47's. They even have small airplanes; I seen 'em in Sinaloa."

"Yeah, I know. They even have submarines now, you know the small kind you can't see from a helicopter."

"How many guys in your 'program?'"

"I've just started to recruit; so far there's just me and my friend Sebastián. I'm hopin' to come up with three or four more."

Jesús scowls. "That ain't many. How you gonna get to these guys when they's surrounded by all them guards? How you even gonna know where to find 'em?"

"We have an informant; she's really good. We done a few tests already and so far she right every time."

"Right about what?"

"About where to find the target."

"Okay, so you know where they are; how you gonna get 'em? How you gonna get through all them guards?"

"We wait until they're in a place where they ain't many guards to protect 'em...like a restaurant or somebody's house. Probly at night; that' gonna be our best time to attack."

Eduardo can tell from Jesús's eyes that the boy is interested.

"What d'ya have for weapons?"

"About anything we need...AK-47s, pistols, rifles, grenade launchers, you name it."

Jesús's eyes widen. "Where you gonna get all this stuff?"

"Can't tell you that now. You just have to trust me."

"So, what d'ya want me to do?"

"Come back to Juárez with me; I can get you a place to live…and a small allowance for food and other stuff. Once I got everybody on board, we gonna train together…then when our informant locates a capo for us, we pounce…(*pause*)…Sound like somethin' you wanna be part of?"

"Yeah. When do we go?"

"Tomorrow morning. Meet me at the church at 8:00. I'll get you a plane ticket."

"Okay. But I wanna say goodbye to Father Garcia first."

"Sure, I do too."

"He done a lot for me."

"I understand."

Before leaving Oaxaca, Eduardo sits down with his brother and relates what happened at breakfast with Jesús…and ends by asking him if he too might be willing to join the team. Manny laughs. "I sympathize with your goals, Eduardo, but my calling is here at the church. As long as the people of Oaxaca need me, I want to stay here. But thanks for the offer." Eduardo and Jesús leave for Juárez later that day.

On the following Sunday, the Zapas post an announcement on the door of the Catedral de Oaxaca, Manny's church.

When did the priests ever help you? Come to People's Church on Hidalgo…free food and clothing. Service at 10:00 Sundays… Z

People stop to stare at the announcement; some get close enough to read it. There's just a Z at the end, but it's obvious what it stands for. One parishioner, a woman particularly devoted to Padre Garcia, rips the sign off the door and throws it into a nearby trash basket. She is unaware that she has been seen by a man sitting on a bench on the other side of the plaza. When the woman leaves, the man rises slowly, follows her through the zocolo…and waits until she turns the corner, then grabs her from behind, pulls her into an alley and slits her throat. As she lies dying, he uses the knife to cut a large Z on her forehead. Before the police can be summoned, the assassin runs down the street and disappears into a crowd of vendors. Headlines in the next day's papers lament the sacrilege; photos of the dead woman appear on television; some include the Z on her forehead.

The public is furious and demands action. Manuel, who counted this woman among the most devout of his parishioners, is crushed. When he visits her family to pay his respects, he is at a loss to explain how God allowed it to happen. Briefly, he even struggles with his own beliefs, some doubts appearing at the edge of consciousness. Gradually over the next few days, his sadness turns to anger…then fury. Unwilling to share his feelings with anyone else, he calls Eduardo up in Juárez.

"Did you read about Sofie Amarillo?" he asks.

"Yeah…I was gonna call you and see if yir okay"

"Well, I'm not okay; I'm so frustrated I can hardly eat or sleep. I need to do something but I don't know what to do."

"Well, Manny, my offer is still open."

"I've got to do something. I'd like to join you but there are all kinds of complications here at the church…(*pause*)…Let me think about it. I'll call you back when I've made a decision."

"Okay. No rush. The Z's aren't goin' away any time soon."

Three days and three sleepless nights later, the padre calls. "I've decided to join you, Duardo, if you'll still have me."

"That's great; when can you come up here?"

"I've already notified the bishop…took a while to convince him it was the right thing to do…but he gave me his blessing. I can pack a few things today and get a flight to Juárez tomorrow morning. There's one flight that arrives there at 11:20 A.M. Could you pick me up then?

"No problem. I'm really happy we're gonna be workin' together on this thing."

"I'm with you on that. By the way, how's Jesús doing? You get him a place to stay?"

"Oh yeah. He's got an apartment over on the east side; there's actually room enough for two, if you're interested? Of course, if you'd rather have a place of your own…"

(*Interrupting*) "The apartment sounds fine. Jesús might enjoy a little company; after all, the kid has been on his own for months now."

"I'll pick you up at 11:20 tomorrow."

"Great. One other thing. Have you managed to get the 'supplies' from your friend over in El Paso?"

"They're already sittin' in my garage…pistols, rifles, AK-47's…even grenade launchers."

"I've given this operation a little thought. How about night-vision goggles? They could come in real handy."

"Good idea. I'll order some. If you think of more we need, jis' let me know. My guess is that you're gonna be real good at this stuff."

"Thanks. See you tomorrow."

Chapter 10

The Video

Sebastián is sitting at his desk when the phone rings. "Hello, PGR, how may I help you?"

The woman on the other end asks, "Who is this?"

"My name is Sebastián Salazar." Silence. "You want to talk to someone else?"

Her voice is quivering. "I don't know."

"Are you in trouble?"

"What do you mean?"

"Well, we're a drug enforcement agency. Does your problem have anything to do with drugs?"

"I'm not a drug user, if that's what you mean."

Sebastian takes a deep breath. "Okay. So, you're not a user. Good. We couldn't help you if you were. That leaves several alternatives, all related to drugs: trafficking, assault, theft, and murder. Is it one of those?"

(*Sighing*) "No."

"Well. then, what is it?"

(*pause*) "I'm afraid to say."

"Why"

"I didn't call the police because I don't trust them. I'm not sure I can trust you."

"Hmm. What do I have to do to get you to trust me?"

(*Whispering*) "Tell me your mother's name."

"O.K...Reyna."

"Where does she live?"

(*Voice rising*) "What d'ya want to know that for?"

"I want to call her and ask her about you."

"For Christ's sake, lady, my mother doesn't want to get involved with my work here in the office."

"Yes, I know. But it's just a little call. I won't do it again."

"What are you going to say to her?"

"I'll just talk to her mother to mother. I'll ask her if you're a good boy...things like that."

(*Stifling a laugh*) "Well, okay, but please don't say anything to scare her. She hasn't been well lately."

"I promise."

"Okay. Her phone number is 353-1890."

"Thank you. If I find out I can trust you, I'll call back and tell you my problem."

"Alright. I'll be here for another three hours."

Sebastián is a year out of law school. His job at PGR is a relatively menial one given his education. He sees it, quite accurately, as a stepping stone to a policy-making position higher up in the Attorney General's office. The fact that he speaks fluent English as well as his native Spanish is a definite plus. Being tall and handsome is no handicap either. In the office, he is regarded as a rising star, on board for a year or two before moving on to better things. With his law school degree he could have worked just about anywhere in the government he wanted to. His choice of a drug enforcement agency reflects his deep concern about the mess his country is in and his desire to do something about it. Not everyone in the office at PGR agrees that Mexico is falling into chaos, but that doesn't keep him from arguing his case with anyone who will listen.Twenty minutes later the phone rings. When Eduardo goes to pick it up, Sebastián waves him off. "This is for me, a real weirdo. She called earlier…refused to tell me her problem until she talked to my mother."

"What?"

"Yeah, real crazy, huh? But who knows; it could be something interesting."

He picks up the phone. "Hello, Sebastián here."

"Hello, it's me again. Your mother was very friendly, said you've never been in trouble and that you have a good heart."

"Hmm. That was nice of her to lie like that."

(*Alarmed*) "Lie…what do you mean?"

"Relax…I was only kidding."

"Kidding…at a time like this? My son has been kidnapped. I just received a video…(*starts sobbing*)…"

"I'm sorry…tell me about it."

"It's a video of Artémio getting beaten by a man with a whip. He's in his shorts and has red welts all over his body. In the video he says, "Mama, please give them what they want; I want to come home.""

"What do they want?"

"One million dollars U.S. The voice says unless we give him the money, they're going to cut off Artémio's fingers, one by one."

"Did he mention a deadline...you know, a date by which you have to come up with the money?"

"Yes, next Friday."

"That gives us just five days."

"The voice said if we go to the police, they will kill my son and send us the body to prove it."

"That sounds like Zapa's work."

"It must be. They painted a Z on Artémio's forehead...with a magic marker or something."

"Well, that definitely makes it a drug-related case...so you've come to the right place Mrs...."

"Do I have to give you my name?"

"We can't proceed without it."

"How can I be sure these people won't find out I've told you?"

"I'm only going to share this information with the few people I can trust. I guarantee you they won't pass it on to anyone else."

She starts crying again. "They're monsters. Only someone without a soul would do something like this. My husband and

I can't bear to look at the video again; I've never seen my son so scared. And his fingers…they're threatening to cut off his fingers."

Sebastián shakes his head before continuing. "It's hard to believe someone could do that to an innocent kid. But hang on; we're going to find your son. Now, who have you told about the video besides your husband?"

"Nobody…just you."

"O.K. First thing I want you to do is promise you won't tell anyone else. This is extremely important. And I'm including anyone else in this office. If you need to talk to me again, do not…I repeat…do not leave a message with one of our secretaries. Try later or wait until I call you. Now tell me your name and how I can reach you."

"My name is Gloria, Gloria Lorenzo; my husband is Carmelo. I already told you our son's name, Artémio. We live at 31 Zaragoza Calle; you know where that is?"

"I can find it. But before we can go any further, I'll need a recent photo of your son…several photos if you have them. Okay?"

"Yes."

"Attach them to an e-mail and send them to me at Sebastián. Salazar@PGR.gov. Got that?"

"Yes. I wrote it down. But why do you need pictures of my son?"

"I can't tell you exactly, except to say they will help us find out where he is being held."

Gloria sighs audibly. "You must act quickly. He's in danger, right now."

"I understand; I'll make it top priority. That's a promise. In the meantime, it will help if I can see that video; it may contain clues about your son's whereabouts. Can I come to your place tomorrow morning and take a look?"

"Of course, but please don't wear your uniform. Someone may be watching."

"Good idea. I'll come by around 10:00; is that okay?"

"Yes, the earlier the better. My husband will be home too."

That night after dinner Sebastián withdraws to the living room. The kidnapping of the Lorenzo boy makes it impossible to think about anything else. As Sebastián watches his five-year old son, Miguel, play with his model cars, his earlier conversation with Señora Lorenzo returns to haunt him. In his imagination, it is his own son now who has been kidnapped. He pictures Miguel shielding his eyes, then screaming as a masked man lashes at him with a whip. The scene is brief but real enough to be terrifying. He leaps from the couch and takes the boy in his arms. His action is so sudden that it evokes a startled response from Ana, his wife.

"Sebastián," she shouts from the doorway, "What's the matter?"

Sebastián continues hugging his son but doesn't answer. Much better at reading minds than her husband is in concealing feelings, she asks, "Did something happen at work today, something awful?"

He hesitates, then yields to her question. "I can't tell you the details, but it was really scary. There's a woman who called… well, her boy is in trouble, real trouble. Let's leave it at that."

"You mean from the drug people?"

"Probably, yes."

"What kind of trouble?"

"I can't say…it might put you in danger if I told you."

"You're scaring me Sebastián. If it concerns our family, I think I have a right to know."

"Yes, but not if it puts you in danger."

"Is Eduardo involved in this too?"

"He will be, yes."

"Does his wife know about it?"

"Just general stuff, nothing specific. But he and I were talking about it the other day…before this phone call came in today… and we agreed that it might be best if our families spent some time with relatives, away from Juárez."

"So, it's that dangerous, dangerous enough to send us away."

"Yes. It could be."

"Well, I can take Miguel to Abuela's for a while…but how long do you think we should stay?"

"I don't know…maybe a few months…even a year or two."

"A year or two? That's crazy. When are we going to see each other?"

"Your mother's place is only an hour away; I can visit you on weekends."

"Sebastián, this is getting scary." She bites her lips. "Honey, you don't have to keep this job at PGR; with your law degree, you could get a safe position in Mexico City, no?"

"Probably, but there's not going to be any safe places left in Mexico if our government collapses. And that's possible. This is a real insurgency; the narcos are at the gate. They've already broken through in places. If we don't stop them now, they're going to turn Mexico into a jungle where everybody's got a gun and it's eat or be eaten."

Ana shudders, then turns and heads back into the kitchen. Early the next morning, Sebastián pays a call to the Lorenzo's home. The house is a large one, situated in the richest suburb of Juárez. It makes sense that the kidnappers asked for as much as they did. Gloria turns out to be a very pretty, petite woman of about 45; her husband, a darker-skinned man at least 6'4" and 300 pounds, towers over her. Sensing Sebastián's curiosity, Carmelo explains that years ago he emigrated to the U.S. from Jamaica to play football in the NFL. "I played for 10 years, mostly for the New England Patriots, then retired while I was still in one piece. That's when I met Gloria at a dinner party. So, I began spending summers in Mexico with her, finally moved here in 2000."

Once the formalities are out of the way, Sebastián asks to see the video. As soon as the disk is inserted in the DVD player, both parents retire to the kitchen. Just as Gloria said, the boy is in his underwear; there are red marks on several parts of his body. He is cringing as a man, his face concealed, gets ready to lash him with a whip. *This is hard to believe,* he murmurs, as the hideous drama unfolds on the TV screen. Half way through, he reaches out and turns the sound down so that the parents won't hear the boy's cries. As soon as it ends, he plays it again, looking carefully this time for evidence that might indicate where the scene was shot. The smallness of the room and peeling paint around two windows are suggestive of a lower-middle class neighborhood. There are also hints of other people in the room besides the boy and the man with the whip. He turns off the player and calls out to the parents: "Is it okay if I take this back to the office? We've got a guy there who is good at analyzing things like this. I'm sure he'll be able to tell us something about where the video was shot."

"Of course," Señora Lorenzo answers, returning to the living room. "But I hope you don't have to leave so soon. We have more to talk about."

"Oh no, I didn't mean to go…just wanted your okay about the video."

"So, what else would you like to know?", she says, taking a seat on the couch.

Sebastián pauses before continuing. "Well, for one thing, do you have any other children who might be at risk?"

"I have another boy from an earlier marriage…Felipé," she answers, clasping Carmelo's hand. "But he's a lot older than Artémio."

"Does he live here in Juárez?"

She hesitates, then looks at Carmelo. "Yes."

"Really…I didn't know that," her husband says, turning to face her. "Why didn't you tell me?"

"Well, it's another man's son, so I thought you might not like knowing too much about him."

"But I am interested. After all, he's my step-son."

"Well, what would you like to know about him?"

Carmelo pauses. "I know that you gave him away when he was three and that you saw him a few times after that."

Gloria begins sobbing, then turns to Sebastián. "I was so poor back then; my first husband left me and I couldn't feed

Felipé, so I gave him to a friend who was married and lived in a nice house." She leans back in her chair, her eyes half-closed. "I promised not to interfere, not even to see him…but I couldn't help it. Many times I waited outside his new mother's house and tried to talk to him but he just pushed me away. Later, when he started school, I waited for him in the playground but he still wouldn't talk to me. All he said was, 'Leave me alone.'"

Carmelo pats her hand. "He was still angry that you gave him away?"

"I'm sure that was it. So, I stayed away, at least I didn't try to talk to him anymore. Instead, I bought little things for him and left them on the front porch where he lived. I hoped that as he matured he would see that I had to give him up…for his sake."

"Did he eventually forgive you?", Carmelo asks

"Not really. In all these 19 years, he has never spoken to me." (*Trembling*) "He doesn't know that I follow him around sometimes, watching while he plays soccer or baseball over at the Santara playground. I even followed him in my car one day, just to find out where he lives. It's way out in the country. He doesn't seem to have a wife or girlfriend. That makes me sad… you know, that maybe he can't trust a woman anymore."

"Where does he work?", Carmelo asks.

"At the police station. I don't know what he does there; I've never seen him in a uniform."

"Sounds like we don't have to worry about Felipé," Sebastián offers.

"Well, no," Gloria replies. "It's Artémio we're worried about."

Carmelo takes her hand again. "So, Sebastián, what should we do? I don't like the idea of giving up a million dollars after breaking my neck for 10 years to earn it, but I'm ready to hand it over if that's the only way to get our son back."

Sebastián shakes his head. "There's no guarantee you'll get Artémio back in one piece even if you give them the money. These guys are not human; there are no limits to what they're willing to do…(*pause*)…Give us a chance to find out where they're holding him; if we can't come up with anything by Friday, stall them. Tell them anything, but get us a few more days. What we need most of all is time…especially time for our informant to find out where they're keeping the boy. Once we locate him, we have the means for going in there and taking out his captors."

(*Squinting*) Carmelo asks, "How is she going to find out where he is?"

"She has her ways. For one thing, she'll take a careful look at the video and draw some conclusions from that."

Carmelo shakes his head. "Now that Artémio's in the hands of those savages, every minute counts. Friday's only three days away."

"I know. Back at the office, we've already started our search. This video should give us more clues. I'll call you as soon as we've got something to report. In the meantime, as I told your wife earlier, it's best if you don't try to call me…you know, for security reasons…unless you have some new information."

Carmelo asks, "What do we do if they contact us again?"

"Tell them you're getting the money together and should have it soon. Stall them. Remind them it takes time to get a million dollars together; you have to sell stocks and bonds, redeem CDs, etc."

Sebastián rises and goes to the door. Carmelo follows, then extends his hand, "Thanks for coming."

"Good to meet you two," Sebastián replies. "Keep your chin up. We're going to find your boy."

"I hope you're right," Gloria whispers. "I pray every day. I hope you do too."

Sebastián, a confirmed agnostic, is about to shake his head, then changes his mind. "I'll do my best," he answers, then leaves.

Chapter 11

Peaches

Later in the day Sebastián shares everything he knows about the kidnapping with his partner Eduardo Garcia who immediately calls Dunwoody to arrange a meeting. Although he has never met Eduardo's friend, Sebastián is invited to come along. That evening the three of them go over the photos of Artémio that Gloria e-mailed. Once everybody has a good idea of what the boy looks like, they turn on the DVD player and insert the disk. Before hitting the start button, Sebastián warns Bob that this is not something he would want his kids to see. Acting on Sebastián's advice, Bob asks his wife to take the two boys upstairs. The three men then play the video in complete silence. By the end of the disk, heads are shaking but nothing is said. As they play it a second time, Bob points out some of the same things that Sebastián saw back at the Lorenzo's house…physical signs of a working class setting. That can be used to rule out certain neighborhoods when talking to the informant. When they play it a third time, Sebastián stops the disk, runs it backward for several seconds, then says, "Do you see what I see…that thing on the guy with the whip? They were careful not to include his face, but his hand and lower arm are showing. He's got a tattoo on his right arm, just above his wrist. If we could magnify it, we might learn what it says…(*pause*)…anybody know how to magnify a video?"

Bob shrugs his shoulders. "Well, I've got a magnifying glass in my office. Want me to get it?"

"Eduardo shakes his head. "Naw. Your office is too far away…we don't have enough time now. Maybe tomorrow."

"No," says Dunwoody. " I mean my home office upstsairs. Let me get it."

When they examine the tattoo with the magnifying glass, they agree that it's a snake, probably meant to be a rattler. Bob looks at the other two, then asks, "What kind of guy would have that inked onto his arm, right where people can see it?"

"Somebody who's not all that anxious to make friends," offers Sebastián.

"An ornery prick, I'd say," adds Eduardo. "He's sendin' a message, 'Don't mess with me. I can bite…and my bite is poisonous.'"

Well," says Bob, "it certainly fits what he's doing in the video, whipping that poor kid. Okay, our next step is obvious…get in contact with our informant, give her the info we've uncovered and let her zero in on the kid's whereabouts. Trouble is, I have no way of contacting her; we have to wait until she calls me." The meeting breaks up with Bob promising to call Eduardo as soon as he hears from the informant.

Jessica is reading the evening newspaper when the phone rings. The caller I.D. indicates it's Ned. "Hi Jess, it's yours truly. Did you see the report about the CEO who was kidnapped and had four fingers cut off before the police nabbed the guys who did it?"

"I was just reading about it, Ned. It's horrible?"

"Yeah, it looks like the Zapa's are branching out into kidnapping…like they aren't making enough money with narcotics. I hear they're moving into the extortion racket as well…you know…making business people pay for 'protection.'"

"Protection against what?"

"Rival gangs, I guess. It's gotten so bad in Juárez that lots of owners have stopped asking the police for help. The Zapa's are now providing the protection that the police are supposed to provide." "Yes, that's scary. Lloyd says it's a sign that law and order are breaking down in Mexico."

"I agree. Mexico is on the verge of descending into chaos… of becoming a failed state."

"I just hope it doesn't spill over into our country."

"So far it hasn't, but it's going to be hard to keep the violence out…(*pause*)…Would you and Lloyd like to come over for dinner tomorrow night?"

"Sure. What are you serving?"

"I don't know; we'll dig up something."

(*Laughing*) "What's the matter; your refrigerator broken?"

"Nope…just forgot to pay the bill last month."

"Oh dear. We better have a burger before we come over."

(*Chuckling*) "I understand. Just leave a little room for dessert."

"Okay. See you at the usual time?"

"Sevenish?"

"Thanks."

With nothing else demanding her attention, Jessica returns to the paper and rereads the article about kidnapping. The story of the man who lost his fingers is so vile as to turn her stomach. When she finally calms down, she closes her eyes and begins murmuring, *Where are you, Mata? Where are you?* Minutes later, an image forms before her. She can see a bed…someone lying down…maybe someone next to him. In vain, she looks for other clues. Frustrated, she shouts, "Is this a home…a hotel…I can't tell. I know you're there but where is it?" Startled by her own words, she opens her eyes, then reaches for the phone and dials Bob Dunwoody's number. Before he can answer, she slams the phone back down. "No, not from my home," she cries. "I've got to find a public phone." Just as Lloyd is entering the house, home from his day at the university, she dashes out the door, shouts a hasty hello and jumps into her car. A half an hour later, she is on the phone with Dunwoody. "It's got to be some kind of hotel or maybe his home. I don't know."

"Hmm. That's really not enough to go on, I'm afraid. But look, there's something more important that deserves your attention."

"More important than finding Mata?"

"Yes…at least right now. A boy has been kidnapped, probably by the Zapa gang, and the thugs who took him threaten to kill him if the parents don't come up with a million dollars by next Friday. They're already torturing the kid with a whip. You can see it all on a video they sent to the parents, showing the boy covered with welts and bruises and crying for his mother."

"Oh my God. How can I help?"

"We need you to locate the boy for us before this goes any further. I guess I didn't mention that they're going to start cutting off his fingers, one by one, until the parents pay."

"Oh, those poor parents. They must be beside themselves."

"Yes. Look, is there some way I can get photos of the boy to you; the video too? The video probably contains clues as to where the kid is being held."

"You certainly can't send them to my house, but there may be somewhere else where I could pick them up without being seen."

"Just tell me where. I can have them there either tonight or early tomorrow morning. We don't have much time."

"Let me think…(*pause*)…How about somewhere in the park? You know, Addison Park near mid-town El Paso."

"Okay. Where?"

"There's a grove of trees…piñon pines I think…right behind the big fountain where all the paths meet in the middle. Do you know the place?"

"Yes. I've been there many times with my kids."

"Alright. To the…let's see …north of the fountain, there's a big tree with a message carved into its bark. It says 'J.F. loves G.H.'"

"How far from the fountain is it?"

"Well, the grove of trees starts about 20 feet from the fountain, and the tree I'm talking about is a few feet further in from the edge. Leave the package right behind the tree. Nobody will see it." "

"Got it. I'll go up there first thing in the morning and drop the stuff off. When can you pick it up?"

"Is nine o'clock too late?"

"No. Perfect…(*pause*)…One little question: those aren't your initials on the tree, are they?"

"Good heavens, no. I just happen to remember them from my high school days. They were both friends of mine. Now, I've got one question for you. You aren't going to stay behind and follow me, are you?"

"Of course not…scout's honor."

"Were you a boy scout?"

"No. But my sister used to sell girlscout cookies (*chuckling*)."

"Oh, that's very reassuring."

"Look it…I know damn well that if you found out I was following you, you'd stop helping us. I can't take that chance since you represent the best chance, maybe the only chance, we have of finding this boy before they start cutting off his fingers."

"Well, you're right. The minute I get the feeling you're trying to find out who I am, you and I are finished."

"Okay. Call me when you've come up with something on this boy. By the way, his name is Artémio, if that's any help."

"It might be; I don't know."

"Another thing: I'm aware you don't want me to know your name and I respect that, but I need some kind of handle for you when I'm discussing your input with my associates. So, how shall I refer to you?"

Jessica pauses. "How about Peaches?"

(*Chuckling*) "Okay. Peaches. Bye for now."

Chapter 12

A Call

"**H**e just called," Gloria whispers, her voice still trembling.

"The kidnapper?" asks Sebastián.

"Yes. He reminded me that we've got two more days. He said that if he didn't get the money by Friday noon, they would start cutting Artémio's fingers." When she breaks down, sobbing, Carmelo can be heard whispering something to her in the background. She stops to blow her nose. "Oh, and if that wasn't bad enough, the man went on to ask if Artémio was right-handed or left-handed. I was afraid to answer…how you answer a question like that knowing what they might do? So, I didn't say anything. He waited, then said, 'Okay. If you ain't gonna tell me, we'll start with his right hand.' I gasped, almost fainted I think. That's when Carmelo grabbed the phone and shouted something at the man…said he was going to kill him with his bare hands. The man said nothing at first… Carmelo held the phone so I could hear too…then came the words I dreaded. He said, 'Sounds like he's right-handed. We don't wantcha to think we're cruel or anything, so we're gonna start with his left hand.' Carmelo yelled again, 'What are you, some kind of savage? He's just a kid, an innocent kid.' I could hear the man better this time, He said, 'If ya don't get the money to us by noon on Friday, we're gonna make you a little present. Go to St. Paul's church at the corner of Monteño and Rio. On the lawn outside, near the statue of the angel, you gonna find a small plastic bag. It's a gift; take it home and put it on the kid's dresser.' Then he hung up."

Sebastián waits until the sobbing stops. "This guy is really sick…to say something like that…I mean, he's not even human. Now I've got a couple of questions. First, where did he say to leave the money?"

"He didn't. He said he'd give us directions when we're ready to hand over the money."

"What did you say about the deadline?"

"Carmelo told him he's still working on it."

"Okay, second question. What did the man sound like? Could you tell anything from his voice, his accent, the kind of language he used?"

"He sounded kind of rough; you wouldn't hear people in this neighborhood talk that way."

"Where would you be likely to hear that kind of language?"

"Well, I'd say he talked the way men talk back in the village where I used to live."

"You mean, where you lived with your first husband."

"Yes. It was a pretty rough neighborhood. Lots of violence. You had to be careful where you walked."

"So, the voice was familiar…I mean, the way he talked, the way he pronounced words."

"I'd say so, yes."

"Okay. We're getting ready to move…just waiting to hear from our informant. Should be any time now."

"Why don't you just call him?; maybe he doesn't realize how urgent this is."

"I can't call; it's too dangerous. We just have to wait. I'll let you know the minute we hear. It can't be long now."

"Are you praying?"

"I'm working on it. Goodbye Gloria."

It's Commandant Mendoza for you, sir. Do you want to take the call?"

"Yes. Put 'im on."

"Hola, Bob, Luis here. Catch any banditos lately (*chuckling*)?"

"A few...always room for more though...why, you got somebody you want to hand over?"

"Not right now...but maybe soon. But hey Bob, you remember I ask you about makin' a recording of that woman's voice."

"I remember."

"Well, you ready to do it next time she calls?"

"Okay. If you think it's really necessary."

"Well, it seems like she right sometimes, wrong sometimes. I wanna know where she gets information; is she workin' undercover for somebody...or maybe freelancin', you know, workin' alone, doin' it for money."

"I don't know how you're going to figure that out from listening to her voice, but I can record our next conversation if you think it will help. Right now, I don't know any more about her than you do, even though I've talked to her several times."

"Gracias, Bob, much appreciated. Just put it on CD and send it over. I'll recommendyou for Purple Heart."

"You get a Purple Heart when you're wounded in battle."

"Okay. So, make it bouquet of flowers, yes."

"You're too kind, Luis,"

"My mama's influence. She was saint. Goodbye Bob."

"Bye Luis."

Dunwoody's secretary announces that there's a woman on the phone who won't give her name. "Don't worry; I won't listen," she adds (*giggling*)."

"It's hardly that," her boss replies, then waits until he hears her put down the phone before identifying himself to the caller.

"Dunwoody here…Peaches?"

"Yes. Is this a good time to talk?"

"It is. But before we start, I have a little favor to ask of you. We have someone in the Mexican drug enforcement community who is trying to find out who you are. We are convinced that he's on the Zapa's payroll…so we don't want to tell him anything important. But we need to string him along, make him believe that we're cooperating with him. Given his curiosity about you, one way to do that is to let him hear a recording of your voice."

"I can't do that, Bob. He'll hear what I say about Mata and warn him."

"Not if we make a special recording, which we can do today, in which you concoct a fictitious report about Mata's whereabouts."

"You mean, just make up something?"

"Yeah. Then, afterwards, you can call me back and we'll talk about real stuff. Okay?"

"I guess so, although I don't feel comfortable with all this secrecy."

"Because?"

"Because he might use the recording to find out who I am and where I live. That sort of thing."

"I don't see how that's possible. The only thing real will be your voice; everything else is a charade."

"Hmm. Have you ever played charades?"

"Not really…just heard about the game." "Well, I played it a lot when I was a kid and you can tell a lot from a person's gestures. My guess is that a voice can be just as revealing. But maybe I'm being paranoid. Am I?"

"A little perhaps."

Jessica lets out a long sigh. "Alright. Let's do it. Do you want me to call you back right now?"

"Yes. Make up a phony story about Mata…you know, where he is, and so on. You can even let on that you got this information in a trance. He won't know what to do with that."

"How shall I identify myself when I call?"

"Just say it's Peaches. That'll really throw him off."

"Okay. I'm going to hang up now."

"Yup. Just remember to call back when you've finished so we can have a real talk that won't be recorded."

Minutes later, the phone rings. "Hello Bob, it's Peaches. I've got something for you."

"About Mata?"

"Yes. It was definitely Mata in the trance."

"Okay. Let me hear it."

"Right now he's in a car heading west out of Juárez."

"What road.?" " I can't be sure…but it could be Highway 73. It looks like he's heading for Tijuana."

"Hmm. That could mean he's meeting with the Obregon Bros."

"Is that important?"

"Yes, it's possible they're tired of fighting each other and have agreed to divide up the territory between Juárez and Tijuana. Good work. I'll pass this on to Mendoza as soon as we get off the phone."

"Okay. Always glad to help. By the way, do you want the video back? I have no further use for it. What they did to the boy made me sick. I couldn't watch it a second time."

Dunwoody grimaces. "Ah no, chuck it. It's not important."

"Okay, bye."

Thirty seconds later, Bob's phone rings. It's Peaches again.

"Did you shut off the recording?"

"Yes."

"Was I okay?"

"You were great, at least right up to the end. What you said about Mata was terrific. As far as I could tell, you didn't give him anything of value; in fact, you probably sent him off a wild goose chase. … (*pause*)… It probably would have been better, however, if you hadn't mentioned the video. Let's hope Mendoza has no idea what you were referring to. It's unlikely that he knows anything about the kidnapping since there's no reason for the PGR to get involved."

Sorry about that. I just wasn't thinking. Now, do you want to hear what I originally called you about?"

"Of course, but first, did the photos and video help at all."

"They did."

"Pretty gruesome, I mean the video."

"Really gruesome. I almost threw up."

"I understand. I had a similar reaction. You say you have some new info for me?"

"Yes. I haven't been able to think about anything else since I saw the video. My first attempt to locate Artémio produced nothing, but I did get something on my second try. I saw a small square building with windows…most likely a house… and behind the house was a larger building with no windows but a huge door. Right next to the large building was a tower of some sort."

"You mean pointed like the Eiffel tower?"

"No, rounded like a cylinder."

"Hmm. Could it be a silo…you know, the kind of thing they store grain in?"

"Could be. The whole scene was more rural rather than urban."

"Like a farm or ranch."

"Possibly, yes."

"Well, it might be safer to hide somebody out in the sticks than in town where you could be seen…(*pause*)…Anything else?"

"No, That's it. I'll keep trying. If I pick up anything new, I'll call you."

"Okay. Thanks."

Chapter 13

The Raid

Still excited about his call with Peaches, Dunwoody calls Eduardo and arranges a meeting for tonight. "I've got some new info," he says. "It could be interesting. Bring Sebastián over to my place and we'll talk."

Eduardo tightens his grip on the phone. "How about if I bring our two new members...my brother Manny and his friend, Jesús?"

"You're willing to vouch for these guys? "

"Absolutely."

"So, you now have a team of four?"

"Yeah. We need at least one more guy, maybe two."

"How about right now? Can the four of you move on this info I just got?"

"Depends. As long as nobody knows we're comin', the four of us could be enough."

"Well, these guys who kidnapped Artémio are probably well-armed. There's no way of knowing how many will be there, but even if there only a few, getting the kid out of there ain't going to be any picnic."

"Let's find where the kid is, then I can tell if four of us is goin' to be enough."

"Okay. Can you get over here in an hour?"

"Sure. See you then."

Eduardo calls Manny and Jesús to tell them the news. "We got a lead on where they're holdin' the kid, you know, the kid on the video. I'll be around to pick you up in a half an hour. Bring your weapons and don't forget your night goggles. We're movin' out." He checks next on Sebastián at the office. "We gotta go right now. Bob's informant just called with info about a target. We're meetin' at Dunwoody's place for a briefin', so you and I gotta get home and pick up our gear."

"What are we going to tell Mendoza? It's only 4:00; he'll think it strange if we leave so early."

"I'll tell his secretary there's a problem at the car pool and we gotta straighten things out."

Sebastián sighs. "Sounds a tad fishy."

"Probly, but nothin' else come to me." As Eduardo rises to leave, Sebastián calls out. "Hey, I need to make a quick call first. I told the Lorenzo's I'd let 'em know when we got our first lead."

"Can't that wait?"

"No, they deserve to be in on whatever we're doing. Don't you agree?"

"Okay. but make it snappy."

"Hello."

"Señora Lorenzo, it's Sebastián at PRG. I can't talk but just wanted to let you know we've got a lead on your son's whereabouts and we're going to check it out right now."

"Oh, that's wonderful. I want to come with you. And Carmelo too."

Sebastián coughs. "I'm afraid that's too dangerous, Señora. If we find the kidnappers, there will probably be some shooting. We don't want you to get hurt. Besides there's not enough room in the van for the four of us and our gear plus you and your husband."

"How about just me? Carmelo can go some other time." Her voice is pleading. "After all, you promised me earlier that I could help." "I did? Well, alright. We'll stop at your house some time during the next hour. Please be ready."

"Thank you, Señor Salazar. You won't be sorry."

"I hope not."

When the whole group (now including Gloria) has been assembled at Dunwoody's house, the host calls them into his living room and lays out the plan. "According to our informant, Señora Lorenzo's boy is being held somewhere outside the city… in what appears to be a rural area. That's not very specific, I know, but there are only two areas outside Juárez that can be considered rural. On the north side of town is the U.S. border… so that's out. And on the East side you've got light industry stretching for at least 10 miles. That leaves south and west. I say we start this evening scanning the area to the south. There's still plenty of light left to make out the size and shape of buildings. According to Peaches…yes, that's what she calls herself…what you're going to be looking for is a small square house with a large barn out back. Next to the barn is a silo…or something that looks like a silo. At this time of day, the buildings should be visible from the road. Any questions?"

Señora Lorenzo is the first to speak. "What are we going to do if we find it?" "Sergeant Garcia and I have already gone over this in some detail. He'll instruct you if and when you find the target. Remember, he's in charge here. You must do what he says."

"But what about me?", she asks. "How can I help?"

"You?...(*chuckling*)...Just stay in the van and don't let anybody steal it. Okay. Time to go. Let's use every bit of daylight we can."

Eduardo and Sebastián take the two front seats...with Manny, Jesús, and Señora Lorenzo in the rear. The men are all wearing black fatigues; each has a pistol saddled with a silencer. The rear of the van is packed with two rifles, a grenade launcher, extra ammunition, and four sets of night-vision goggles. As the van heads south, Eduardo takes the opportunity to go over assignments. "If we find the house, we'll park somewhere outta sight and wait 'til it gets dark. If we see armed guards out front, then we know we got the right place. It'll be up to our marksman, Jesús, to take these guys out with his rifle. (*turning to face Jesús*) Just be sure your sight's attached nice and firm."

"No problema."

Eduardo continues. "But maybe they don't wanna attract attention, so they keep their guards inside the house. In that case, we gotta get up close and peek through the window. What we do next depends on what we see inside. If we see the kid, Manny and Jesús will go in through the front door while Sebastián and I fire through the window. Just wait for my signal before doin' anything."

"You're not going to fire when Artémio is in there, are you?", Gloria asks, making no attempt to conceal her anxiety.

Sebastián quickly answers for his partner. "We'll do whatever is necessary to rescue your son, Señora. I assure you that his safety is our top priority."

For the next two hours they scan one road after the other. Sebastián holds a map in his lap and directs traffic. "The idea is to do this systematically," he says, as he runs a magic marker through each road they've tried.

"Still, no small square house with barn and silo." Manny says, "Most of the haciendas around here have large sprawling casas. A small farm like the one we're looking for may be wedged in between two haciendas….and hard to see from the main road. Besides, a small house like that may have been abandoned when NAFTA came along and everybody had to move to the city."

Eduardo looks back at his brother. "So, you're sayin'…what?"

"That we should drive down some of these small roads… and keep our eyes peeled for something that looks run-down. With nobody around to keep the farm up, the barn may even have collapsed by now."

With that thought in mind, Eduardo begins looking for small side roads that fit Manny's hunch. Some of them are not marked on Sebastián's map, requiring him to pencil in each road they try. After two hours of searching, the light becomes too dim to make out buildings from the road.

"If we go any further," Eduardo announces, "we might miss our target. Better to come back tomorrow and try again."

"I think you're right, Duardo," replies Manny. "I know time is of the essence but since we're only going down each road once, it would be tragic to miss our target because it was too dark to see. Why don't we wait until tomorrow?"

When everyone agrees, they head back to town, stopping to drop off Señora Lorenzo at her house and Manny and Jesús at their apartment. Sebastián accompanies Eduardo to the PGR office where he left his car. Eduardo agrees to pick everybody up again tomorrow night at 5:00.

The following evening, Eduardo makes the rounds again. He waits until the whole group has been assembled before speaking. "Okay…tonight, we try the area west of town. It's all farmin' and ranchin' out there…or at least it used to be. Should be lots of old haciendas…and not many people. Good place to hide if yir up to some kinda dirty business."

Sebastián circles the area on his map and marks the first road to be explored. "Let's try Benito Juárez Avenida; it's the first road on the right after the cemetery. Should have some side roads branching off of it."

As they head for Benito Juárez, Señora Lorenzo taps Eduardo on the shoulder. "This informant…the one you call Peaches…how does she know where my son is? How can a person know something like that? Does she have spies…or is it some kind of magic?"

Eduardo turns to Sebastián. "Your turn, buddy."

Sebastián smiles. "Thanks, friend. Well, some of it's secret. She doesn't want everybody to know how she does it. But I can tell you this: she does it on her own…no spies, no mysterious technology…just intuition."

"How much did you tell her about Artémio?"

"Just that he's 16, still in high school, lives up on Zaragoza Calle…and that he is much loved by you and his father, Carmelo. That's all I really know about him…(*pause*)…Why do you ask?"

"I just wanted to be sure it was accurate. That's all."

"It was, wasn't it?"

"Yes…as far as it goes."

Sebastián turns around so he can see Gloria's face. "What do you mean?"

"Nothing, really. Let's keep looking."

When Benito Juárez Avenida yields nothing of interest, Sebastián looks at his map and points over to the left. Let's try that side road over there. It's pretty long and could have some houses or farms we can't see from here."

The road turns out to be dirt and has numerous potholes, a threat to anyone foolish enough to drive more than 10 miles an hour. Before they can go very far, Gloria stares out the window and shouts, "I know this road; I came here once when I was following Felipé, my older son. I just wanted to find out where he lived."

"He lives here?", Eduardo asks.

"Yes, I'm pretty sure…a little further down, over on the right. But this lady…Mrs. Peaches…she musta made a mistake. I think she got my two sons mixed up. This is where Felipé lives, not where we're going to find Artémio."

Sebastián squirms in his seat. "But how could she make such a mistake, Gloria? I never mentioned Felipé to Bob Dunwoody when we got together to look at the video. It didn't seem important. So, he couldn't have told Peaches."

"Well, maybe she was tryin' to use her magic and got the two sons mixed up. I don't know. But I tell you; we're not goin' to find Artémio here. So, we might as well turn around and look somewhere else."

Eduardo looks over at Sebastián who shrugs his shoulders.

"I don't know, boss; do what you think best."

Eduardo looks back at his brother, expecting some kind of comment. When he hears nothing, he throws up his hands and begins looking for a place to turn around. Jesús, whose experience since leaving home has forced him to think for himself, is unconvinced. As Eduardo begins turning into a driveway, the boy shouts, "Look…over there…at the end of the driveway…d'ya see that white house? It's got a big barn out back…and that thing you put grain in."

"Yes," says Gloria. "Like I told you, that's Felipé's house. But let's not disturb him. I see a car in the driveway, so he's home."

"There's more than one car," says Jesús, looking out the window.

"Yeah. Maybe we better not turn around here…just back up and drive by," says Eduardo. "We don't want to draw any attention."

"But why don't we just go back to the main road and keep looking?", Gloria asks.

Eduardo turns to Sebastián. "What do you think, buddy?"

"Where d'ya wanta go?"

"Why don't we go down this dirt road for a bit, then turn around and park. We wait until it gets dark, then send somebody back here to look around…see if they any guards hangin' around outside…maybe take a peek through a window."

"That's a real impolite thing to do, spyin' on somebody like that," Gloria says. "Besides, if Felipé is in there and sees you, he might think you're a robber. And then what? Remember, he works in the police station, so he might shoot you."

Eduardo smiles. "I don't know. Sebastián is right. We come all this way…maybe we otta take a peek. If we're wrong, we apologize and get outta there pronto."

"At the very least, Sebastián says, "I think we should stick around long enough to check the place out. Peaches was right on when she saw a square house with barn and silo. That in itself is nothing short of miraculous. Maybe Artémio isn't here, but we shouldn't leave without making sure."

Eduardo nods his approval. "So, you wanna go down the road a bit, then turn around and park?"

"Yeah, then wait until it's dark and send a coupla guys up there to look around. All agreed?"

"Sounds good to me," says Manny.

"I wanna be one of the snoopers," says Jesús.

"Yir on," replies Eduardo.

As the van heads down the road, Gloria shakes her head. "Artémio's not there, I know it. We're just going to make trouble."

Without answering, Eduardo turns the van around and parks. Everyone is silent as they wait for the sky to darken. Once the moon can be seen rising in the east, Jesús and Manny get out and creep up to the driveway leading to the small square house. As agreed, Jesús takes the back of the building, Manny the front. Ten minutes later they return to the van to report.

"They ain't no guards anywhere…at least we couldn't see any," Jesús says, his excitement showing.

"Okay," says Eduardo, "time to move closer." He turns on the ignition but keeps the headlights off as the van creeps up the driveway and stops. Conversation ceases as all five passengers peer out the window at the house with a barn and silo out back, now just 50 yards away. There is a light on in the living room; the upstairs is dark.

"Okay," says Eduardo. "Everybody grab a rifle from back of van; make sure the pistols loaded. And take night-goggles if there ain't enough light comin' from the house. Jesús and Manny...take position near front door, jis' to left of the porch. Sebastián...go 'round back and keep an eye on the rear door. I'm gonna sneak closer and peek through the livin' room window; it's the only light on in the house, so if they got the boy, that's where he's gonna to be. And if he's in there, we're goin' in after him."

"Okay, but how will we know when to storm the place?", asks Manny..

"Wait until you hear my shot before breakin' in. I'm gonna fire only if boy is in there and I can take out anybody who's guardin' 'im. Gloria, you stay here in van. Keep doors locked in case somebody comes by."

As Jesús and Manny take up their positions in front and back, Eduardo creeps up to the living room window. When he peers inside, he sees two Latino men, a big beefy guy drinking beer and apparently watching television. His partner, a slender man of about 30 who wears his hair in a pony tail, is thumbing through a magazine. As Eduardo watches, a third man comes in from the kitchen, holding a pastry. He's in his late 20's and wearing a short sleeve shirt. The man appears to have some kind of tattoo on his right arm, just above his wrist. As Eduardo leans forward to see the patch, he almost touches the window. "My God," he whispers. "That looks like the tattoo in the video." He takes the rifle off his shoulder and continues looking for Artémio. When he can't see all parts of the room, he moves to a second window. The view is better but there's still no sign of the boy. He slings the rifle on his shoulder and moves back from the house. When he takes several steps, he stumbles into someone. He grabs his pistol and whirls around to face the intruder. It's Gloria. "My God, you scared me. I told ya stay in the van."

"Yes, but I thought I could help if I came with you."

"How you goin' to help us?"

"If there are some men in there, I can tell you if one of them is Felipé."

"Okay." Eduardo leads her up to the window. "When I looked a minute ago, I see three men."

Before peering inside, she turns to face Eduardo. "I don't think it's right to spy on people like this, do you?"

"Usually, no…but tonight's different. We're tryin' to save your son. If he's in there, we gotta go in after him."

"Alright, let me see." She stands on her tiptoes to take a look. "There are only two men, not three like you said. Felipé isn't there."

As she steps away from the window, a light suddenly goes on upstairs. Gloria grabs Eduardo's arm. "The other man, the one you saw, must have just gone upstairs." They retreat further out onto the grass to get a better view of the upstairs. A man can be seen moving across the room, but he is too far away to identify. It is clear, however, that he is holding a whip.

Suddenly there's a scream from upstairs. Gloria stifles a cry. "Shh," says Eduardo. "They might hear you."

"But it's my boy," she cries. "It's Artémio! I know it." When she begins running toward the front door, Eduardo runs to catch her but slips on the grass. Frantic to get inside, she runs up onto the porch and pushes the door open. On a signal from Eduardo, Manny races to stop her but she's too fast. Once inside, she heads for the stairs and starts climbing.

Her entrance does not go unnoticed. The beefy guy in the living room quickly rises from his chair, reaches for his AK-47, and heads for the stairs. Before he can get there, Manny, who is right behind Gloria, steps into the house, whirls to his right, and fires at the man with the machine gun. The man drops to the floor before he can get a shot off. Awakened by the sound, the man with the pony tail begins firing his machine gun even before he can see the intruder. Manny waits until the shots stop, then spins around the corner and drops the man to his knees with a quick volley. When the man tries to fire back, he stumbles, unable to hold his gun steady, spraying shots all over the wall and ceiling.

The upstairs lights suddenly go out. Alerted by the noise, the man with the whip grabs Artémio by the hand and yanks him toward the staircase. Half-way down the stairs he collides with Gloria and knocks her over. He stands for a moment, staring… trying to figure out who it is. When she looks up at him, she gasps, "Felipé…it's you!" He stops and snarls, "Get outta my way", then turns to go. Immediately, Gloria leaps up and grabs Artemio by the shoulders, pulling him down onto the steps. Felipé clings to the boy's hand, but is forced to let go when Artémio falls to the stairs. Resuming flight down the stairs, Felipé reaches the front door just as Eduardo enters from the yard, pistol held in both hands. Still unseen, Felipé throws himself at Eduardo, hoping to knock him to the floor. As the two men collide, Eduardo's gun goes off, ripping a hole in Felipé's chest. He groans, then falls to the floor, spitting blood. Seconds later, Gloria arrives, screaming, "Why did you shoot him? He was trying to save Artémio."

Eduardo looks down at the man; his eyes fixed on Felipé's right arm. "You see that?", he says, pointing to the arm.

"See what?", asks Gloria, barely able to talk.

"The tattoo."

"Yes."

"Haven't you seen it before?"

"No, never. It's ugly." Eduardo is about to tell her what he saw on the video, then decides to skip it. To himself, he murmurs, *Let her think what she will. She's in enough pain already.* Just then the man coughs. "Hurry…we've got to get him to a hospital," Gloria screams, her voice hysterical. As she bends over to examine his face, her eyes moisten. "Felipé…it's me, your mother." He looks up at her and whispers, "You bitch," then closes his eyes and rolls over dead.

As Gloria sobs convulsively, Manny approaches from the living room, the AK-47 still smoking. "Now we got three dead men. What are we going to do with them? We can't just leave them here."

"Too dangerous," Eduardo answers. "If we call police, they gonna wanna know who we are. And it be crazy to tell 'em. So many cops workin' for cartels now, Z's gonna find out who we are and come after us. Then we all dead meat."

Sebastián nods his agreement. "Eduardo is right. We have to leave them here."

Gloria glowers at Eduardo, "I'm not going to leave Felipé here. He deserves to be buried with a priest at his side…just like anyone else."

"Maybe this best," says Eduardo, "we call police but not tell'em who we are...jis' say three dead men at this address. Once they figure out the names, they call relatives and turn bodies over."

"But they don't know I'm his real mother; nobody does."

"Well, if you go to police and tell 'em you mama of Felipé, don't say your other son was kidnapped. If ya do, they gonna ask how you knew where to find Artémio...and that gonna get us all involved."

"And killed, probably," adds Sebastián. "Just say you read in the paper that Felipé was shot and you want to make arrangements for the burial service." As the group, now including Artémio, piles into the van for the return trip home, all impulses to celebrate are muted out of consideration for Señora Lorenzo. In the ensuing silence, Manny takes her hand and whispers words of condolence. Back in town, Gloria and Artémio are the first to be dropped off, then Jesús and Manny. Before heading to the PRG, Eduardo and Sebastián stop for a drink and a chance to review what happened at Felipe's house. No sooner do they reach the office that the phone rings. Eduardo picks it up, then hands it to Sebastián when the man on the other end asks for him by name.

"Hello Sebastián. It's Carmelo...you know, Gloria's husband."

"Hi Carmelo...how's your wife doing? She's been through a lot tonight." "Well, I'm on my way to the hospital. The people I talked to on the phone say she's probably had a nervous breakdown."

"Whew...I'm sorry to hear that, Carmelo. I mean...after what happened to Artémio...and then to discover that her other son was involved. It's a wonder she even got through it all."

"She's still not sure what part Felipé played in all this. She wants to believe it was the other two guys who did the whipping…and that Felipé tried to stop them…*(pause)*…Do you think there's any truth in that…(pause)…Please tell me what you think. Sebastián. I respect your judgment."

"I can certainly understand why Gloria finds it difficult if not impossible to accept the fact that her older son was involved in kidnapping her younger son. But we know that much is true. The whole truth is actually worse than that… *(pause)*…I don't know if you noticed it, but in the video they sent you, the man doing the whipping had a large tattoo on his right arm…down near the wrist. You could just barely see it in the video."

"And?"

"Felipé had a tattoo in exactly the same place."

"But was it the same tattoo?"

"Yes…a rattlesnake."

"Oh my God! Then it really was brother against brother. But do you think Felipé knew that the boy he was whipping was his half-brother? Was it revenge for being rejected by his mother years ago? If so, that could really send Gloria over the edge."

"I don't know. It may have been a coincidence. Maybe the Z's picked your family because of your wealth, not realizing that Felipé and the boy to be kidnapped were related. We may never know for sure." Carmelo breathes an audible sigh. "I think it's best to let my wife think what she wants to think."

"I agree. It sounds like she might not be able to handle the truth."

"Yes. I'm not going to bring the subject up again, unless, of course, she wants to talk about it. But Sebastián, there is something else I want to talk to you about...something related."

"Fire away."

"Artémio's kidnapping has been extremely painful for us both. Not only painful, but frustrating. At first, I was frightened...for my boy...and my wife. Now that he's back, I find myself wrestling with a different feeling. I want to do something about these drug people; I want to fight back some way. Trouble is, I don't know what I can do. At least I didn't know until a few days ago when the idea came to me of joining you guys...you know, helping you to go after the dealers, the kidnappers, the people who are poisoning this country. I'm not exactly sure what you guys do, but what I've heard about this latest case tells me I'd like to join you. What do you think?"

"I'd have to check with the others, but personally, I think it's a great idea, Carmelo."

"I don't have any great skills...you know...with detective work... that kind of thing."

"Those things we can help you with. What counts most right now is motivation and there's no question that given what happened to your son, you've got all the motivation you need. If you want, I'll bring it up with Eduardo tonight and let you know what he says."

"Thank you. My life right now is kinda empty. I love my son and that takes some of my time...but my football days are behind me. I had a real sense of purpose then...but it's gone now. Joining you guys to fight the drug dealers would give me a purpose that's been missing for the last 10 years."

"I like what you're saying, Carmelo. I'll call when I have something to report."

"Okay. Sebastián. Thanks."

Chapter 14

The Recording

Luis gets a call on his cell phone as he's driving to work. The voice is all too familiar. "I jis' come back from Felipé's house…tried callin' 'im three times. When nobody answered I figured somethin' went wrong with the kid. So, I go over there…and they's all dead…all three of our guys. Now, you tell me… what the fuck happened?"

Luis takes a deep breath before answering. "I don't know; this is the first I heard about it."

"Hey Luis…we're payin' you big bucks to tell us when we're gonna get hit. You never said a fuckin' word."

"What the hell you talking about? I didn't say anything because our department wasn't involved. This is the first I even heard about the kid. Nobody told me about no kidnappin'. If I had known, I woulda done somethin' about it."

"Well then, who dunnit? Somebody killed three of our guys and took the kid we was holdin'. It wasn't the federales; they would'na left those bodies there like that."

"I don't know. Didn't you see anything…something they left behind?"

"Nothin'. Nothin' but three guys with bullet holes in 'em."

"Well, don't blame me. If I knew anything, I woulda let you know. I always do."

"Well, how the hell they find out where the kid is? You tell me that." "I already told you. I don't know. I really don't know."

Before putting the phone back down, Luis wipes it off with a handkerchief...as if cleansing the device of some noxious bacteria. *Where the hell does he get off, treating me like a servant? I need the money but Christ, not if I have to put up with scum like this.* As he settles back into the driver's seat, two questions nag at him. *Who coulda done it...maybe the Gulf cartel...I know they tryin' to move in...but how did they find the boy?* His thoughts switch quickly to the recording Dunwoody sent yesterday. *Ah...the mystery woman. Could there be a connection? A psychic...someone who can see through walls...from miles away. Dunwoody musta sent her a video of some kid, but is it same kid being held at Felipe's house? If yes, he not gonna tell me anything about it. No...if this woman involved with shooting, I gonna have to find out myself.* Back in the office, he plays the recording again...then calls Dunwoody. "Bob, thanks for the recordin'. I can't tell nothin' so far, but it would help if I know where she call from. You get number from the phone company?"

Dunwoody quickly assesses the situation and decides on a cautious approach. "Yup...in the beginning I was curious so I checked. After the first three calls, I stopped checking: it was the same thing every time."

"What you mean?"

"She always calls from a public phone...once from Paseo, once from Sheridan and once from Altira. That's all I know."

Unseen, Luis writes down the names of the three towns mentioned "Yeah, I agree...not very interestin'. Oh, another thing, she said somethin' on the recodiin' about video. What video was that?"

"Oh that. It's a copy of a TV series about the war against drugs. Her husband was interested in seeing it."

"Well, if you learn any more, I appreciate call."

"Will do."

Once the phone is down, Luis begins mumbling to himself. *That video she mentioned on the recording musta been the one kidnappers sent to boy's parents. Somehow, she used it to find out where he is. The only way Dunwoody got his hands on it is if the boy's parents brought it to D.E.A. So, maybe Dunwoody's group had somethin' to do with shoot-out at Felipé's house. And mystery woman is involved somehow. Jesús Christ…what the hell is goin' on here?* He looks down at the list of towns the woman called from. Pulling a map of Texas from his desk drawer, he quickly locates them and puts a red dot next to each. He sits back and looks again. The three dots form a semi-circle…all equidistant from El Paso. He smiles. *So, she lives in El Paso and goes outside city to make calls. Not much of a lead but it's a beginning.*

The next idea comes with a suddenness that makes his eyes pop. *What's his name…oh yeah, Santayana…Juan Santayana… linguist at University of Monterrey."* He begins talking out loud. "This guy's a specialist in regional dialects. Someone tole me he can identify any accent in Mexico…or in the U.S.…he's that good. And he tells lot more from voice alone." Without hesitation, he rings his secretary and tells her to get Santayana on the phone. "Tell 'im it's urgent…and that we'll pay him for his time." He gets up and goes into her office. "Once we have Sr. Santayana's address, make a copy of this recording (*hands her the disk*) and send it to him by express mail. Don't delay for minute."

Two days later Luis is on the phone with Juan Santayana. "Hey, Juan, thanks for taking the time. The CD I sent you is really important."

"What do you mean?"

"I can't tell you the details...just that we gotta locate the woman who made the recording. She's important to investigation we got goin', but we still don't know who she is. So, Juan...now you heard her voice, what can you tell me about her?"

"Not an awful lot. She's an educated woman...articulates her words carefully."

"But where's she from?"

"That's the easy part...Northeast U.S....probably somewhere in what they call upstate New York. You can tell from the flatness of her vowels."

"And?"

"Oh, I'd say she's about 35, maybe 38...(*pause*)...I get the sense she's quite confident, although to a newcomer the softness of her speech might suggest otherwise. Another thing: she sounds quite concerned about the boy on the video. Kind of maternal; to me that indicates she might not have any kids of her own."

"That's it?"

"Yes...sorry I can't say anymore."

"That's okay. I appreciate your help. Send your bill to PGR here in Juárez."

"Oh, no. If it's something for the war against drugs, I don't want any money...just glad to do it. These cartels are a real menace to our country."

Luis suppresses a smirk. "Thanks. Is okay to call you when we get more evidence?"

"Sure…be glad to help."

Although Luis is not accustomed to relying on intuition, especially in important matters, something tells him there's a connection between this mystery woman and what happened at Felipé's house. Carefully he goes over what Juan Santayana had to say about the recording. He tries to picture her now but nothing comes; without a photo he's stuck. Frustrated, he leans back in his chair and lets his mind work freely. He is more rational than intuitive and knows from experience that if he is patient, an idea usually comes to him. What comes now is nothing less than brilliant. *Sure, her heart goes out to kid in video,* he mumbles. *She can't stomach what they doin' to him. She a bleeding heart. So maybe I get to her by appealin' to her maternal instincts…(pause)…how we do that? Well, we put ad in El Paso newspapers sayin' we need psychic to help locate missing child.*

He scribbles a few words, then throws them away. Starting again, he settles on a title…MISSING CHILD…PSYCHIC WANTED. Below the title he sketches some additional information. 'Generous reward. Discretion assured. Call — —'. Satisfied with his work, he bursts into his secretary's office. "Hilda, would ya like to take the rest of the day off?"

Hilda beams. "Of course, Chief? Who do I have to shoot?"

"Nobody…just go home and place this ad with all three El Paso newspapers (*hands ad to Hilda*). In empty spaces insert your own home phone number."

Hilda scrutinizes the text carefully. "Fine…but what do I do if someone calls and offers their services?"

"If a man, say you already found someone. If a woman, tell her you are the mother of the missing child and invite her to come to your house. Tell her it's a boy…an eight-year-old boy…no make that a girl."

"But I don't have any children; I'm not even married."

"No importante. You a woman; fake it."

Hilda re-reads the ad. "What if more than one woman answers the ad?" "See them all until you come to one we looking for. Tell others you call back if you need…"

(*Interrupting*) "…and how will I know Ms. Right?"

Luis bites his lip. "I was gettin' to that…jis' listen for a change. We're lookin' for a woman in her thirties, born in New York, speaks good English and…"

(*Interrupting*) "My English is pretty primitive; how am I supposed to tell how good hers is?"

"OK. Forget that one. Concentrate on what I already tole you… her age and where she grew up. And ask her where she lives now. The one we want probly has home in El Paso."

"And if she says she can do her magical stuff from her own home, what do I say?"

"Tell her it will help if she sees photos of your daughter… maybe handwriting as well…even girl's bedroom."

"And if she comes?"

"Call me right away. I be there in ten minutes."

"What are you goin' to do to her?"

Luis winces. "None of your business."

Hilda nods her acceptance, then sets the ad on her desk.

"And for Christ's sake, don't tell anybody we're lookin' for this woman."

"Okay, but are we talkin' friend or enemy?"

Luis frowns. "Just do it."

Chapter 15

A Romance Blossoms

"So, how's the sleuth business going?" asks Ned on the phone. To Jessica, the voice is a familiar one, especially comforting now that she's involved in this game of cat and mouse.

"I don't know; okay I guess…at least so far."

"You sound a tad nervous; any truth to that?"

"A little bit…no…more than a little."

"How about taking a drive in the country? A nice relaxing drive…just a few hours…it'll get us out of the city."

"Sounds nice…but what about Dolores?"

"She's sleeping."

"In the afternoon?"

"She's depressed; only way to get rid of it is to sleep it off."

"I see. Okay. When?"

"I'll drop by in thirty minutes."

"Fine. See you then."

As Jessica slides into the passenger's seat, Ned's eyes fasten on her white shorts. This is the first time he has seen her bare legs, or more accurately her bare thighs. Slightly tanned from mornings out on the rear deck, they are a stunning complement to her golden hair. As he stares, a question dangles deliciously before him. "Is she trying to turn me on?"

As if reading his thoughts, she turns and smiles. "This was really a nice idea, Ned. I was feeling cooped up inside." Her eyes are sparkling, her lips full with the promise of requited pleasure.

"How long do we have?", he asks as he pulls out of the driveway.

"Well, Lloyd usually gets home around 5:30. Just in case, I left him a note, saying we had gone for a ride."

"So, let's head for Altira; I know a little bistro there. A glass of wine would taste pretty good right now."

"Hmm," she answers. "I like the way your imagination works, Ned."

He is aware that she has used his name twice already, a sure sign, he reasons, of a growing intimacy. On the way out of the city, the conversation turns to her work for the D.E.A. Ned is the first to speak. "I read in the paper about the Lorenzo boy… you know, the one who was kidnapped and whipped. Don't suppose you had anything to do with that."

She pauses. "I guess it's okay to talk about it now. Yes, I got involved after his parents received a video showing their son being tortured. It was the most terrifying thing I have ever seen. I never realized just how cruel humans can be."

Ned shows alarm. "How did you get hold of the video? You're not meeting with these people face-to-face, are you?"

"Oh no, we've been careful to avoid any direct contact. Dunwoody, you know, the D.E.A. head in El Paso, left the video in a secret place. I picked it up later, so we never saw each other. I still don't know what he looks like."

"And he has never seen you, right?"

"Yes, although, of course, he does know my voice. He even asked if it was okay to make a recording of it."

"What?"

Jessica bites her lip. "Well, there's more going on here than meets the eye. I'll tell you…but you've got to promise not to share it with anyone…not even Dolores."

Ned smiles. "We don't share much as it is."

"I need to tell someone; it makes me feel alone if I don't. Lloyd is too interested in what he calls 'the big picture' to get involved in something as messy as this. That leaves you. After all, you're the one who got me started with this spying business."

"So, what's going on?"

"The people at D.E.A. suspect that Dunwoody's counterpart over in Juárez…a man named Luis Mendoza…is working for the Zapa's…or at least one of the drug cartels."

"You mean he's a traitor."

"I guess you could call it that. Anyway, Mendoza is aware that a psychic woman is now working with the D.E.A. and that she has tracked down Mata on two different occasions. That's enough to make him concerned."

"So, he's looking for you."

"Yes. He knows that I talk with Dunwoody, so he asked Bob to make a recording of my voice next time I called. He claimed that if he's going to act on my guesses, he should know something about me. I guess that's standard procedure with informants."

"But don't you think that's dangerous? I mean, these people are notorious for squeezing information out of simple things like handwriting, footprints, background sounds…stuff like that. If Mendoza is working for the Zapa's, his interest in you can only mean one thing…he wants to get rid of you before you upset the applecart. Why else would he want a recording of your voice?"

Jessica grits her teeth. "Yes, you're right, he's obviously up to no good. But we had to string him along; Bob said that a flat denial would have aroused his suspicions…you know…make him wonder if we know he's working for the cartels. So, we made a special recording for him, one that contained nothing that could identify me."

"You mean nothing you think can identify you."

"Well, yes."

Ned reaches over and touches her hand. "Tell me about the Lorenzo boy. What part did you end up playing in that gruesome tale?" Step by step she explains how the boy was found. "Some of the story was left out of the newspapers," she says, "especially the part about Mrs. Lorenzo's relationship with her two sons."

"You mean there was another son involved…not just the twelve-year old?"

"Right. What makes it all hard to believe is that Felipé, the man who did the whipping, was Artémio's half-brother."

"You're kidding."

"No, it's true."

"But did Felipé know he was torturing his own brother?"

"That's not clear…at least as far as I know. But it's possible. Felipé was given away to another family when he was three years old and never forgave his mother for abandoning him. He even shouted something nasty to her just before he died."

"You know what's really frightening about this whole thing…at least for me…is that you've become a major player in a pretty sordid drama. Who knows where this whole thing is going? I feel somewhat responsible I since I was the one who talked you into offering your services to the D.E.A."

As he talks, his voice takes on a new softness. When she turns to look at his face, she detects a moistening in his eyes. *My God; he really cares. He's more afraid for me than my own husband is.* Even with his eyes on the road, he can feel her interest. His heart begins racing. Years of longing, carefully concealed behind a facade of marital propriety, begin bubbling at the surface of consciousness, threatening to explode into reality. He considers turning to look at her; instead, he places his right hand on the shift, then listens to her breathing. It has stopped. Minutes later he moves it again…further right this time…until it brushes against her bare thigh. When she places her left hand on his, his heart skips a beat. Steering with one hand only, he maneuvers the car over into a rest area and stops. In the ten years they have known each other, they have never shared a kiss. Not until now. With the engine still running, he reaches over and pulls her cheek toward his, then places his lips firmly on hers. She does not resist. All pretense of friendship is abandoned when she places her hand on his neck and pulls him closer. The two sets of lips, swollen with years of repressed desire, unite in a blissful loss of separateness. Where there were once two individuals, each lost in its hidden torment of aloneness, there is now but one. The kiss is broken only when a truck pulls up behind them and honks. The driver makes no attempt to wipe the grin from his face.

Quickly, Ned steers the car back out onto the highway. Nothing more is said until they reach the bistro in Altira. There is no more talk about Mendoza, the D.E.A. or her new role as clairvoyant spy. In fact, there is little talk about anything. Both seem content to sip their wine and look at each other. Words no longer satisfy; by now the relationship has reached a point where all they need is their senses. From across the table they make love with their eyes alone. In fantasy they caress each other's cheek; with their fingers they explore noses, lips and ears. To others seated nearby, they appear lost in a world of their own, oblivious to what anyone else might think. When the waitress comes with the check, she leaves abruptly, envious of what she sees and unwilling to break the spell.

On Saturday the Bransons are once again invited to dinner at the Kinsmans. Much of the talk before and during dinner is about the drug cartels and Pres. Calderon's decision to bring in more soldiers. After dessert, the conversation switches to police corruption and the government's inability to stop it. During the discussion, Ned senses that Jessica has something to share in private and invites her to go outside for a walk. Dolores is surprised by the gesture but conceals her anxiety behind a forced smile. Once outside, the two friends, now on the verge of becoming lovers, hold hands while strolling up and down the street. When she sighs contentedly, he puts his arm around her. "I love being alone with you like this. I just wish we could do it more often."

"I would like that," she responds.

"So, tell me what's going on? I know it's something."

She chuckles. "I guess I can't keep anything from you anymore." As they walk, she proceeds to tell him about the ad she saw in yesterday's Evening Gazette. "My heart really goes out to this woman. It's pretty clear that her child has been kidnapped and she's afraid to go to the police. Instead, she's reaching out to a psychic." Ned squeezes her hand. "And you want to help?" "Yes. Although I've never had a child of my own, I think I know what she's feeling."

"I hope you're aware this could be a trap."

"What do you mean?"

Ned clears his throat. "I'm not sure exactly. Maybe if I saw the ad I could say more."

"It said simply that a psychic was wanted to help find a missing child. Oh, and that there would be a reward."

"Phone number or address?"

"Just the phone number."

"Hmm. If you want, we could do a little detective work of our own. I can call that number and offer my services as a psychic…just to see what happens." His voice is soothing. She lets go of his hand and puts her arm around his waist. "What can you tell from that?"

"I don't know…maybe I can get invited to her home, look around…see what I can see."

"But what if she is fooled into thinking you really do have psychic abilities? Won't she be crushed when she finds out that you were only pretending? That could be pretty devastating."

"I agree. Maybe I'll just do the phone call…ask her lots of questions about her child…see if she's lying or not."

"You know how to do that?"

"Hey, I'm a psychologist; I can at least try."

Back in the living room Dolores and Lloyd sit silently. "Do you want to watch some TV?", she asks, trying to relieve the awkwardness.

"Ah, no. I'm okay."

She looks at him closely. His figure is tall and lean; his face strong, almost noble, as if carved from granite. His features are made even more attractive by the wisp of gray hair at his temples. His manner is very different from Ned's; where her husband is bold and talkative, Lloyd is quiet and unobtrusive. Things are very different, of course, when the two men are discussing politics or philosophy; there, Lloyd can be forceful, even domineering. But here, alone with her, he seems shy, apparently waiting for her to take the lead. The thought evokes a smile, even a hint of excitement. While this is not a role she is accustomed to playing, there is something tantalizing about it. She offers him some tea. When he accepts, she bounces up from her chair and heads for the kitchen, newly aware that her depression has lifted. She returns a few minutes later with both tea and cookies and sits down next to him on the couch.

If Lloyd were more observant, he might notice that her face, typically gray and lifeless, has become animated. There is a new sparkle in her eyes. Instead, he listens for her words...or more accurately the sound of her voice. If anything, he seems mesmerized by the music of her speech. He feels no urge to contribute to the conversation; he finds it more satisfying to sit back and listen...the way a baby might listen to a mother's soothing song. As she rattles on about nothing in particular, he is conscious of a growing warmth in his loins. When she notices the change, she takes a deep breath. It has been years since Ned showed any real interest in her. The slight reddening of Lloyd's cheeks is enough to remind her that men can still find her attractive, that she is more than a ball and chain around the leg of a husband who remains with her only because he feels sorry for her.

Sensing Lloyd's receptiveness, she reaches out and places her hand on his knee. Although nothing is said, their eyes meet in an undeclared confession of mutual interest. The thought of taking her hand never occurs to him. Instead, he waits for her next move, aware only that he wants her to do more. By now she knows the rules of the game. It is up to her to be bold, to take the initiative, then wait to see his response. Unlike Jessica who despises the game and plays it only out of sexual frustration, Dolores relishes the chance to assert herself. For years she has yielded to the power of Ned's personality, particularly when they are in bed. She is aware that her very sense of self, the certainty of being a separate, independent person, is threatened whenever he initiates sex. At those times, love-making not only ceases to arouse desire; it becomes a battle to keep her identity from being obliterated, a battle she wins only by shutting down all feeling.

With her hand still on Lloyd's knee, she looks around at the two empty chairs. The possibility that Ned and Jessica are falling in love does not escape her attention. While hurtful, it is in a way relieving; if he is attracted to someone else, he'll be less likely to insist on sex at home. She closes her eyes and takes a deep breath, emboldened by this unexpected turn of events. *Just a hint of freedom*, she murmurs to herself, *but perhaps there is more to come.* As she turns to look at Lloyd, the front door opens. Ned and Jessica have returned.

Several days later Ned and Jessica repeat their drive into the country. Again, she wears shorts, lavender this time with a white blouse revealing ample cleavage. He too is wearing shorts… eager to show off his recently tanned legs. Without soliciting her assent, he heads for the same rest area where they first kissed. As they pull in and park, she smiles silently at his obvious intention. Within minutes they are embracing, her lips warm and welcoming, his tongue eager to invade. The spell is broken only when she withdraws long enough to ask, "What about the bistro? I could use a glass of wine."

Startled by her comment, he pulls back, turns on the ignition and heads out of the rest area. He says nothing but continues obsessing. *Did I do something wrong? My God, I can't get enough of her.* Reaching for the CD player, he considers apologizing, then changes his mind. Still inflamed with their kisses, he places his hand on her bare thigh and begins sliding it up and down. As they speed down the highway, he inches his way to her shorts, then boldly tucks a finger under the hem. When she squirms, he withdraws his hand, kicking himself for being so aggressive. It comes as a shock when she takes his hand and puts it back where he had it. Speechless, he continues driving with his left hand while simultaneously using the other to probe the area around her sex. She opens her legs slightly to accommodate his exploration. When he slides his index finger into her labia, she sighs, signaling surrender. Without hesitating, he takes her clit between his finger and thumb and massages it. Neither looks at the other. Five miles up the road, she suddenly shudders, closes her legs, and gasps. He presses hard, then withdraws.

Contented that he has pleased her, he takes her hand and presses it to his lips. Repeatedly he kisses it, unwilling to let go. There is no room for words now; all doubts have been consumed in an inferno of mutual desire, a desire that can at last be acknowledged openly. As they head for the bistro and the promised glass of wine, they realize that doubts will return later…when Dolores wakes from her fitful sleep demanding to know how her husband spent the afternoon…or when Lloyd retires early after dinner and leaves his door open, shyly inviting his wife to his bed. For each, anxiety about what is to come draws them into the here and now where nothing exists but lips kissing, fingers touching, and eyes aflame with the promise of love. Tomorrow is another day; que será, será *(what will be, will be)*.

Ned smiles as he steps on the accelerator. When the car responds, he takes her hand again, holding it to his cheek. "Is it okay if I adore you…a little?", he whispers.

She smiles and fluffs her hair. "Just a little?"

Chapter 16

The Mustang

"You think it's the same place as before...the Mustang restaurant?", Bob asks.

"Yes, it's the same shape building, the same pictures on the walls, the same horse outside," she answers. "And the image is quite clear...unlike several I've had lately. It's Mata alright."

"Okay. This time we're going to get him."

"You're not going to tell Mendoza?"

"No. We have other ways to get the job done...stuff I can't share with you."

"Because you don't trust me?"

"Oh no...there's no question about that. I don't want to burden you with info that could make you vulnerable. Besides, there's no need for you to know."

"That's fine with me." As she hangs up, questions arise. *Three times now I've told him where to find Mata. And still the man is out there, butchering innocent people. What's wrong?"*

Within minutes, Eduardo is notified and in turn calls the other members of his team. For Carmelo, this will be his first raid. He kisses his wife and son goodbye and heads for the rendezvous point…a cemetery at the east end of Juárez. As he piles into the van along with Jesús, Manny and Sebastián, his eyes focus on the weaponry in back. "Grenade launchers?", he comments, clearly surprised.

"We're probly goin' to need 'em," responds Eduardo. "Now here's the situation. Peaches says he at the Mustang…right now. We know when he goes out to eat, he's gonna take armed thugs with him. When they enter the restaurant, they take everybody's cell phones, then give 'em back when the boss is done eatin'."

"Makes sense, Carmelo suggests, "A customer could secretly call the police or military and get the guy arrested."

Eduardo smiles. "Apparently he makes up for this by payin' for everybody's meal."

"So, the guy's got a heart," says Manny. "I've heard that he's actually well-liked by the locals. That's hard to believe when he's responsible for cutting up his enemies and dissolving their bodies in a barrel of acid."

"They say he hands out free food and medicine," adds Sebastián, "sort of like a social service agency."

Mnny nods. "I suppose when people are really poor, they'll turn to anyone who gives them a hand. But that hardly justifies the savagery we read about in the papers."

"Okay, we gotta go," interjects Eduardo. "We can be there in fifteen minutes."

"But Duardo, we can't go bursting into the restaurant with guns firing," protests Manny. "There are bound to be innocent people in there."

"I agree," his brother is quick to answer. "Not only would a lotta innocent people get hurt; we'd probly get killed ourselves.

Mata's not foolish enough to go in there without protection."

"He'll probably have some thugs outside as well," adds Sebastián. "We'd never have a chance."

Eduardo nods his approval. "That's why we got the grenade launchers. Our best chance is to get him as he's leavin' the restaurant."

"You mean right outside, like on the sidewalk?", asks Jesús.

"No, that too dangerous…better to wait until he in his car and headin' outta town."

"You mean we gonna wait by the side of the road and pop his car with a grenade?", the boy responds cheerfully. Eduardo nods. "That's the plan unless anybody can think of somethin' better."

"Sounds good to me," says Carmelo, "especially if we can find a place with some tree cover."

"But don't you have to be pretty close for those things to be accurate?", asks Manny.

"Never used one," says Duardo, "but accordin' to instructions, they accurate at 100 yards...maybe even 200. If we hide in trees just off road, we can get 'im as he goes by."

"But how are we going to be sure we have the right car?", asks Manny.

Silence.

Sebastián turns to Eduardo. "How about dropping me off near the Mustang before you go to the attack point? I can call you on my cell phone when I see him coming out and describe the car he's getting into. From what I've heard, he typically rides in a three-car caravan. I might even be able to tell you which of the three he's in."

"I hear ya, but with them launchers," Jesús says, "they ain't gonna be a problem. Why don't we jis' pop all three?" Manny lowers his head. "I don't know. It would be a sin if we ended up getting the wrong car."

Eduardo looks around. "Lookit, if three cars stay together, it don't matter which one Mata is in. His top dogs gonna be in one of 'em. They all wanted for murder, arson, kidnapping…you name it."

"I suppose you're right," Manny offers, "but how do we know which road they're going to take when they leave the Mustang?"

"The Mustang's on Macedonia Calle, right?", says Eduardo. "The road goes north and south. Now, he ain't goin' north to U.S. border this time a night. So, south is our best bet…a spot two or three miles below restaurant. We drop Sebastián off a few blocks from Mustang…and then drive to attack point where we set up shop in trees off road…*(pause)*…Any questions? Okay, time to get movin'."

With no further discussion, Eduardo turns on the ignition and heads the van into town. Once Sebastián is dropped off, they drive to a spot several miles out of town on the road going south. Eduardo eases the van into a turnaround and points to a grove of trees just off the road. "This look perfect. Manny, you and Carmelo set up launchers around 25 yards back toward restaurant. I gonna leave van here. That way when we leave, we don't hafta drive past a lotta fire and smoke…*(pause)*… Give Jesús one of the rifles, but be careful, they already loaded. Carmelo, get a launcher and set it up next to Manny. Careful, they mucho heavy."

"I thought we were gonna use two?", the big man answers.

"Okay. You probly right. We need both…and don't forget the magazines."

As Carmelo opens up the rear of the van, Eduardo watches in awe as the former defensive tackle picks up a grenade launcher in each hand and heads for the target site like he was lugging bags of groceries. Back in town, Sebastián begins a slow walk to the Mustang. He waits until he gets to a place ten yards from the restaurant, then calls Eduardo. "He's definitely in there."

"You sure?"

"Well, for one thing, I can see four thugs outside, each with an AK-47. Inside there's a long rectangular table; the guy I think is Mata is seated at the far end…like he's the host or at least the most important guy there. There must be at least eight of his henchmen seated at the table; at the near end is another thug with a machine gun. The guy is turned around so he's facing the front door."

"You mean he not supposed to do any eatin'?"

"I guess not; apparently he's there for protection only."

"What's Mata look like?"

"Well, from here, I can't be sure, but he seems to have a thin mustache…not at all like his hero Zapata. He's definitely Indian; you can tell from his high cheek bones and dark skin. He's seated, but he looks kind of small…not tall like a Mestizo. Other than that, I don't know. But the way the waiters are fawning over him tells me he's the boss. And if Peaches says Mata is in the Mustang, that's gotta be him; there's nobody else in there except a few regular people eating dinner."

"Okay. Be sure to follow 'im when he come out. Call me right away and tell me the kind of car he gets into…and how many cars in caravan."

"Okay, but I don't want to get too close and arouse suspicion."

"Got it."

Inside the restaurant, Mata is busy congratulating himself on the success of their latest shipment of crystal meth into the Houston area. His voice is deep and hoarse as he looks up and down the table. "We don't hafta buy meth from the Columbians no more; just make the shit right here in Juárez. And those fat-cat gringos up north are gonna eat it all up…every bit we can feed 'em." No details are given; the word methamphetamine is never used, at least not here in the restaurant. But everyone around the table knows why their capo is smiling. After all, they're here to celebrate. They've just completed one of the biggest drug transactions ever. Later, back at the local safe house, proceeds from the sale will be distributed. Even the lowest member of the gang will receive thousands of dollars. No one is likely to complain if Mata keeps a half a million for himself. There's plenty of cash to go around.

"There jis' one problem," the capo continues. "El Gordo thinks he can move into Juárez and grab some of our business. I'm tellin' ya right here, that ain't gonna happen. It's taken three years to build up this plaza and no peasant from Sinaloa is gonna take it away from us." The others nod; some even clap slightly. "We may hafta roll a few heads to convince that son-of-a bitch we mean business…but we ain't exactly amateurs in that department, are we?" On cue, the others break into unrestrained laughter. Mata stops to take a sip of mescal. "Angel, find out where some of his guys are holed up. Then take your best hit men…José, Pedro, Alfonso and others…make sure you take enough people…and go in after them. Make it look bad…you know, take off some heads, leave body parts all over the place. Let 'em know they ain't exactly welcome in Juárez. Okay?"

As dinner winds down, some of the thugs head for the door to check out security before leaving. From across the street, Sebastián watches, then ducks into a convenience store that's still open for business. He pulls out his cell phone and calls Eduardo. "You all set up there?", he asks.

"We just waitin' on you. What's he doin'?"

"He's getting ready to leave. Some of his men have just come outside to look around. I don't think they suspect anything. Two of them are heading for a black sedan parked right outside the restaurant. In fact, there are two sedans and one van, all black. The two sedans are late model Ford Explorers; the van is one of those big Chrysler models…(*pause*)…Okay, one of the guys from the restaurant just got into the lead Explorer and started the engine. Oh, and here comes Mata with the rest of his gang. He's getting into the middle vehicle…the second Explorer…along with three men. The others are piling into the van in back…(*pause*)… Let's see if they move out together."

Eduardo coughs. "They better; it gonna get messy if they leave at different times."

"Okay. So far, so good. The two sedans have moved out; the van is a bit behind. They're heading your way…(*pause*)…Jesus Christ!."

"What happened?"

"When a silver Honda tried to squeeze in between the second Ford and the van, somebody in the van fired a shot in his direction. The poor slob backed away…so now all three vehicles are together and headed south."

"They don't fool around, do they? But, hey, nice work. We're ready. Wish you was here with us…but there ain't no way to get you up here in a hurry. We gonna circle around and pick you up later. Jis' lay low for a while, okay?"

"Will do."

As Mata's caravan moves south along Macadonia Calle, Eduardo's men get ready. Suddenly, Jesús yells, "Here they come. All three together."

Manny and Carmelo squat and pull their launchers into position. "Wait a minute, hold on," Manny shouts to his partner. "There's another vehicle in there."

"I see it," says Carmelo. "He's tryin' to pass the van."

Eduardo cranes his neck. "That's the silver Honda Sebastián tole us about. Hold your fire!" Manny and Carmelo drop their hands. By now the caravan is within 100 yards of Eduardo's group and approaching fast. All eyes are on the Honda as it pulls up alongside the black van.

"Holy Christ!", Carmelo shouts as a hail of bullets from the van sends the Honda careening into a ditch.

"Okay," yells Eduardo, "get ready. All clear now."

As agreed upon, Carmelo takes the lead Explorer, Manny the one just behind. Jesús, the sharp-shooter, is responsible for picking off anyone fleeing from the wreckage.

When the lead Explorer reaches a point just yards in front of Carmelo, he pulls the trigger, sending a grenade screaming across the road. One of the thugs sees the flash in the woods and yells. It's too late. A second later the grenade buries itself in the Ford, flipping it onto its side and turning it into a fireball. The car behind, the one carrying Mata, is going too fast to stop. As it collides with the lead Explorer, it bursts into flames and rolls off the road into the bushes. Manny moves his launcher slightly to the left and fires. The van, now stopped, takes a direct hit. Metal, glass and body parts are thrown into the air as the vehicle explodes. Jesús scans the area for anyone who might have escaped. When he sees no one, he dashes out onto the road to have a better look.

Eduardo waves desperately, "No…Jesús, come back."

The boy is not to be stopped. As a lone figure emerges from the middle car and stumbles toward the bushes, he raises his rifle and fires. The shot spins the man around. Even from a distance, Eduardo can tell: it's Mata. The capo, clinging to his shoulder, takes three more steps and falls to the ground. Again, Eduardo yells to Jesús. "Get back here." The boy takes a final look at his target, grins, and heads back to the group. As he crosses the road, a pickup passes, swerving onto the shoulder to avoid contact with the burning vehicles. The driver, at first mesmerized by the flames, takes a quick look at Jesús before moving ahead.

"He seen you," Eduardo yells as Jesús returns to the side.

"So what?", the boy asks.

"Whatd'ya mean, 'So what'?" Eduardo fires back. "Maybe the guy in the pickup see your face and identify you. That would put us outta business."

"I don't get it," the boy responds sullenly.

"You don't see it?" Eduardo yells, now furious. "Everybody is gonna be after us…Mata's gang, El Gordo, the police, the military…the whole goddamn country. We can't let that happen. We gotta stay secret. Comprendes?"

As the two rejoin Manny and Carmelo, Eduardo announces, "Okay. I think we got 'im. So, let's get outta here, pronto." As they pile into the van, he adds, "First we gotta circle around and pick up Sebastián. Then we all go home."

Manny, aware of Jesús's sensitivity, gives him a pat on

the shoulder. "I guess we got the head honcho. If our little sharpshooter here hadn't picked him off, he might have gotten away." "Yeah," chimes in Carmelo. "Nice job Sús." Jesús beams, then turns away.

"You all did good," says Eduardo from the driver's seat. "The world is gonna thank us for what we done tonight."

The next morning's headline screams the news, "Mata killed in fire fight on Macedonia Calle." The article speculates on who might have been responsible, the leading candidate being El Gordo's gang which is known to want a piece of the Juárez action. The article concludes with a prediction of more violence as the two cartels vie for dominance in northern Mexico.

As he heads for work in his new Infiniti, Mendoza turns on the car radio. The news is all about Mata and last night's fire fight outside the Mustang restaurant. Once the news has sunken in, he has a premonition. *I'm goin' to get a call right now from one of those thugs in Mata's gang, asking why I didn't warn them. But how the hell am I supposed to tip 'em off when the PGR wasn't even involved?...(pause)...So who the hell did it? Something tells me that woman, the psychic, had somethin' to do with it. I wonder if Hilda has gotten any calls yet. We gotta move on that right away.*

Mendoza is wrong about two things. The call doesn't come until later...and it's not from one of Mata's thugs. It's from El Gordo himself. Fully aware of Luis's importance as a voice within the Attorney General's office, the capo has decided to make the call himself. After introducing himself, he says that now Mata is out of the way, the Sinaloa people will be taking over the Juárez plaza and need Mendoza's help in keeping the PGR off their tail. When El Gordo asks how much Mata has been paying him, Mendoza doubles the amount. El Gordo not only agrees but ups the payout by another 25%. Before the conversation ends, Luis asks an important question. "Were you guys behind last night's action outside the Mustang restaurant?"

El Gordo pauses. "I wish I say yes. That was nice piece of work. We hopin' you tell us who did it."

"I don't know. It certainly wasn't us."

"You got ideas?"

"Just one. There's a woman who's been supplyin' D.E.A. with info on Mata. Apparently, she's a psychic and works alone. She could be involved."

"Get on her, pronto."

"I already made a move…should pay off in next few days."

"I like you attitude. Call me when you find out somethin'."

"Okay, boss."

Pleased with the conversation, Luis heads back to his office, more convinced than ever that Dunwoody's informant is the key to what happened at the Mustang. *But if she is, how come Bob didn't run the operation through me? Don't he trust me anymore?* His doubts quickly give way to more pleasant thoughts about his new boss, the one known as El Gordo…or the Fat One. According to the newspapers, El Gordo was born into a peasant family, somewhere in the rural hills of Sinaloa, although his speech suggests a more refined upbringing. The explanation, again according to the media, lies in his unusual intelligence, a fact borne out by his phenomenal success as drug lord. Forbes, a conservative financial magazine, reports that over the years Gordo has pulled himself out of abject poverty to become one of the world's richest men, with net assets in the billions. All of his success has come from his ability to manage a vast empire of drug dealers, distributors, guards, informants and hit men. It is said that while generous with his associates, he can be savage toward those who get in his way. Not many have stood up to him. The few who have were cut down and beheaded, sometimes in front of their wives and children. Others have had fingers, ears or testicles removed. Some say he does it in order to send a message: "Cross me and this will happen to you." Others see it as an expression of his narcissistic personality, a personality shaped by a dog-eat-dog environment back in Sinaloa where only the strongest survive and cruelty is accepted as a way of life. Starting as a grade school dropout working in his father's marijuana field, El Gordo went on to serve kingpins like El Major and El Azul who, once they were assured of his organizational skills, gave him responsibility for the crystal meth part of their business. Later he took over the whole organization, killing off anyone who wouldn't submit to his authority. Finally caught in Guatemala, the billionaire drug lord whose operations had by that time become global in scope, was sentenced to 20 years in a maximum-security prison. After eight years of a pampered existence behind bars, he escaped by bribing not only the guards but the warden himself.

Regarding his name, El Gordo, it is only partially true that he is overweight. Chubby, yes…but since his second marriage, he can no longer be described as fat. Judging from photos in the newspaper, he could actually qualify as handsome. His face lacks the Oriental cheekbones so typical of rural Mexico; his eyes, nose and mouth actually have the aristocratic bearing of a figure from 16th Century Florence. Now in his forties, he has lost none of his overarching ambition. His goal? To completely dominate the drug business in Mexico. Nothing less will satisfy.

Luis smiles as a picture of his new boss falls into place. Having grown up in the lap of luxury, the PRG leader tends to look down at anyone lacking the social graces of an affluent upbringing. While El Gordo fits the image of an uneducated campesino (*farmer*), his wealth and power make him someone of substance. Luis is aware that his new boss demands and deserves respect; one false step and he could find himself on the wrong end of a bullet…or worse yet, having his head delivered in a box to his official boss, Colonel Contréras. But there is no need for worry; years of dealing with the underworld have taught him how to sidestep trouble. He relaxes now as thoughts of his pay raise come back. With this extra money, perhaps he can repurchase the family hacienda outside of town, maybe even hire a few laborers to work the fields. In time, assuming the drug business lasts for a few more years, he can re-establish himself as patrón of an estate that rivals any throughout Meso-America. As the image of his family home returns, he turns on the radio. *Now, if I can just find this woman; that would really make El Gordo respect me…and get me another raise.*

Chapter 17

The Switch Begins

Ned and Jessica continue to see each other daily after Ned's afternoon class. While the two have clearly fallen in love, there is a difference. When Ned calls, his voice is thick with longing, his words not as poetic and orderly as he would like. Sometimes he is actually incoherent. On one occasion, he called her during a playing of Wagner's Tristan und Isolde…a definite mistake. He felt so ensnared by the libido-saturated music that after saying "hello," he couldn't continue…just held the phone to his ear in silence. Jessica, not surprisingly, found his behavior strange. While she feels much of the same affection, she doesn't obsess over him the way he does over her. It's true that she is happier than she has been for years…even Lloyd can notice the difference…but it is a joy unburdened by the weight of love sickness. Everything seems lighter, easier…almost as if it were happening by itself. She is aware that the meditating she's been doing lately may be contributing to this new peace of mind. Every time she has attempted to locate Mata, she has first gone to her bedroom, sat down and cleared her mind of all thoughts. From the very beginning, this experience of 'emptiness' has been an enjoyable one, so enjoyable that she has repeated it even when she's not trying to locate Mata. Her attempts to share the discovery with her husband, however, have met with skepticism, even derision.

"Thinking is what separates us from the apes," he is fond of telling her. "Getting rid of all thoughts may bring you peace of mind, but it comes at the sacrifice of your humanity. When you meditate, you regress to a point in evolution where you're operating on instinct alone. Do you really want to be that primitive?" She knows better than to argue.

For Ned, being in love is more complicated. While exhilarating in its impact on body and mind, it has all the trappings of a disease. From the moment he wakes up in the morning, he obsesses over the object of his affection; he literally can't think of anything else. Privately he frets over her every word…her every gesture…looking for signs she still cares…the sparkle in her eyes, the trembling in her voice…the desperate clinging during an embrace. And then there are the things he dreads…the half-smile, the kiss that fails to linger, the rebuke at a sexual overture. He goes over their last time together, reliving the touch of her hand, their final kiss at the door, her response when he confessed how much he loved her. He counts the hours until he can see her again. Evenings that should be devoted to preparing lectures are spent instead inventing new ways to tell her how much he loves her. At school, things are no better. He sits in on faculty discussions, but can't concentrate on what the others are saying. In his classroom lectures, he reads from his notes rather than risk looking like a fool who can't remember what he was saying. Dolores knows something is troubling him; it's obvious from his lack of appetite, his inability to relax, and the way he tosses and turns in bed. She is aware that he is seeing more and more of Jessica, but never having been in love herself, she fails to associate Jessica with her husband's strange behavior. *At least, he's not pestering me for sex*, she murmurs, smiling at her new freedom.

Having defended herself against Ned's sexual advances for years, Dolores is confused when she begins entertaining thoughts of love-making with Lloyd. What makes the idea appealing is his apparent willingness to let her take the lead. With Ned, being made love to has always aroused the fear of being totally obliterated. When he mounts her, she feels suffocated by his kisses, invaded by his manhood; as he climaxes, her very existence hangs in the balance. For years now, aware that some sex is required, she has experimented with different ways of blunting his thrust. She smiles now as she recalls one of her favorite techniques. It takes the form of a question, best offered as he prepares to mount her. "Does peener want to pay a visit?", she asks. Sometimes it works. With the question presented so demurely, his fantasy of 'conquering' her no longer fits. His only option is to pull back and accept the less intrusive idea of 'paying a visit.'

With Lloyd things might be quite different. At least, she is willing to entertain the idea that with him sex could actually be enjoyable. In all her 38 years, she has never had an orgasm, either with a partner or alone. When she brought the subject up recently in a therapy session, the therapist offered an explanation. "In orgasm, we lose our sense of self," he intoned, "at least for a few moments. If you're not sure who you are to begin with, that can be a terrifying experience." She had to admit the explanation made sense, but it did little to relieve her frustration. *Maybe it would be different with Lloyd,* she murmurs. *He doesn't frighten me the way Ned does. But I mustn't get my hopes up. After all, we're just friends.*

Lloyd typically wastes little time fantasizing, preferring to spend his considerable brain power on issues that lend themselves to logical analysis. Lately, however, he has caught himself reminiscing about Dolores. Jessica's increasing lack of response to his 'open-door' strategy has left him frustrated and receptive to the idea of a closer relationship with Ned's wife. Not strangely, he finds that thinking about Dolores helps to allay the jealous feelings that have crept into his otherwise orderly consciousness. For a man who prides himself on his freedom from emotion, jealous feelings are hardly welcome. They are in fact so unwelcome that they have become the focus of his thoughts. In time, he begins to obsess not over Dolores but over his own discomfort. *Jealousy is a primitive emotion,* he mutters.

I thought I had left that behind years ago. Here I am, the department head of philosophy at a major university, a person who has devoted his whole life to the intellect. It doesn't make sense that I should be having such primordial feelings; it's shameful…no, it's disgusting.

The only time he gets relief from his obsession is when he's with Dolores. As a result, he finds himself looking forward more and more to their meeting; to everyone's surprise, he even takes the initiative in arranging such meetings. When he and Dolores are actually together, however, taking the lead is the last thing on his mind. Without exception, he waits until she makes a move, then yields. It is the only way he knows. Although they haven't had sex yet, he can already picture the way it will happen. Most likely, he will be sitting on the couch while she is in a nearby chair. Gradually she will draw closer, using words to mesmerize him with hints of intimacy. She will tease him with her eyes and lips. For her, much of the excitement will lie in playing the role of seductress, a role unheard of in her relationship with Ned. For Lloyd, it is exactly the role he wants her to play. He is most aroused when he can lie back and wait for her to start something. It could be an act as simple as touching his knee or loosening his necktie. Then again, it could be something more dramatic, like moving next to him on the couch. His heart begins to race now as he pictures her leaning against him, then getting on top of him…looking down at him as she unzips his fly and takes his manhood into her warm hand.

For Dolores, such an act, unimaginable only a few weeks ago, now seems realistic; she can even visualize the more intimate act of sliding his member into her sex. Intimacies she has never even dreamt of now fill her girlish imagination. As yet unknown to her is the similarity of Lloyd's own fantasies. For both, the ideal scene is the same: he is lying on his back while she rides up and down on top of him with his penis inside her. She looks down at his face, contorted now with inexpressible pleasure; she smiles and drives harder until he explodes inside her. That's what they both want…separate dreams, yes, but borne of a mutual desire, a desire too long denied.

Over the following weeks, the new relationships ripen to the point where Lloyd and Ned agree to spend a night with each other's wife; after huddling in private, the women give their assent. According to the plan, the men are to leave their own homes at precisely 11:00 P.M. and drive directly to the other's home where they will spend the night. Because they both take the same back road, the two cars pass each other around 11:15, Ned going east to Jessica's, Lloyd on his way west to Dolores's. At that time of night, there are no other cars on the road. In the enveloping darkness, each honks shyly as they pass.

When Ned arrives at Jessica's house, she greets him warmly at the door, her ample breasts clearly visible through the off-white gown that hangs precariously from her shoulders. Because of the hour, they pause only briefly for a kiss before ascending the stairs to her bedroom where two candles have been lit. With Ned leading the way and Jessica gladly acquiescing, their love-making, up to now the stuff of fantasy, bursts into reality as image and dream give way to the sensations of touching and tasting.

For Ned, a temporary peace comes with orgasm, but fear soon follows. He knows the fear to be irrational but can't shake it off. *Why am I so afraid?*, he asks silently. *I know she loves me; why else would she be so affectionate? I see the love in her eyes, in the way she touches me. Why, then, am I so afraid of losing her?* Sensing his doubts, Jessica tries to reassure him of her love with kisses. When his fear persists, she resorts to words. "I've waited so long for you, Ned. I don't think I've ever been in love until now, although I've thought about it often enough." When he forces a smile, she responds with, "If you love me half as much as I love you, you will make me a very happy woman."

For her, the love-making is very different. There is no fear, no worries about being abandoned, just the joy of surrendering one's self to another. In that union, no words are necessary; it is sensations that count...his cheek on hers, the caress of his lips, the thrust of his penis inside her...all signs of an intimacy she has longed for but never had.

At Dolores's house, love-making with Lloyd takes place on the living room couch...exactly as envisioned in their complementary dreams. As she rides on top of him with his member swollen inside her, she can't believe her transformation. No longer filled with dread of intrusion, she does everything she can to make it happen. Fear gives way to desire as thoughts of being obliterated yield to a craving for more. In the midst of jockeying, she stifles a giggle as she considers how surprised Ned would be if he were watching.

This is all new for Lloyd as well...but in a different way. With Jessica he has always felt inadequate, knowing as he does that she wants him to be more assertive, even dominating. His guilt at failing to be the man she wants him to be has tarnished whatever pleasure he gets from their love-making. With Dolores there is no guilt, perhaps even a hint of pride that he, a man, has the courage to let a woman take the lead. He smiles at the thought as he looks up at her now, her delicate beauty never more apparent.

When all four meet the next day at the Bransons, the idea of a joint divorce and remarriage arises. Ned is the first to suggest it. "We can remain a close-knit group," he argues, "even keep our present houses. There are no children involved, so nobody loses."

"Yes, but what are people going to think?", Dolores counters. "Switching partners isn't exactly a common practice here in El Paso. I don't want to be seen as a social deviant." As the words pour from her mouth, she is astonished by her boldness, having spent years sitting quietly while others do the talking. She is not the only one to be impressed. Lloyd immediately rallies to her side. "Maybe it would be enough if we spent a lot of time together…you know, Ned and Jessica doing one thing, Dolores and I doing something else."

"But what about the love-making?", interjects Ned, unable to conceal his anxiety. "We can't go on 'dating' forever; we need a more permanent solution."

"Like?"

"Well, like I suggested…divorce then remarriage. Jessica and I could live here while you two take the other house." Jessica nods. "Ned is right. Any arrangement other than remarriage sounds shaky; I know I would be uncomfortable having to get everybody's agreement before deciding who's going to sleep with whom every night. All sorts of things could go wrong. Let's say Lloyd is feeling sick and wants me to pamper him while Dolores insists that he sleep with her…or maybe Ned has been away at a conference for a week and is anxious to reunite with me while Dolores and Lloyd are having a fight and can't stand being together in the same room. It could easily become an emotional nightmare. In my opinion, switching partners may draw glares from our neighbors, but it sounds like the only practical solution." After countless discussions over the ensuing weeks, the group decides to take Jessica's advice. Ned and Lloyd consult their lawyers about drawing up a separation agreement and filing papers for a formal divorce. It is agreed that the new marriages will take place soon after both divorces are granted. According the Texas law, that should take about four to six months.

Chapter 18

The Ad

Hilda's ad appears in all El Paso newspapers every week for three weeks running. Not surprisingly, the first calls are from men whose repeated questions about the reward leave little doubt as to their motivation. She politely declines them all. When Ned, who has been looking for the ad, spots it in a daily midway through the second week, he calls the number listed. He speaks in English. From the woman's speech, it's obvious she's Latina. When he tells her he has read the ad and wants to help, he is told she already has someone else. Ned congratulates her on finding help so quickly, but insists he can help as well…and is not interested in the reward money. "There's no harm in having more than one psychic on your side," he adds. Before she can hang up, he asks about the missing child. "How old is he…or is it a she?"

Hilda hesitates. "Why you want to know?"

"The more info we have on the child, the easier it will be to find him." "But I tell you; I already have other person."

Ned acts as if he didn't hear her. "What school does he go to?"

When she doesn't answer, he asks, "Was that the last place you saw him? Kidnappers often grab kids coming out of school."

Hilda pauses. "I not sure he kidnapped. Maybe just lost."

When he realizes she's not going to tell him anything, he

thanks her and hangs up, then immediately calls Jessica. "It sounds pretty fishy to me, Jess. She wouldn't even tell me whether the child is a boy or girl." Jessica responds quickly. "But the poor woman is suffering from grief, Ned. To lose a child, maybe her only child…well, I can't imagine anything more devastating. In this state of mind, she is bound to be distrustful toward strangers. I'm not at all surprised she refused to tell you anything about the child. I would probably act the same way." Ned, anxious to prove his worthiness, is crestfallen; unseen, he hangs his head. "I was just trying to help," he murmurs. "I hope I didn't get in the way. If so, I'm sorry." Jessica immediately picks up on his mood. "Oh no, I really appreciate your efforts, Ned. But it's best if I take it from here."

"So, you're going to call her?"

"Yes…sometime soon. I'll let you know what happens… okay?" When Ned is slow to respond, she adds, "That was really sweet of you to call her, Ned. You might be right to doubt her. I'll certainly be careful." "Okay," he says, making no attempt to conceal his disappointment.

Three days later Jessica calls Hilda. She mentions the ad and introduces herself as a concerned person but does not give her name. "I'm so sorry," she says. "You must be beside yourself." When she asks for the child's name, Hilda says she would rather give information face-to face. "I'm sorry, but I must be careful. As a woman you understand."

Jessica says she understands and agrees to meet despite her suspicions. "Shall I come to your house?", she asks.

"Oh no, somebody see you," Hilda replies.

"At a restaurant? Would that be better?"

"Too many people see us…maybe kidnappers…think you police or something. Better in place where no people."

"Like?"

"Maybe Red and White supermarket…the parking lot."

"But that's very busy."

"Not at 5:00 in morning."

"Hmm. Okay. What day?"

"Is Friday good for you?"

"Fine. I'll see you in the Red and White parking lot at 5:00 Friday morning."

"Bueno. What I call you?", Hilda asks.

"You can call me Peaches. And you?"

"Hilda."

When Hilda reports to Mendoza, Luis immediately calls his Sinaloa contact and insists on speaking directly to El Gordo. While waiting for his boss to pick up the phone, he rehearses his lines. Five minutes pass before he hears a voice.

"Francisco here; what dya want?"

Aware that his new boss is in a bad mood, Luis tries to moderate his excitement. "The trap is set; Hilda and the mystery woman are going to meet at the Red and White parking lot early Friday morning…like 5:00."

"Okay. Where this Red and White store?"

"You know, right here in Juárez…the big one at the corner of Paseo and Montero." He pauses, waiting for some sign of appreciation, a 'good job' or something to that effect. When it doesn't come, he takes a deep breath and asks, "What do you want me to do?" Gordo growls, "Nothing. I'll take it from here. Jis' keep your mouth shut."

"Okay."

When Jessica fails to show up at home that evening, Lloyd calls Ned to see if he knows anything. Ned, quickly alarmed, tells him about the newspaper ad…and shares his suspicions that it could be a trap. Lloyd can hear the panic in Ned's voice and considers offering some reassuring advice, but stops in mid-sentence when nothing comes to mind. Instead, he offers to call the police where he is told to file a missing persons report if she doesn't show up by Wednesday. Early the next day, Ned, unable to think about anything else, calls in sick, then tracks down the street address of the number given in the Psychic Wanted ad and pays the woman an unannounced visit. After introducing himself, he asks if a woman named Peaches came to see her yesterday. Hilda hesitates, then says yes. "But why you want to know?" she adds, her lips visibly trembling. When Ned raises the possibility that Peaches may have been abducted, Hilda denies any responsibility. It is only when Ned threatens to call the police that Hilda admits that two men came to the Red and White parking lot early in the morning and took her away. "But I don't know those men," she cries. "I not know why they take the woman." Ned again threatens her with police intervention if she doesn't tell all she knows. He specifically wants to know with whom she shared information about the meeting at the Red and White parking lot. When Hilda refuses to say, he asks her where she works. "PGR."

"And your boss's name?"

"Mendoza. Luis Mendoza."

Ned freezes when he hears the name. Just days ago Jessica confided that Dunwoody suspects Mendoza of working for one of the cartels. As soon as he gets home, he decides to call Dunwoody and tell him about Jessica's disappearance. In the ensuing conversation Dunwoody laments the loss, but is cagey about Mendoza. As they continue talking, he lets on that if Luis is selling out, it may not be with the Zapas now that El Gordo has moved into the Juárez area.

"Okay," replies Ned, making no effort to hide his anxiety, "let's say it's El Gordo's group that abducted her. Where might they take her?" "No question about that," Dunwoody answers. "The safest place for them would be somewhere in the Sierras… probably high in the remote hills of Sinaloa where the capo has his headquarters."

"Oh no", Ned cries, clenching his fist. "We can't let that happen."

Silence.

Neither man speaks until Ned, with head down now and voice quivering, adds, "but thank you for the information." Dunwoody is quick to warn him. "They have men armed with AK-47's all over those hills. You're going to get your head blown off if you go poking around in there."

Back home, Ned and Lloyd discuss their findings and come to the conclusion that Jessica is probably still alive. "If they were going to kill her," Lloyd reasons, "why wouldn't they do it right there in the parking lot? Why bother to take her all the way back to Sinaloa or somewhere else deep in Mexico?"

Ned finds Lloyd's logic convincing and decides right there that, come what may, he has no choice but to go looking for her. With that in mind he calls the Dean's office the next morning and applies for a six-month sabbatical leave.

Chapter 19

A Prisoner's Life

When he agreed to Jessica's abduction, El Gordo had no idea how beautiful she was. Now that he gets to see her every day in his Sinaloa stronghold, he quickly falls in love with her…to the consternation of his wife, Maria, who withers at the lack of attention. Weeks, then months, go by without any love-making between husband and wife. "You haven't made me feel like a woman for ages," she complains finally. "I see how you gaze at this new woman. Do you like her blonde hair? Are you tired of Mexican women's black hair? What kind of husband are you that little things like that can change your heart? I am your wife, Francisco, not just a friend you can discard when you meet someone you like better."

When he can no longer stand his wife's complaints, Francisco arranges to have her sent to her parents' house in Culiacán for a lengthy visit. To the man known as El Gordo, it's not just Jessica's blonde hair that dazzles him. Every chance he can get, especially when she's not looking, he studies her whole frame, from her sparkling blue eyes and gracefully-shaped lips to her long, slender legs and petite feet. To someone accustomed to short, black-haired, dark-skinned women of Indian ancestry, this new member of the household has all the earmarks of a goddess. Her behavior, too, has an Olympian air about it; she's always serene, never ruffled, suggesting a woman at peace with herself, a person of immeasurable depth and substance. But much of this assessment is conjecture on Francisco's part since Jessica spends most of her time alone in her bedroom, reading or meditating.

When he can't stand the frustration, he insists on taking meals with her. At the dinner table, she says nothing. Even when he goes to great lengths to entertain her, she remains mute. In an attempt to please her, he brings her books to read, most of them cowboy and Indian novels he found at a local bookstore. When he asks her if she liked them, she confesses that she didn't read any of them. His temper flares, "These are stories about your own people. You not interested in your own country? You have no feelings." She starts to explain but gives up when he walks away. A few days later, he has one of his henchmen deliver a Mexican-style armoire for her clothes. The large mirror on the door is surrounded by crudely drawn images of farm animals. When Jessica objects to the ornamentation, Francisco gets upset. "You need place to hang your clothes, no?"

"But those animals are really ugly," she answers. "Can't you find something simpler?"

"This is people art…not fancy stuff like in museum. If you want to learn our ways, you must learn to like what our people paint."

Jessica refuses to back down. "Who said I wanted to learn your ways? Maybe I want to learn *about* your ways…but that doesn't mean I want to imitate your tastes. Those animals are ugly." When she looks at him again, her voice softens, "I'm sure Mexico has some very good painters but I don't think they waste their time ornamenting armoires."

Later that day, without consulting her, he has the armoire removed and a simple coat rack put in its place. Hanging from the rack is a peasant-style blouse and skirt, the kind traditionally worn by women from the Sinaloa region. But this is no ordinary attire. The blouse is adorned with tiny sequins cut from mica and silver; the black woolen skirt is covered with brightly-colored orange, yellow and pink flowers.

When Jessica emerges from her room the next morning wearing some of her old clothes, Francisco stops her. "You no see the blouse and skirt I bought for you?"

"Oh, I saw them alright," she replies.

"Why you no wear them?" When she says nothing, he asks, "Wrong size? I punish tailor."

"I didn't even try them on," she says. "It's just not my style… much too flowery. I like more conservative things."

"But you not in America now; in Mexico you dress like Mexican woman."

She studies his face, looking for an opening but finds none. She settles for a brief reply, "No thanks."

My God, she murmurs, once safely back in her bedroom. *This man cannot accept the fact that people are different. He thinks everybody should be like him…talk like him, eat like him, think like him. How can I get him to see that I don't want to become like him?"*

An opportunity comes the very next day. When she leaves the table without touching her breakfast, he growls, "What's the matter? You no like squid I order for you?"

Her reply is brief. "I don't like squid…especially for breakfast."

"Why you no like? Everybody in my family like squid. Is very expensive. You learn to like it."

She considers her options, then replies, "Why can't I order my own meals? I'm the only one who knows what I like and don't like." When he begins to sulk, she adds, "You and I are different. I don't expect you to feel the same way about things that I do. It's okay that we're not the same. I may not like it, but I accept it. And I want you to accept that I have different feelings and opinions than yours. So…please stop telling me what I should or should not like." Francisco appears flustered, turns to leave. At the door he barks, "Alright…I no bother you."

When it becomes obvious that her Spanish is elementary, he hires a tutor to improve his English. A natural aptitude for language allows him to progress rapidly. When they are together, he doesn't hesitate to correct her Spanish, but gets defensive whenever she corrects his English. She is aware of his efforts to please her, but cannot forget that she's here as a prisoner. He accepts her silence as the price he must pay for keeping here against her will. *In time*, he murmurs, *she loosen up, show more life…and want my attention. For now, I be patient friend, not demand much. Hey, I overcome every other challenge in my life…why not this one?*

For Jessica, being walled up in this compound high in the Sierras has all the hallmarks of a prison. She is allowed to walk up and down the main street that runs between Francisco's headquarters and the billets of his followers…but that's it. The huge forest just outside the compound is off limits, a restriction enforced by the two armed guards who remain at her side whenever she comes out of her bedroom. She is not allowed to communicate with anyone outside the compound, either by telephone or mail. Even inside the compound, Francisco has made it clear that he will "put a hole in head" of any male who tries to get close to her. It is obvious to his associates that Francisco hopes to starve her of human contact, thus making interaction with him all the more desirable. In the two months she has been there, however, there is no sign she is coming around. She continues to dwell on her relationships with Lloyd and Ned, wondering if the planned switch will ever take place now that she has been kidnapped. *I may never get out of here…at least alive. Now that I'm no longer a threat to the cartel, is there any point in their feeding me? I can tell that Francisco wants to get close… but that would be like climbing into bed with a rattlesnake. I don't see any chance of escape. So, what can I do?*

The first sign that she might be changing occurs when he invites her to a fiesta in the little town of Badiraguato where every month he distributes a truck load of free food (mainly rice, beans, cheese, and milk) to the poor people who live there. It's an event eagerly awaited by families whose meals often consist of nothing more than a tortilla laced with salt. El Gordo likes the gathering because he is treated like a god, a welcome change from the harassment he typically receives at the hands of the police and military. To make the contact even more personal, he insists on handing out the food himself rather than leaving it to one of his henchmen. Having grown up in this part of Sinaloa, he knows most of the families by name and can knowledgably inquire as to their health, their children...even their farm animals. To some he is known as El Gordo; most, however, call him Francisco. As they take their life-giving gifts of food, they offer kisses (the women) or a hug (the men). The children are shy; some just nod with their heads while others neither say nor do anything. When the truck has been emptied, Francisco waves to the remaining few and assures them he will be back with more next month. "Viva El Gordo," they shout as he drives off. "Gracias, Señor."

This is the first time that Jessica has seen the softer part of her captor's personality. Without intending it, she smiles at him often, a reaction duly noted by her ever-watchful keeper. When he reaches out to touch her hand, however, she quickly withdraws it and looks the other way. Outwardly he winces, but inwardly smiles. *So, maybe I make discovery. She like me if I do nice things for people. Hmm. I make that happen.*

On the way back to the compound, he turns to her, saying, "You like what we do today?"

She nods.

"Next week we make foundation for new school in Badiraguato. Now children must go to school far away in Culiacán. Soon they have school near houses. We have big fiesta...lots of food and drink...many people be there...(*pause*)...

You come with me." When she fails to nod her approval, he looks at her, squinting. At the door he mutters to himself, *What wrong with this woman? I make nice day for her and she not thank me. Maria not give me trouble like this one.* At dinner that night, their conversation centers around the school and the monthly gifts of food in the park. Just as he is warming to her interest, she asks, "With all the money you make selling drugs, you could do much more. Just think of all the poor people in Mexico who need your help. Why do you limit yourself to people you know?"

He frowns, clearly uncomfortable with this turn in the conversation. Speaking slowly, he says, "They are family... brothers, nephews, cousins, grandparents; some not family but people I grow up with in town. In Mexico...maybe not in U.S... families and neighbors help each other. I just do what everybody else do." Jessica puts down her fork and stares at him. "Don't get me wrong, Francisco, I think that's a great idea. I just wonder why you don't take the idea further...you know, do the same things for people in other villages. After all they're your fellow countrymen."

The gist of her argument is lost in the ringing of a single word...'Francisco'. *She say my name...for first time,* he murmurs. *And she look at me different. She never look at me like that before.* It's all he can do to remain in his chair. When she notices the look in his face, she excuses herself and retires to her bedroom.

Still brimming with excitement at Jessica's use of his name, Francisco goes out to one of the grassy park-like areas in the compound where he can think while he walks. One of the things getting in the way is her name. Jessica is not a Spanish name; it's not only foreign but hard for Hispanics to say. The obvious answer: she needs a new name, a name that rolls easily off the Mexican tongue. He turns around at the little fountain at the end of the path, the one dedicated to Guadalúpe, a deity who came to earth back in the 16th Century and asked to have a church built on the site where she appeared. On the way back through the compound, it suddenly hits him. *Why not Guadaúpe…a name Mexicans know and trust. Yes, Guadalúpe…(pause)…much better than Jessica. For nickname, she will be Lúpe? (LOO-pay) I tell her tomorrow at breakfast.*

At breakfast, Francisco waits until his prisoner is seated and served. He watches carefully as she places her napkin in her lap and reaches for her juice. No squid this morning, just cereal, milk, and fruit…with toast and coffee. With eyes sparkling, he leans forward and raises his glass of jugo de naranja, "I have surprise for you…a new name." She scowls. Before he can say anymore, she asks, "What's wrong with my old name. Is Jessica too hard for you to say?"

"Not a good Mexican name…has funny sound. We say 'J' like gringos say 'H'…so comes out Hessica. Not good. Make people laugh. I have better name for you…Guadalúpe."

"I like my name. Besides, Guadalúpe is a saint…someone people pray to every day. Why would you want to call me a saint?"

"Is common name in Mexico…like Jesús. Doesn't mean you a saint…just beautiful name." She squints. "I don't like it; it's too religious. I don't want people to think of me as a spiritually gifted person. That's not me at all."

"But maybe you really spiritual person, just don't know it. You beautiful on outside; maybe you beautiful on inside too."

She shifts uneasily in her chair. "Well, thank you, Francisco, but I prefer my real name, Jessica. Call me Hessica if you want to but please not Guadalúpe."

Francisco sits back down. "Okay. We give you nickname… Lúpe. You like?"

"That's a little better...although it sounds like a disease... or a wolf. How about using my last name...Branson? Is that too hard to say?"

Francisco shakes his head. "Not easy. How you say... Branesin...Brawnsin?" He laughs. "No do. Lúpe better name for you. I tell everybody call you Lúpe."

Chapter 20

Culiacàn

Given the mounting evidence, Dunwoody decides it is time to pull the plug on Mendoza, even though this means taking his chances with Luis's superior at PGR…Col. Contréras. The gamble pays off. With the Colonel's support and testimony from Eduardo, Sebastián, and the self-serving Hilda, Mendoza is caught and arrested. While a quick call to El Gordo brings the bond money he needs to post bail, the evidence against him makes conviction a foregone conclusion. News of his arrest floods local and country-wide media. As far away as Mexico City, newspapers blare: 'PGR INFILTRATED, MENDOZA CHARGED WITH TREASON.' Despite his denials, Luis is quickly seen as a traitor who sacrificed soul and country for the sake of money. In grief, he flees to his former hacienda, wanders out into the fields where his laborers once worked and puts a pistol to his head.

Without Peaches to help them locate suspected targets, Eduardo's group disbands. Manny returns to his role as priest in Oaxaca; Carmelo applies for an equipment job with the Denver Broncos. At a get-together in town, Eduardo and Sebastián prepare to say goodbye to Jesús who plans to head back to Sinaloa where he grew up. The decision to do so is fraught with anxiety since he hasn't seen his family in two years. Nor have there been any letters or phone calls. At this point, he's not even sure if his family still owns the small hillside farm where he once tilled fields of tomatoes, squash and marijuana. From what he reads in the news, he's certain that El Gordo is still kingpin of the Sinaloa drug cartel. That means, in effect, that he and his underlings rule the whole area. Of concern to Jesús, now 19, is whether El Gordo remembers his botched attempt at extortion. That was the time, recorded indelibly in the young boy's memory, that he was sent into a local grocery store to collect protection money, but chickened out when he saw his girlfriend there. His boss, waiting in the car, exploded when Jesús returned empty-handed. Furious at the boy's ineptness, the gunman stormed into the store and shot both the girl and her uncle...and then took the owed money from the register. Under threat of lethal punishment from El Gordo, Jesús fled the next day and hasn't been back since.

When asked why he wants to go back now, he cites two things...a desire to see his parents again and frustration with a life of drifting. Besides, there is nothing he really wants to do, no career to pursue, no places he wants to visit. But these are the easy answers. From deep within his psyche, in a place not yet conscious, a more basic force is at work. Here, beyond the reach of reason, Sinaloa lips its seductive call, like a mother calling a lost child to her breast. It is a power he is helpless to resist...He leaves for home the next day.

As he makes his way from Juárez down Mexico's Pacific coast to Sinaloa, he stops to take odd jobs, stays a few days then moves on...guided each step of the way by instinct...careless of what lies ahead, like an aging salmon drawn to its spawning grounds even in the face of certain death. He heads south from Juárez, then west over the Sierra Madres until he reaches Culiacán, the town where he attended secondary school. Sensing that Culiacán is a safer place to stay than Badiraguato, the town where he got into trouble, he rents a cheap studio apartment and moves in. After only two days of looking, he lands a job as a night-time janitor at a large sports goods store. While the work is dull and unchallenging, it gives him a chance to examine the equipment on display, including rifles, shotguns, hunting bows, fishing rods, and stuff for camping. Of particular interest is the wide selection of bows and arrows.

Putting down his broom one night, he picks up a small wooden bow similar to the one his uncle gave him on his 12th birthday. Now nineteen and muscular enough to handle a bigger, stronger bow, he puts it back and picks out a larger compound bow made of aluminum-carbon alloy. It has pulleys at both ends and wire cables connecting the two, a design that, according to the accompanying brochure, increases both trajectory speed and accuracy compared to the traditional longbow. He has seen pictures of such a bow before, but has never tried one or even touched one. He looks around to make sure he is alone, then tries pulling on the main string. It requires all his strength to draw it all the way back. Once the string has been readied to shoot, however, the two pulleys absorb the tension and make it easier to hold the string in place until it is time to let go. He smiles at his discovery and tries again. Each time he tries, the process becomes more comfortable. Reassured that no one can see him, he places a metal arrow in the string and draws it all the way back. Still holding the arrow against the string, he moves over to the practice area where a straw target has been set up for customers who want to try out the equipment. He looks first to make sure the night watchman can't see him through the window, then lets the arrow fly. Although it lands at the edge of the target, far from the bull's eye, the thrill he feels is palpable. He retrieves the arrow and tries again...getting a little closer to the center this time. After three more tries, he puts the bow and arrow back in their original places and resumes sweeping the floor. The work is no more interesting than it was a few minutes ago, but something has changed. As he turns to look at the archery display again, he is energized. What he feels is akin to what he felt back in Sinaloa when he shot his first rabbit. That was with a rifle, he recalls, but the thrill was the same. As he moves on to sweep the next room, he mentally replays what happened with the bow and arrow. Secretly, he begins laying plans for buying a set for himself. He doesn't stop to ask why he needs a bow and arrow...or under what circumstances he is going to use such a weapon. This is not a time for reasoning;

the decision has been made in his unconscious where it feels not only right but necessary. Events will justify the purchase. Of this he is certain.

Over the next weeks he denies himself all food other than the tortillas and frijoles he eats at his apartment. At meal times he drinks water rather than his favorite soft drink…Coca-Cola. He volunteers for work on Saturday which is usually one of his two days off. He even takes a second job bussing at a nearby restaurant on Sundays. By the end of the month, he has enough to buy the compound bow and a set of twelve arrows. Not wanting to carry around a full-sized bow, he opts for the kind that folds in half and is small enough to fit into a large backpack. The owner is so pleased with the work of his young janitor that he throws in a leather release that makes drawing the string back easier on the fingers.

Eager to master his new weapon, Jesús spends every morning out on the archery practice range at the edge of town. There he finds fellow archers who have much to teach him. Why he is so motivated to learn is still not clear, either to him or his associates. All he can be sure of is that it has something to do with Sinaloa. Right now, that is all he needs to know.

When he has put aside a little money for extras, he plans a bus ride to Badiraguato where he grew up and where his parents presumably still live. He is aware that this could be dangerous. Who knows how long El Gordo's memory is? It's been two years now since he botched the assignment at the grocery store. Does the capo who despises failure on the part of his subordinates still hold a grudge? Before leaving his apartment he takes a long, hard look in the mirror. What he sees is reassuring…the cheeks filled out, the thin mustache, the more muscular shoulders…a man who many in Badiraguato will not recognize as Jesús Celestino, son of Carlos Celestino, the hillside farmer. To make it harder for people to recognize him, he wears a hooded jacket and sunglasses. His plan is to visit his parents whom he has not seen or heard from in two years…and visit the grave of Lili, the girlfriend who was shot in her uncle's grocery store.

In Badiraguato he leaves the center of town and heads up a dirt road into the hills where his parents live. Along the way he stops to look at the fields where poppies have replaced the tomatoes, squash and marijuana that used to grow there. At his house, he pauses to lower his hood and remove the sunglasses. When he hears someone coming to the door, he reaches out with his arms. The expected hug never comes.

"Who the hell are you?", the man growls..

Jesús gasps. "I…I…ah…I'm lookin' for the Celestinos."

"Well, they ain't been here for two years now. That's when we bought the place."

"They sold the farm?", Jesús asks, struggling to make sense of the news.

The man smiles. "They didn't have no choice. Kept losin' their crops. Had to move into town."

"Losin' their crops…but why? Used to grow lots of things here…tomatoes, squash, onions, and corn. The soil is good; they was careful to rest the land every five years."

"Got nothin' to do with the soil (*pointing to the field out front*). We don't have no trouble growin' jis' about anything we want. No, they made the wrong folks angry…and got their crops burned out."

"Angry…what folks were those?"

The man looks around. "I don't wanna get into all that. Jis' take it from me that as long as they stayed here, they couldn't grow nothin'.

The other folks wouldn't let 'em. So, they had to sell the farm. Now I gotta go." He prepares to slam the door in the boy's face when Jesús yells, "Where'd they move to? Can you tell me that?"

"From what I hear, they moved to that apartment buildin' down behind the Pemex station. You know where that is?"

"Yeah, I know. Thanks." Still shaken by the news, Jesús heads for the Pemex station. Once he finds the right apartment, he again lowers his hood and removes his sunglasses. This time it's his mother who opens the door. He falls into her arms.

"Oh my God, it's you," she gasps.

When he takes a step inside the apartment, she blocks his way. "You can't come in here, Jesús. You'll get us all in trouble. We been warned not to have anything to do with you if you ever come back to Badiraguato."

"Who warned you?", he asks, knowing full well who it is.

"You know, the man who sent you into that grocery store. They ain't never forgiven you for makin' El Gordo look bad. There's no question about it; they're the ones who burnt our crops and forced us to sell the farm. And then they tell us we can never have anything to do with our son." When she starts sobbing, Jesús instinctively moves to hug here. "No, Jesús, you gotta go before anyone sees you here." With that, she backs up and starts to close the door.

"But what about Papa?", Jesus cries out. "Is he okay?"

"Yes, he's okay," she whispers as the door closes. Through the crack, she speaks her final words, words that she never thought it possible to say to her own son, "Now, don't come back."

Speechless, Jesús stumbles down the walkway and past the Pemex station. Disbelief that his mother could talk to him that way alternates with fury at the men who put her up to it...the same men presumably who burned his parents' crops and made them move. Weakened by the emotions raging inside, he heads for Paradiso Park and the tranquility of its fountains. There, on a bench by himself, his feelings begin to sort themselves out. With thought, anger toward his mother gives way to forgiveness. What choice did she have but to reject him? No, he murmurs, the blame lies elsewhere. As an image of El Gordo arises, fear of the man who drove her from her home yields to bitterness, then to fury and a thirst for revenge. He clenches his fist and pounds the bench. When he rises, his jaw is set, his lips curled. There are plans to be made, options to be considered. But first, he must pay a visit to Lili's grave.

At the cemetery Jesús looks around until he finds the Cardénas family plot. Lili's grave is marked with a wooden cross, bent now by summer rains and tilting to one side. As he approaches the gravesite, he is alarmed to see someone there, a boy his own age. Afraid of being recognized, he pulls his hood down over his forehead and puts on his sunglasses.

"Jesús, is that you?", comes the unexpected greeting.

Jesús steps closer before responding. "Raffi...yeah, it's me."

"You look different," Lili's brother says, looking up at his old friend.

"Yeah, you do too. Two years is a long time."

As Raffi rises to shake hands, his knee buckles, spilling him to the ground.

"What happened to your leg?"

"It ain't my leg really; it's my knee. Drinkin' too much mescal, I guess."

"No, I'm serious," replies Jesús. "What happened to ya?"

Raffi beckons Jesús over. "Well, I'll tell ya but you can't go blabbing it around town" "

"I promise."

"I fell off a bicycle…smashed the knee cap on a rock."

Jesús chuckles. "Glad it wasn't your head."

"Thanks."

As he sits, Jesús is flooded with thoughts about Lili whose grave is now just a few feet away. Raffi recognizes the look and asks, "You two could probly be married by now, don't you think? She really liked you."

"Yeah, well I liked her too."

"Enough to get married?"

"Yeah, I think so. We talked about it a few times."

Silence.

Raffi shifts his legs to get more comfortable. "The guy who shot her, you know, Fernando, he's still around…moved up in the cartel…kind of a big shot now…has two bodyguards with him all the time."

"How do you know that?"

Raffi flashes a boyish grin. "I follow him around sometime… to keep tabs on him."

"How come?"

Raffi looks around. Reassured of their privacy, he says, "Ever since the day he killed my sister, I dreamt of payin' him back. It's gonna be hard with them bodyguards around, but I think it can be done. I jis' haven't figured out how to do it yet."

The two boys lapse into silence as afternoon shadows break across Lili's grave. Like marble sculptures, they lie on their backs with hands folded behind their heads, minds spinning with thoughts not yet ripe for sharing. When several minutes have passed, Jesús is the first to speak.

"This guy Fernando, he's the one who told El Gordo about me screwin' things up at the grocery store; that's why I had to leave town. This morning, I found out he's also the one who sprayed my parents' field with poison, killin' all the plants and forcin' them to sell the farm." He shakes his head. "I can't even go to my parents' apartment now; they afraid Fernando will find out and do somethin' to 'em."

"You mean he's still lookin' for you…after two years?"

"Yeah, I guess El Gordo wants me to pay for my mistake."

Raffi sits up. "He ain't satisfied that he drove you outta town for two years?" "I guess not. He wants my head."

"No wonder you goin' around with that hood over your face… and those sunglasses. Dressed like that, you is one scary dude. Glad I know you ain't really nothin' but a a wimp." Both boys laugh hard, Jesús going so far as to kick his feet up in the air. When the laughing subsides, Jesús speaks. "Serious, though, you want to get this guy Fernando…I mean, kill 'im?"

"I ain't stopped thinkin' about it for two years now…'specially when I come here to visit Lili's grave. Every time I come, I promise her I'll get 'im."

Silence.

"Maybe we could do it together, Jesús. What d'ya think?"

"I'd like to," says Jesús, "but I don't know how to do it. I don't even have a rifle anymore. Mama says they took that along with my other things. The only thing I got now is the bow in my backpack. And that ain't gonna stand up to an AK-47."

"A bow…can I see it? I ain't never seen one up close."

"Sure." Jesús opens his pack and pulls out the bow…and unfolds it with a snap."

"You any good with it?"

"I been practicing over in Culiacán. They got a nice target area there…lots of guys gettin' ready for huntin' season."

"Can you really take down a big animal like a deer with that thing?"

"Oh yeah. You jis' gotta get the arrow goin' where you want it to go."

"How far can you shoot it…you know, like accurate?"

"With this compound bow, probly fifty yards, maybe more with a metal arrow."

Raffi shouts, "Wow…that's pretty far. How about a little demo? That tree over there (*pointing*) is about twenty-five yards from here. Can you hit it?"

Jesús sighs. "I dunno. It's pretty skinny. Let's see." He takes an arrow from his pack and carefully inserts it into the bow string. After stretching out his left hand, he uses his right hand to pull the string back all the way, then pauses long enough to line the tip of the arrow up with the tree. When he lets go, the string makes a slapping sound as it leaps forward, sending the arrow on its way.

WHACK.

"You got it," Raffi exclaims. "Right in the middle of the tree."

"Okay, but twenty-five yards is pretty easy; fifty'd be a lot harder. You gotta keep everything steady. Even with these metal arrows, you get some wobble and that can throw you off… 'specially at long distances."

Raffi limps over to the tree to inspect it more carefully. "This here arrow went in at least two or three inches. That's enough to kill somebody, ain't it?"

"Probly, depends on where you get 'im. But no matter what, it's gonna hurt."

Raffi squints. "Have you ever…you know… killed anybody with it?"

"Nope…not yet at least."

"You think maybe you could get Fernando with it?"

"I dunno. We'd have to be in a perfect place, you know, somewhere where the bodyguards can't use their machine guns on us. But they're with 'im all the time, ain't they?"

"Yeah."

Silence.

"You jis' said 'us'. Do you see me helpin' out somehow?"

"Hey, I don't know what to think. I need some time to get used to the idea."

"But it's a possibility…ain't it?"

"Maybe. Let me sleep on it."

"Can we get together soon…I mean like tomorrow?"

"Don't know why not. I got nothin' else to do. I'm not even sure why I came to Badiraguato, except to see my parents. And I can't even do that now." Raffi looks puzzled. "You didn't come back to get even with Fernando?" "I don't think so. Maybe it's El Gordo I'm after. I can't be sure. All I know is somethin's gnawin' at me inside. Whatever it is, it's pullin' me back here no matter what I say. Seein' how strong it is, I figure there's no use me fightin' it."

Chapter 21

Fernando Gets Whacked

In the days that follow, the two meet often, usually in the woods behind Raffi's house in Culiacán. "Since our talk in the cemetery," Raffi says," I've been keepin' a close eye on Fernando. I know one thing for sure…his favorite hangout is the Sonora Bar and Grill on Crespo Avendida…right here in the middle of Culiacán."

"How often he go there?" Jesús asks.

"Two, maybe three, nights a week…usually around 7:00. Gets somethin' to eat at the bar, watches some telly, and keeps drinkin' until his bodyguard takes 'im out to the car around 10:00. By that time he's usually pretty tipsy; you can tell from the way he walks. If his guard don't hold 'im up, he don't make it to the car."

"I thought you said he had two guards."

"He does; one goes inside with 'im while the other waits outside near the door."

"Sounds like he's got somebody watchin' 'im all the time he's in there."

"Most of the time, yeah…but not when he's done drinkin' for the night and ready to go home. That's when the outside guard has to go get the car."

"Where's the car parked?"

"Down in back of the restaurant; they got a parkin' lot there."

"So, Fernando has jis' one guard with him when the other one goes for the car."

"Yeah…and that's when we can get 'im."

"Well, how? The guard that's with 'im has a machine-gun, right? How we gonna stand up to that?"

Raffi smiles. "I think I got that figured out. Before the outside guard goes to get the car, we get in position behind some trees down in the parkin' lot. When he opens the car door to get in, you plug 'im with an arrow in the back. Then we take the car up the street and wait for Fernando and the other guard to come outta the restaurant."

"Sounds okay so far, but it's still gonna be a bow and arrow against an AK-47, no?"

"Yir forgettin' one thing; the guy you plug in the parkin' lot has an AK-47 too; so, we dump his body next to the car and take his gun with us when we drive up to the restaurant."

Jesús nods his approval. "Okay…so we park outside the restaurant as Fernando and the other guard come out. Now what?"

"You drive; it'll be dark so they won't notice anything wrong… and I'll be in the back seat with the machine-gun. When they get close enough, I'll roll down the window and blast away."

"You know how to use that thing?"

"I seen one up close; all you gotta do is switch the safety off. I can figure out how to do that on the way up from the parkin' lot."

"Whew! You give this lotsa thought. But what happens after we get Fernando? Gordo's goin' to be pretty mad, ain't he? You say Fernando is now one of his top guys. How we s'posed to handle that?"

Raffi pauses. "I dunno. I guess we'll hafta figure somthin' out."

Silence.

"Okay, let's give it a try." As Jesús reaches out to shake hands, he adds, "When's a good time?"

"Why not tomorrow night; he goes there every Friday."

As agreed, Jesús and Rafáel meet across the street from the Sonora restaurant at 6:30. They huddle in the shadows outside a gift shop until Fernando arrives.

"There he is," Raffi whispers, pointing to the black Infiniti.

Jesús checks his wrist watch…7:15…right on time. Raffi adds, "Now we gotta wait here until Fernando goes inside and the guard takes the car down to the parkin' lot."

"Okay…then what…we gotta go down there and hide behind some trees for the next three hours?"

"Yeah, but let's wait until the driver comes back up and takes his position outside the front door."

"Right."

When they see the driver coming up the driveway, they cross the street and head down into the parking lot. Seeing that the lot is already half full, Jesús says, "There could be a problem...you know, if somebody parks next to the Infiniti on the driver's side. How am I s'posed to get an open shot at 'im?"

"You jis' hafta get closer...creep around back of the other car and pop the guard from behind as he's openin' the door. He'll never see you."

Jesús nods. "Yeah, okay. I think I can do it. But for now, we gotta hide behind some trees, right?"

"No rush; the driver won't be out for three hours. We could even go get somethin' to eat." Jesús shakes his head. "You go if you wanna; I'm too nervous to eat anything."

"Okay; I'll bring you back a torta jis' in case you get hungry." With that, Raffi leaves and heads down the street for a vendor hawking tortas and soft drinks at the corner. He returns thirty minutes later and offers his partner the promised meal. By now Jesús's nerves have settled down and his appetite improved. In between bites of the torta, he jokes about what the newspapers are going to say in the morning. "I can see the headlines now... 'FERNANDO RUÍZ KILLED AT RESTAURANT'. Down below it'll say somethin' like, 'City mourns as outstanding citizen is brutally murdered. Hundreds expected at funeral....blah...blah...blah'"

"Yeah, El Gordo tells 'em what to write. If he don't like it, he shuts the paper down...or jis' pops the guy who wrote the stuff."

At 10:10, Raffi suddenly points to a burly man coming down the driveway. He's carrying an AK-47. By now, there is someone parked on both sides of the Infiniti. As the gunman heads into the space between the Infiniti and the Toyota on the driver's side, Jesús readies himself to pounce. When he hears the car door open, he goes into a crouch and circles behind the Toyota. It's now or never. He stands, pulls the string all the way back, and aims at the driver's back. It's a big target. The man is solidly built, 5'6" and over 200 pounds. At this range, it's impossible to miss. As the driver bends over, the arrow buries itself deep in his flesh. The AK-47 drops to the ground as he gasps…then falls, half inside, half outside the car. He moans softly, then rolls over.

Jesús drops his bow and rushes to pull his victim from the car and grab the keys. Raffi looks first to see if anyone is watching, then, reassured there's no one else is in the parking lot, limps to where Jesús is standing and picks up the machine-gun. "D'ya get the keys?", he whispers

"Yeah, right here. Lemme get in and unlock the back door."

When he hears the familiar click, Raffi opens the rear door and slides in, holding the AK-47 on his lap.

"I think he's still breathing," Jesús' whispers, the anxiety evident in his voice.

"Don't matter," blurts out Raffi. "We gotta get up there before the other guard thinks somethin's wrong."

Jesús nods, then steps over the guard's body and slides into the driver's seat.

As they head up the driveway, Raffi, now in the back seat, leans forward, "Make sure you park so the passenger's side is in front of the restaurant. That way I can get 'em while they're standin' on the sidewalk."

Jesús says nothing but nods. When they reach the street, he turns right, advances a few yards, then backs up until the passenger's seat is directly opposite the restaurant. Fernando and the guard are already there, waiting. The guard, even fatter than the one back in the parking lot, looks in at the driver and says, "Where the fuck you been?"

Jesús holds up his right arm to conceal his face and says nothing. Raffi quickly rolls down the back window and readies the gun. At the sound, the guard turns to look. When he sees the barrel of the AK-47 pointing directly at him, he screams to his boss, "Get down." It's too late. Before Fernando can act, a volley of bullets explodes from the rear seat of the Infiniti, sending both Fernando and guard toppling over backwards. A second blast tears into their bodies when they hit the sidewalk. Jesús waits long enough to see a pool of blood forming before hitting the accelerator. "You got 'em both," he shouts as he heads the car down the street. "Now what?"

"Jis' head outta town," Raffi answers. We gotta ditch the car before the police come lookin' for it."

"Too bad," Jesús responds, already relaxing. "Such a nice car; wish we could take it for a spin."

"Yeah, well everybody knows this car; we wouldn't make it five miles before somebody spotted us." He pauses. "So, get off this main road as soon as you can. Take a right on the first dirt road you come to; we can ditch it somewhere up in the woods."

"Then what?"

"I don't know about you but I'm gonna walk home through the woods and watch some soccer on the telly."

"Ain't you nervous?"

"Sure, but who cares? We jis' knocked off one of El Gordo's right-hand men. And he happens to be the thug who killed my sister."

"You gonna tell your parents?"

"I dunno, probly. It'll make 'em pretty happy...(*pause*)...You gonna tell anybody?"

"Naw. There's nobody I want to tell...at least down here. Maybe if I was up in Juárez, I'd want to tell Eduardo and the other guys. But that's okay. I feel good, jis' like you. We got the guy we wanted. Now we jis' hafta lay low for a while." A mile up the dirt road, Jesús points to a smaller, more primitive road to the right. "How about in here somewhere?"

"Let's try it."

The road has deep ruts left over from summer rains, making headway slow and difficult. "What about over there?" Raffi shouts, pointing to an open space surrounded by a grove of pines. Jesús brings the car to a halt and gets out to look around.

"Yeah, I don't think we'll find anything better. We can always cover it with some branches."

"Let's leave the machine gun here," adds Raffi as he gets out to inspect the area. "We can always come back and get it."

"What about the car key?", asks Jesús. "You wanna take it home?"

Raffi pauses. "Naw. Let's hide it somewhere here in these trees. That way we gonna be the only ones who know where to find it."

Once the key is hidden in the crotch of a young mango tree, the two break off a few pine boughs and cover the roof, hood and trunk of the Infiniti. Satisfied with their work, they head back through the woods.

"I don't think anybody saw us…so we should be okay," says Jesús. "Outside the restaurant I covered my face so nobody walkin' by could see me. I think it worked…(*pause*)…anybody see you?"

"I was too busy blastin' the pricks to notice. It'll be all over the news tomorrow, but nobody's goin' to know who did it."

Jesús nods. "Yeah, besides, they don't even know I'm in town."

With a final handshake and promise to stay in touch, they go their separate ways, Raffi to his parents' home, Jesús to his apartment.

Chapter 22

The Collectors

Three days later, as Jesús is finishing up his shift for the night, he is approached by Sergio Martinez, the sports store owner. "Hey, Jesús, can I talk to you for a minute?" His smile does little to allay the fear bred by such a question. Once they are both settled in his office, he smiles again. "I heard on the news the other day that Fernando Ruiz and a bodyguard were gunned down in front of the Sonora Bar and Grill… and another guard was ambushed in the parking lot by someone using a bow and arrow." He cocks his head as if waiting for an answer.

"Yeah, I read that too."

Sergio continues. "The newspapers are even referring to it as the 'Tarzán case'." He pauses, clearly looking for a response from his young janitor.

"Yeah, I saw that too. Kinda crazy, huh?"

Sergio leans back in his chair, hands behind his head. "Any chance you had something to do with that, Jesús?" When no response is forthcoming, he sits up and says, "The reason I ask is that the other day two men dressed in suits and vests and driving a black Infiniti came here wanting to know if we sell arrows similar to the one used in the bodyguard killing. When they showed me the arrow in question, I said yes, 'We sell that type here…and others as well. Why do you ask?' The one with the thick glasses said, 'We're lookin' for the guy who did it. We want the names and addresses of everybody who bought arrows like those ones.' When I hesitated, the other guy, the one with the cauliflower ear, said that if I didn't give them the information they wanted, they'd call in the police and make me do it. So, I said, 'The only names and addresses we keep are for customers who pay with credit cards. I can give you those if you want.' As I said it, I was reminded that you paid for your bow and arrows in cash, so there would be no record of either your name or address on our books."

Jesús nods, "Yeah, right...cash only. I ain't got a credit card."

"Well, I gave them the names of two men who purchased a metal arrow recently. Having gotten what they wanted, they left without further trouble. I thought I'd let you know about this just in case you had something to do with the parking lot incident." He waits, staring at Jesús, but still smiling.

Silence.

"Well, did you?", he says, careful to lower his voice.

Jesús pauses for a moment, then tilts his head forward.

Sergio smiles. "Well, you can be sure I'm not going to tell anyone. I'm on your side in all this. It makes me sick to see our town handed over to a bunch of thugs. They run everything now...the mayor's office, the police department, the newspapers, the courts... just about anything you can think of. And they're not satisfied with just the drug business; recently they've begun running a protection racket that's poisoning our business community."

Jesús nods quickly, indicating that he is aware of the latter.

"And that's the other thing I wanted to tell you about. The same two men who wanted to know about the arrows came in last

Thursday with a message I've been dreading to hear. As they put it, I can sign up for 'protection' at a cost of $6,000 pesos ($500 US dollars) a week…or suffer the 'consequences'. When I declined the offer, they said they would be back in a week…that's this coming Friday…to see if I had changed my mind. Jesús, I know I'm taking a big chance, but I can't afford to pay $300,000 pesos a year. That's more than half my profits. I have to say no."

"D'ya tell the police?"

"No, because they might be in on the deal. I've read about cases where owners who refused to pay had their businesses burned down. The police were called but arrived an hour after the owner called for help."

"Yeah, I heard about stuff like that. There was a big fire up in Monterrey where some guys burned a casino down 'cuz the owner refused to pay for protection. The cops was too late to do anything about it."

"Of course. Everybody's heard about that one. People say it was the Zapas who did it; they ended up not only burning the casino to the ground but killing fifty customers in the process."

Silence.

"D'ya think that could happen here…to this store?"

"Well, yes I do. That's what I wanted to talk to you about. You need to be aware that it could happen any day now…and when it happens it would probably be at night when you're cleaning up."

"What d'ya want me to do?"

"If they come, they'll come with several armed men, so there's really nothing you can do…except get out of here as fast as you can. Use the emergency door in the back of the building. But call me first on your cell phone. I can be here in ten minutes."

"And the police?"

"Yeah, I guess there's no harm in that...but call me first. I'm going to call the fire station today...tell them to be on alert just in case."

Silence.

"What are you gonna do if they burn the place down?"

"I'm not sure. I have the place fully insured, so I won't lose any money. But I'd have to start all over. It would take at least a year to find another building, set up show cases, and order new supplies...(*pause*)... I'd probably go to another town and start over there."

"Yeah...I hope they don't come. But you don't hafta worry about me; I can take care of myself."

"I know you can, Jesús. But look, in case something does happen, I want you to have a little gift from me. On your way out of the store, go over to the archery display and pick out two sets of metal arrows, the kind you like. You don't have to go to the register...just take them. I don't want you to pay for them. Who knows, they might come in handy."

Jesús nods his appreciation. "Thanks. Them's my favorite kind. The aluminum helps 'em to fly straight...much better than the wooden kind."

Starting that night, Jesús leaves his small radio at home, not wanting the music to interfere with his ability to hear someone entering the store. The only one other than the owner and himself who has a front door key is Rey, the security guard. Sergio is aware that the drug people are in a position to pay Rey a lot more than he's making at the store, but the recommendations he came with convinced him that the man can be trusted.

Jesús is not so sure. Throughout his shift, he makes a point of keeping an eye on the security guard. While sweeping the downstairs, he constantly turns to check the front door where Rey can be seen walking back and forth outside. To be on the safe side, each time Jesús goes upstairs to do more sweeping, he leaves the downstairs lights on, just in case there's trouble.

The trouble starts on Friday night, just hours after Sergio has given his final answer to the two collectors. Convinced that the owner means what he says, the men leave without protest but with a menacing smirk on their faces. At about 1:00 A.M., while Jesús is cleaning the upstairs showcases, he hears a metallic sound at the front door. Dropping his broom, he tip-toes down the stairs just far enough to get a look at the front door. His heart begins racing as Rey opens the door and lets two men in. The shorter man in front is carrying a red can and a pistol; the one in back has a flashlight and some kind of firearm tucked into his belt. Rey returns to his post outside as soon as the intruders are inside the door.

From his position on the stairs, Jesús has to think quickly. First, he takes out his cell phone and dials Sergio's number. "They're here," he whispers. "Two of 'em. Rey let 'em, in."

Sergio is startled. "On no, Rey? You say Rey let 'em in? Holy shit. Okay. I'll be there in ten minutes." When Jesús asks if he should call the police, Sergio says he'll do it from his car. "They might hear you making the call. So, just get the hell out of there before it's too late." After putting the phone back in his pocket, Jesús goes to the switch on the nearby wall and turns off the downstairs lights, then races down the steps and across the main aisle to the employee's room where his backpack is stashed.

His steps are heard by the taller man in the rear who aims his flashlight at the fleeting figure. "Did you see that?", he asks his companion.

"See what?", Miguel replies.

Oscar puts his finger to his lips. "There's somebody here… probly the janitor."

"Yeah, Rey told us about 'im."

"Okay," the boss responds, "We gotta get this fire goin' and get outta here before he can make any trouble."

Once he has his bow in hand, Jesús puts the quiver around his neck and pulls out an arrow. He quickly assesses the situation. The intruders have a flashlight but he has the advantage of knowing the layout of the store. Dropping into a crouch, he makes his way to the tent display and stands up. He can see the shorter man unscrewing the cap on the gas can. In the dark, the man has no idea that he is being watched. When he tilts the can, ready to start pouring, his associate yells, "Not here you jerk. You wanta get your feet soaked?" When there is no answer, he adds, "Go to the end of the aisle (*pointing*) and pour out the gas on your way back. I'll light it from the doorway."

Jesús is close enough to hear everything being said. Still unseen, he places an arrow in the bow string, grasps the arrow between his fingers, and pulls the string all the way back. The two men are now illuminated by the taller man's flashlight which he moves nervously back and forth across the floor. Suddenly, there is a thud, then a sharp cry…'aarrgh'…as the man with the gas can collapses. When his partner reaches down to pick him off the floor, he quickly pulls his hand back. Dumfounded, he tries again…then shouts, "What the fuck?" as his fingers grasp something long and slender. "Goddamn…it's an arrow." Then, turning quickly to the door, he yells. "Rey, com'ere. Miguel is hurt…help me get 'im outta here."

When Rey arrives, Oscar takes one of Miguel's legs, pointing for Rey to take the other. Together they begin dragging the corpulent Miguel to safety. At the store entrance, Rey drops the leg he's dragging and steps back to open the door. As he turns the handle, he hears a thud as a second arrow pierces Oscar's neck, sending screams reverberating throughout the store. He freezes, torn between running away and pulling his accomplices to safety. As he stands motionless at the door, he sees the headlights of a car coming into the parking lot. It's Sergio. When the owner jumps out of his car and comes running toward him, Rey backs away to let him inside.

Buoyed by his boss's appearance, Jesús leaves by the emergency door in back and races around the corner of the building toward the parking lot in front. When he gets there, he finds himself directly behind Rey's parked car where he has a clear view of the fire engine now entering the lot. With sirens blaring, the engine comes to an abrupt stop at the store entrance. As men in protective jackets jump from the truck, Rey who has been standing just outside the door, makes his move. He steps back quietly, waits until all the firemen are inside, then bolts for his car. When Jesús sees him coming, he stands up and places an arrow in his bow. In his haste to escape, Rey never considers Jesús's whereabouts. Just ten feet from his car, he gasps as an arrow tears into his chest, inches from his heart.

Convinced that he has hit his target, Jesús folds the bow back into his backpack and dashes up the street. By the time he turns to check on Rey, there are several firefighters standing over the body. He allows himself the luxury of a brief smile, then heads for his apartment.

When he hears what happened at the sporting goods store, Francisco screams, "What? Two more dead…and a security guard to boot? What the fuck is goin' on? I want this Tarzán kid whacked now." Jorge, the messenger, lowers his voice. "They say his real name is Jesús Celestino. Parents live in an apartment down by the Pemex station."

Francisco squints. "The name sounds familiar. Do I know the family?"

"Probly. The kid messed up an assignment two years ago, a grocery store collection; Fernando had to go in and finish the job." Francisco breaks into a grin. "Oh yeah, I remember now; the kid left town right after that."

"Yeah," replies Jorge. "So, we took it out on the parents… made 'em pay for the kid's mistake."

"Right, they had to sell their farm and move out, no?"

"Well, boss, the kid's back…with a vengeance. Already he's taken out five of our guys…all with a bow and arrow."

Francisco scowls. "Not exactly; he had help at the restaurant. Didn't he and another kid steal one of our machine guns and use it on Fernando and his bodyguard?"

"Yeah, you're right. He did have help that time."

"So, how we gonna get 'im…any ideas?"

Jorge who has already given the matter considerable thought, leaps at the chance to impress his boss. "I think the way to get 'im is through his Mama and Papa. We kidnap the parents and bring 'em up to the compound, then spread the word that the kid's got three days to give himself up before we start cuttin' up the parents."

Francisco beams. "I like the idea. That should bring the little bastard runnin' in a hurry."

"He ain't so little anymore, boss. People who have seen 'im up close say he's grown up a lot, put on some weight…tain't the skinny brat he usta be."

Francisco scowls again. "What's the difference? We got guns, don't we? For Christ's sake, you ain't scared of the little shit, are you?"

Jorge reddens. "Of course not, boss. I just meant we gotta be careful."

"Okay, go get the parents and bring 'em in. Once we got 'em locked up, put the word out on the street. Get people whisperin'. If he's anywhere in town, he'll hear about it."

"Got it."

Chapter 23

The Capo Takes Revenge

"What are ya hearin' on the street?" Jesús asks when he and Raffi are alone.

"The whole town is buzzin' about what happened at the sport store. Ever since the newspaper called you Tarzán, that's the name folks are usin'. Tarzán this, Tarzán that."

"But how do they feel about it? Whose side they on?"

"Well, some folks I heard seem glad someone is standin' up to the cartel. Knowin' it's one of us kids makes it even better. Other people I talked to are worried that El Gordo is gonna get mad and stop givin' 'em free food. Some of them are also worried that innocent folks may get killed if this whole thing continues. So, a mixed bag, I'd say."

"Anything else?"

Raffi drops his head. "I hate to tell ya this, but yir parents are in trouble, deep trouble. The word is out that once the store owner identified you as the janitor, El Gordo sent his guys to their apartment and pulled 'em out. Apparently, they're up in the compound now."

Jesús keeps staring. "Yeah, what else they sayin'?"

"They sayin' that if you don't turn yourself in to Gordo by next Saturday, they gonna start cuttin' up your father, then your mama."

Jesús glowers at his friend. "Is this true…or jis' made up?"

"How do I know? It's what people are sayin', that's all."

Jesús closes his eyes to think better. "Okay…let's do this. Go down to the apartment…you know, snoop around a little…find out if my parents are really gone."

"Okay. I'll go right now. Let's meet back here at my house in a couple of hours. I'll tell you everything then. Besides, there's somethin' I wanna show you." At noon, they meet again. As he approaches, Raffi is shaking his head. "Gone, all the neighbors I talked to say your parents are gone…ain't been seen for a whole day, which is unusual."

"Yeah, my parents stick pretty much to their apartment except to buy food."

"So, it looks like Gordo's taken 'em to his compound. No way can we get 'em outta there without a whole fuckin' army behind us."

Jesús says nothing, apparently lost in thought. Then suddenly, an idea. "You ever play chess?"

"For Christ's sake, Jesús , what's that got to do with getting yir parents back?"

"When I worked on this team up in Juárez, my friend Manny the priest taught me a little about chess. One thing I remember is that if you want to save your queen, the best thing you can do is threaten to take the other guy's queen."

"So?"

"It ain't clear?"

"Nope, sorry."

Jesús tilts his head back. "What if…" he stops…then starts again. "What if I sneak over to Gordo's mother's house in Badiraguato, you know, the fancy house he built for her…and kidnap the old lady. I could bring her back here, then let one of Gordo's thugs know that she's gonna die if anything bad happens to my Mama and Papa."

Raffi brightens. "Wow…that sounds great. But would you really kill her if they did somethin' to your parents?"

"Absolutely. Hey, if you're gonna survive in a world of cutthroats, you gotta act like one yirself."

"Well, Jesús, if you want my two cents worth, I think it's doable…as long as you can git past the guards at her house. I've heard she's got two beefy goons protectin' her at all times."

Jesús reaches around back and pats his pack. "I think I can handle that."

Early the next morning, with the sun barely over the mountains, Jesús sets out from Culiacán to Badiraguato, being careful to use footpaths through the woods where he won't be seen. Half way there, he stops to eat the torta he bought the night before. As he leans back against a tree, images of his parents arise. He sees armed men at the farm house door; he sees a field full of crops burning; he sees a man and a woman in tears as they leave their ancestral home…(*pause*)…then he sees them banished to a tiny apartment in town. As his heart begins to pound, a final image appears; he sees them taken from their home at gunpoint and dragged to Francisco's compound in the hills.

He shakes his head and goes back over the whole thing. The image that keeps returning is that of crops burning. According to what Raffi told him, every time his father planted a crop of marijuana or tomatoes or squash, El Gordo's men would come and spray the field with a weed-killer, making it impossible to grow anything for sale. *He pictures the scene now…his father looking out the window as days of back-breaking work go up in flames…a whole season wasted, a way of life lost. And then comes the realization…if they aren't allowed to grow anything, what else can they do but sell the farm… the farm that has been home to the Celestino family for three generations?*

When he opens his eyes, he feels a smoldering in his chest, a fire so intense that it that threatens to ravage his whole body. To calm himself, he removes his backpack and checks his bow. Everything is in its place. As he runs his fingers across the bowstring, the fire in his heart subsides. With the bow in hand, he leans against the tree and pictures what he is about to do. An eye for an eye…a queen for a queen…that's the plan. As he ponders his strategy, an idea suddenly erupts from deep in his psyche, an idea startling in its vividness. It comes to him with the certainty of a divine revelation. "Oh yes," he cries as the image looms in stark detail. "Gordo's mother's house, the one he built for her in Badiraguato; it's goin' up in flames." Taking a rarely used path through the woods, Jesús arrives at El Gordo's mother's house and takes up a position in the bushes. Scarcely ten yards from the steps, he watches as the two bodyguards play cards and sip mescal up on the porch. In deference to the woman they are guarding, the men talk in whispers, although tempers flare when someone is suspected of cheating. Quietly, Jesús opens his bow and places an arrow against the string. When he inadvertently steps on a twig, the noise alerts the guard sitting closest to him. As the man reaches for his pistol, Jesús lets an arrow fly. It strikes its target in the back just below the heart, knocking him forwards onto his partner. As both guards fall down the stairs, Jesús rushes forward, bow at the ready, and shoots an arrow into the stomach of the second man. The man twitches briefly, then opens his mouth to shout. Nothing comes out. As Jesús watches, he clutches his stomach, then closes his eyes with his mouth still open.

The mother is known around town as La Rara (*The Flake*), although no one dares use that name in public. Eccentric is the more acceptable term. Her real name is Madi, which only close friends are allowed to use. Her relatives, of which there are many, call her Mama, Tia or Abuelita, depending on age and relationship. She is in her late fifties, short, bow-legged with wide hips, severe facial wrinkles, and graying hair pulled back in a pony tail.

Just as Jesús is putting the bow in his pack, she appears at the door with two mugs of coffee, looking for her two protectors. When she sees the one called Paco curled up at the bottom of the stairs, she smiles. "I guess he's tired. I'll save their coffee for later." As she turns to go back in, Jesús comes out from behind the bushes and confronts her.

"Who are you?", she cries, clearly alarmed. Jesús says nothing… instead brushes past her on his way into the house. Once he is sure that no one is there, he pushes the fireplace screen to one side, grabs a poker, and pulls a burning log out onto the rug. When the mother yells, "What are you doing to my house?", Jesús grabs her by the arm and drags her outside. Stepping over the two bodies, he takes her across the lawn to the edge of the woods where he turns to watch. As flames appear at the living room window, the mother cries out, "Oh, my poor house. Francisco will be upset. You know he built it for me; it cost a lot of money…but I guess he'll build me another one." She reaches for a tissue to wipe away the tears. "I really don't want another big one: a little one like my neighbors have would be fine with me. It was Francisco's idea to build such a big house. I tried to tell him the neighbors would be jealous but he wouldn't listen. So, there it goes…everything…even my wedding photos. You can't replace things like that, can you?" She seems troubled, but not at all hysterical like Jesús feared. Together, they remain seated at the edge of the forest until the house is fully ablaze. Assured that the fire cannot be stopped, Jesús pulls her to her feet and onto the path. As he tugs on her wrist, she asks, "Where are you taking me?"

"Don't worry; I'm not gonna hurt you," he replies.

A hundred yards further into the woods, he drops her arm and says, "We got a little business to do with your son."

"What kind of business?", she asks, squinting.

"Sit down and take out your cell phone. I saw it in your apron pocket."

She scowls, then takes out the phone and gives it to Jesús.

"No," he says, "you keep it. Dial your son's number."

Madi dials the number. "José…that you? It's Madi…I need to talk to Francisco." A minute passes while José goes to get his boss. Madi begins to tremble.

"Ma, what's up," comes the voice on the other end.

"Francisco, this boy wants to talk to you."

"What boy? Where are you?"

"What's your name, sonny?", she asks, turning to Jesús.

Jesús pauses. "Tell 'im it's Tarzán."

"The boy's name is Tarzán," she says.

"Tarzán, what the hell?"

Jesús takes the phone from her hand and speaks, "Francisco, we got a little business to do, you and me. You got my mother and father up at your place; I got your mother right here next to me. We make a trade. You let my parents go and I do the same with your mother. But I'm not gonna wait forever." He looks at his wrist watch. "It's now 11:15. I'm givin' you until 2:30 to take my parents to the Culiacán bus station and put 'em on the 3:00 bus to Oaxaca. You buy the tickets…they don't have any money. And give them a cell phone…and yir mother's number. They gonna need the phone to call this number once they get on the bus. When they call to say they on their way to Oaxaca, I let your mother go."

Silence.

Before handing the phone back to the mother, he says, "If I don't hear nothin' by 3:30, your mother's gonna get whacked."

"Lookit punk, if you do anything to my Mama…you even touch her…you gonna wish you was never born."

"I ain't afraid of you. Jis' get my parents to the station in time for that bus or you gonna be one motherless fat boy."

Gordo growls, "Nobody talks to me that way…and lives to tell about it." "Yeah, well this is the first."

He gives the phone back to Francisco's mother. "It's me again", she says.

"Where are Paco and Dimitri?", Francisco shouts.

"Oh, they're curled up by the steps," she replies. "I hope they wake up before the fire gets to them."

The son barks, "What fire you talkin' about?"

"My house, it's on fire. Can't you see the smoke from where you are?"

"Your house is on fire? Jesús Christ, why didn't you tell me? Have you called the fire department?"

"No, do you want to?"

"For Christ's sake, yes. I'm gonna hang up now so I can call them. But where the hell are you?" Madi looks around. "We're in the woods somewhere; there are trees all around us. But I don't know where we are."

"You don't remember?...*(pause)...*which direction did you go from your house?"

"I can't tell. Tarzán spun me around."

"Okay, I gonna hang up now and call the fire station. But tell me first, did the kid hurt you?"

"Oh no, he's a nice young boy…reminds me a little of you when you was his age."

"How old is he?"

Madi turns to Jesús. "How old are you, Tarzán?"

"Eighty five."

"He says he's eighty five."

"Yeah, I'll bet. What's he look like?"

Madi turns to look at her captor. "What's he looks like… well…?"

Jesús grabs the phone. "That's enough. I got another call I hafta make." For privacy, he retreats to a bare spot behind a large palmetto tree. When the operator asks what he wants, he says, "Gimme the number of the Catedral de Oaxaca in Oaxaca." Once he has the number, he dials it and asks for Father Garcia. Two minutes pass while the padre's assistant goes to find him.

"This is Father Garcia. How may I help you?" The voice is warm and familiar.

"Hi, Manny. It's Jesús Celestino."

"Sús...what a nice surprise. Where are you?"

"I'm over in Culiacán...you know, in Sinaloa."

"Ah, I thought you might end up back there. But that's not exactly safe, is it...I mean, given what happened to you a few years ago?"

"Yeah, I have to be careful. I'm not too popular with certain people."

"By the way, did you hear that Mendoza, you know, the head of the PGR where Eduardo and Sebastián work, was arrested and charged with treason. As soon as he got out on bail, he drove to the hacienda where he used to live and shot himself."

"Wow. No, I never heard about that. Are Eduardo and Sebastián okay?"

"Yes. Eduardo was promoted to chief of the PGR; I'm not sure but I think Sebastián is still there too. Peaches, of course, is still missing. Looks like they might have killed her. After all, she was the one responsible for bringing down Mata...and then later, the gang that kidnapped the boy in the video. But if she's still alive, she's probably down in your neck of the woods. It's pretty clear that El Gordo's gang was behind her kidnapping. So, if you see anyone who looks like her, let me know. Maybe we can do something."

Jesús pauses. "What does she look like?"

"I don't know for sure since none of us ever saw her. But right after the kidnapping, there were pictures of her in the El Paso and Juárez newspapers. I'd say she's quite tall for a woman, maybe 5′6″

or 7". She has curly blonde hair, blue eyes and an attractive figure, although I'm not supposed to notice things like that."

Jesús chuckles. "I may have seen her, I don't know. There's a gringo woman who came to the park with Gordo last Saturday; that's when he gives away free food. A tall good-looking woman was right there next to him. She even handed out some of the food herself."

"What color eyes?"

"I dunno…didn't get close enough to see."

"It's worth checking out. That could be her. Try getting closer next time, unless, of course, that's going to put you in jeopardy."

"Okay, I'll try. But what do I say if I get close?"

Manny pauses. "Just say 'Peaches' and see how she reacts. If it's not the person we're looking for, she'll just look away and continue what she's doing. If it is Peaches, she'll be startled and want to know who you are."

"So, do I tell her?"

"Well, why not, I don't see any harm in that. You can tell her you were part of the team that took down Mata, using her info. Maybe you can plan to meet her again somewhere safe… then ask her how we can get her out of there."

"If it's Peaches, it's gonna be pretty hard to get her outta here. The woman I seen at the food giveaway is with Gordo all the time…and he's surrounded with thugs carrying AK-47's. Nobody can git close to either one of 'em."

"How about the local police or the military? They obviously know where his hideout is. Why can't they go in after him?"

"People say Gordo has informants everywhere…like in police and military. So, when they go after 'im, he hears about it ahead of time and escapes. He's been doin' it for years now. Nobody's caught him yet."

"Well, it might not be Peaches after all…so be careful. Don't go sticking your nose in where it's not wanted."

"Manny, before you go, I got a favor I need to ask ya."

"Hey, fire away, amigo."

"My parents are gonna be takin' a bus from Culiacán to Oaxaca this afternoon. I need somebody to pick 'em up in Oaxaca and find 'em a place to live. I know that's a lot to ask but it's the only way I know how to protect 'em from Gordo."

"What are you saying?"

"Last week I took out the guy who killed my girl friend two years ago. Now Gordo's tryin' to catch me and he figured the best way to do that is to kidnap my parents and threaten to whack 'em if I don't turn myself in. So, I kidnapped his mother and offered him a deal…let my parents go and I'll do the same with your Mama."

"Wow. Sounds like a good move. Did it work?"

"I dunno. I hope so. But I don't trust this guy. I want my parents outta here…you know…so they can start a new life somewhere. That's when I thought of you and Oaxaca. I'm hopin' you can pick 'em up at the bus station…the one down in Central Oaxaca…and find a place for 'em to live while my father looks for work."

"What kind of work does he do?"

"Well, before Gordo burned down our crops, he was a farmer. So, probly somethin' to do with food…helpin' out on somebody's farm or maybe workin' in the big Mercado in town."

"Yeah. I can help. I'll have my assistant meet them at the bus station. What time does that bus arrive?"

"It leaves Culiacán around 3:00…so I'd say around 9:00 tonight."

"Okay…consider it done. But give me your number so we can stay in touch."

"Yeah, wait a minute." Turning to Madi, "What's the number on this phone?" Madi closes her eyes: "463-7894."

"What's the area code?"

"951".

Jesús repeats the number to Manny.

"Okay. I'll get to it right away. And hey, be careful. Call me if you find out anything about this woman you saw with El Gordo. It could be Peaches."

"Yeah, I will. And thanks Manny for lookin' after my parents. I feel better already."

"Okay Sús…good talking to you."

By 3:20, the call he's been waiting for comes. "Hello, Mama, is that you?"

Silence.

"I can't hear you. Can you hear me?"

"A little."

"Move the phone around until my voice gets louder."

"Okay Jesús…there it is."

"Are you on the bus to Oaxaca?"

"Yes. I don't know why we're going to Oaxaca but that's what the ticket says."

"Are you okay?"

"Yes, we're okay. But we didn't have enough time to pack everything. Of course, we don't have that many things anyway, but I hated to leave my favorite mops and cleaning supplies back there. At least we got our clothes, dishes, and photographs."

"That's good. Did the man who took you to the bus station tell you somebody's gonna meet you in Oaxaca.?"

"No, he didn't say anything like that. Who's going to meet us?"

"He's a friend of mine…the padre at the biggest church in Oaxaca. His name is Manuel Garcia. I worked with him on a job up in Juárez. We talked earlier today; he said if he can't come himself, he gonna send his assistant. They're gonna help you find an apartment too."

"But why Oaxaca?", she exclaims. "We've never even been there."

"Because that's where my friend lives. I think you gonna like the city; it's far from all the drug business. Hang onto this phone number; I want to talk to you again soon."

"Okay, Jesús. Are you alright? Not in any more trouble I hope."

"I'm fine, Mama. Tell Papa I love 'im. Bye for now."

Assured that his parents are safely on their way to a new home in Oaxaca, Jesús turns to Madi and tells her she can go back to her house now.

"To do what?", she asks. "The house is still burning."

"Go to a neighbor's house and call your son from there; tell him yir alright and need somebody to pick you up. I'm gonna keep your phone, so you'll have to use your neighbor's."

"He's going to be very angry; I don't want to be around him."

"He'll get over it."

"Well, he won't get over you. He has a terrible temper...so you better watch out."

"I gonna be careful. Bye now." Jesús waits long enough to see Madi off, then heads for the woods behind Raffi's house. It's no longer safe to go back to his little apartment. *Maybe Raffi will have some ideas. I can always sleep in the woods...jis' need a blanket and a piece of plastic if it rains."*

Chapter 24

Looking for Peaches

When he meets Raffi, Jesús starts by filling him in on what happened at El Gordo's mother's house. Raffi responds quickily. "Once Fat Boy gets his mother back, he's gonna come after you. Everybody in town is gonna know that he's gunnin' for you. If someone sees you, all they gotta do is get in touch with El Gordo and they'll get a big reward."

"Yeah, but I can disguise myself pretty good. A lot of people seen me today but so far nobody's turned me in."

"But where are you gonna stay? You can't go back to that apartment. It's too risky."

"I'll sleep in the woods; nobody's gonna find me there."

Raffi throws up his hands. "I gotta a better idea. About eight years ago my papa built a tree house for us kids in the woods not far from where we are right now. We used it a lot back then but nobody's usin' it now. It's got a ladder for climbin' up to the house. The house has a roof to keep the rain out…and there's a mattress you can sleep on. The place may need a little cleanin' but you can stay there if you want."

Jesús nods approvingly.

"You want to see it? It's back there (*pointing*)."

"Yeah, sounds good, as long as the rent's not too high."

"We'll give ya a special deal…no rent as long as you don't snore too loud."

Jesús laughs as they walk through the woods. When they get to the tree house, he exclaims, "Hey, Raffi this is perfect. It's even got a window so I can see if anybody's comin'."

"Yeah, you can shoot 'em before they get too close."

Together they climb up into the house and look around. As Raffi warned, the place is a mess…used styrofoam cups on the table, ants on the mattress and dead leaves all over the floor. The look on Jesús's face prompts a quick offer from his friend: "I got a broom in the house you can use. And my Ma will give ya a coupla sheets. We can git the old house lookin' sharp in a few minutes."

Jesús nods. "For meals I guess I'll hafta go into town…jis' gotta be sure to keep my hood pulled down and wear sunglasses."

"Don't worry about meals. My Ma and Pa are on your side in this, so we can probly supply you with food most days…you know, leftovers, that kinda thing. And there's a jug in the house you can have for water. That means you won't hafta go into town too often."

"When can I move in?"

"Why not right now?"

The next day Jesús wakes up in his new home when he hears a loud bird call from just below. It's Raffi with some breakfast.

"I thought you was some kinda bird."

"Well, some people say I really am…but not today." He pauses, looking up at the tree house. "Hope you like these muffins; my Ma made 'em special with you in mind."

"Hey, I can already smell 'em. Let me come down and get a few."

"They're all for you Sús. We already had all we can eat."

Down on the ground, Jesús grabs a muffin and shoves it whole into his mouth.

Raffi steps back in awe. "You look kinda hungry. When's the last time you ate?" Jesús waits until the muffin reaches his stomach. "Can't remember. Maybe a year ago…(*laughing*)…at least it feels that way." Raffi stays until all five muffins are gone, then turns to go. Before he can leave, Jesús asks, "D'ya hear anything in town…about me and Gordo's mother?"

Raffi stares. "Did I hear anything? You gotta be kiddin'. Everybody's talkin' about it. Some of the kids want to hear the story over and over…you know, how you stuck it to the fat man by burning down his old lady's house. Most of the older folks are scared; they think there's gonna be more violence now."

"There ain't gonna be no violence unless they find me…and now that I got this house in the woods, that's not gonna happen."

"Let's hope not."

"Anything else?"

"Well, they're also talkin' about a new guy, a gringo who's goin' around askin' questions about some woman he's lookin' for. Maybe his wife; I dunno. But he's headin' for a heap of trouble if he keeps it up. Gordo don't like snoops."

"Did the gringo stop you?"

"He did. He wanted to know if I've seen a tall, blonde woman… maybe late thirties…American…real pretty."

"What d'ya tell 'im?"

"I said I saw a woman like that last Saturday at the food giveaway. He wanted to know if there's gonna be another giveaway next Saturday. When I said yes, he wanted to know where they give the food away. So, I told 'im…over in Benito Juárez Park."

"The guy's crazy. He'll be dead by Saturday night."

As soon as the fall term ends and his sabbatical leave begins, Ned Kinsman heads immediately for Sinaloa to begin searching for Jessica. When he learns that El Gordo's stronghold is located in the hills above a village called Badiraguato, he goes to the nearest city, Culiacán, to make inquiries. It is there that he learns about the food giveaways in the park. When further inquiries reveal information about a good-looking, blonde, gringo woman who helps out at the giveaways, he is convinced he has found the woman he is looking for. The hardest thing about his quest is waiting for Saturday to come around. Every day he takes a taxi over to Badiraguato where he roams the main street, asking questions of anyone willing to talk…unconscious that he is making himself visible to the wrong people. When Saturday finally comes, he mingles with the crowd gathered in front of the platform near the center of the park. Of the hundred or so people there, he is the only gringo, all the others being shorter, of darker skin and black hair and dressed for work in the fields.

By the time the food truck arrives at 11:00, his heart is pounding. He inches forward in the crowd until he is only a few yards from the platform where the food is to be handed out. First to be seen are two assistants who are lugging crates of tomatoes and onions from the truck to the stage. Still no Jessica…until suddenly from the side of the platform nearest the truck, a woman strides up the steps onto the stage.

Ned stares…cranes his neck …then waves frantically. There can't be any doubt; it's Jessica. When he calls her by name, she stumbles, drops the tomatoes in her hand, then looks up. When she sees Ned waving, she waves back, then quickly withdraws her hand when she sees Francisco coming up the steps. When Ned goes so far as to take out his camera, she cringes. Gordo, whose eyes never wander far from his captive, sees her biting her lip. He rushes up the steps and demands to know who she was waving to. Startled, Jessica admits that he is a friend, a professor at UTEP, like her husband.

"What is UTEP?", he asks brusquely. She explains. When Gordo wants to know if they've slept together, she fires back, "That's none of your business."

Not satisfied, he orders José to confiscate the man's camera. José strides over to the gringo and rips the camera from his hands, then gives it to his boss. When Gordo displays the shots recently taken, he discovers several shots of Lúpe. Reddening, he drops the camera to the ground and stomps on it, then gives José a jerk of the head which Jessica, in her anxiety, interprets as an order to kill.

"If you do anything to hurt him," she screams, "I will never, never speak to you again. Is that clear?"

Francisco backs off; instead, he tells his lieutenant to escort the intruder to the airport and put him on a one-way flight back to El Paso. Within minutes, he is gone.

Ned, convinced now that it is Jessica and that she is being held prisoner by El Gordo, checks his luggage only as far as Mexico City, where he buys a ticket back to Culiacán. By noon the next day, he is in Culiacán, holed up in a cheap motel, and sporting a floppy beach hat, a hooded jacket and horn-rimmed glasses. He also shows the beginnings of a beard. When he looks in the mirror, he is pleased to see someone he barely recognizes.

For her part, Jessica is both thrilled to see Ned and fearful for his safety. To relieve her anxiety, she goes to Francisco for assurance he will do nothing to harm him. When Francisco tells her that her friend is already on his way back to El Paso, she relaxes. When they return to handing out food, their arms sometimes touch. Francisco's heart leaps when Jessica remains close instead of moving away. The intruder from El Paso is quickly forgotten as they hand out crate after crate of fresh vegetables, cooking supplies and milk. Predictably, they are both showered with hugs and 'gracias' from the adoring crowd.

As the giveaway continues, Jessica senses a growing softness in her captor and asks him about the possibility of expanding the free-food project. "With all the money you've accumulated," she says, "we could do a lot more than we did today. There are so many poor people in Mexico...especially in the south. I've read that Oaxaca and Chiapas are the two poorest states in Mexico. We could start there, try out some programs...then apply what we've learned to other areas."

Francisco has little interest in such programs, but is aroused by her use of the word 'we.' He beams at this latest sign of a growing intimacy. "You like helping people, yes?"

"Yes. I never knew just how much until now. It's really a beautiful thing to see the smiles on people's faces when they get a carton of milk or sack of potatoes."

"Is good feeling, yes."

She smiles warmly. "I know you feel the same way; I can see it in your face."

Francisco has all he can do to keep from hugging her. "Lúpe, you make me happy man." As they continue handing out food, Lúpe asks if he would be willing to accompany her to other cities, starting with towns nearby...like Durango. While thrilled that she would want to travel with him, he declines, saying that it is dangerous. "Too many people out there want to see me dead."

"What about me going alone?", she replies. When his smile disappears, she is quick to add "with a bodyguard, of course."

"Why you not run back to Texas?"

She takes his hand. "I give you my word that I won't run away."

Francisco scratches his head. "We talk about it later, okay. Is new idea."

Lúpe nods her understanding. A few minutes later, she returns to another subject, "Does it bother you...that people want to hurt you?"

"No...must expect it if you want to be top dog. Always other dogs waiting to take you down. Just like jungle, to survive you hafta kill other dogs before they kill you."

Lúpe shakes her head. "But aren't you afraid of dying?"

"When I young, yes...but no more now. I already live 40 years; in this business, that is long life. I no expect to live much longer."

Chapter 25

Bad News from Oaxaca

Jesús pulls his hood down over his forehead and slips into the crowd as residents line up for their weekly handouts. From a position in the middle of the throng, he trains his eyes on the woman on the platform, the woman who could be Peaches. As he elbows his way forward, he reviews Manny's newspaper description: "Tall for a woman, maybe 5'6" or 7"…with curly blonde hair, blue eyes and an attractive figure." When he looks again, the description seems to fit. He inches his way toward her, careful to keep an eye on Gordo. After watching her for several minutes, he makes his move. Turning slightly so that Gordo can't see his face, he walks up to the platform where Lúpe is giving out cartons of milk.

"Peaches", he whispers.

Instantly she turns to face him, mouth open, eyes staring. "What did you say," she whispers, clearly startled.

Jesús comes closer. "Are you Peaches?"

"Who are you?", she gasps. Before she can say anything more, Francisco comes over to check on her. Jesús sees him approaching and quickly turns away. By the time Francisco gets to Lúpe's side, the boy is lost in the crowd. Off by himself, he again goes over Manny's advice: "If it's Peaches, she'll be startled and want to know who you are."

Jesús nods his head, "Holy shit, that's jis' what happened. I gotta call Manny and tell 'im."

Overtly, Lúpe continues to hand out cartons of milk; in private she wrestles with what she just heard. *Who is this person who knows I'm Peaches? The only time I ever used that name was with Bob Dunwoody at D.E.A. He's got to be part of the group that shot down Mata...and rescued the boy in the video. So, what's he doing here?* She pauses to say hello to Rocio Martinez, one of Francisco's friends from his school days. *Are the other members of that group here too? Are they going to try to rescue me?* She stops to look at herself. *Rescued? Yes, they may be here to rescue me... (pause)...So, why aren't I excited? What's the matter with me?*

When Francisco and Lúpe reach the compound later in the afternoon, he senses this is a good time to ask for a favor, a favor that's been on his mind all day.

"I want you use your power to find kid who kidnap my mother."

Lúpe takes a deep breath. "It's been a long time, Francisco; I don't know if I still have the ability...(*pause*)...You sound really anxious to catch him."

"How you feel if someone kidnap your mama?"

"But I've heard that he did it because you kidnapped his parents and were holding them in the compound."

Francisco sighs. "Yes, but I make him come out in open."

"So, he outsmarted you."

"What you mean?"

"He got you to release his parents by doing to your mother what you did to his parents."

Francisco reddens. "My mother safe now; all I have to do is find this kid and...."

"And what? What are you going to do to him if I help you find him?"

"He needs to pay."

"You mean killed...or 'whacked' as you say?"

"Of course. How else I send message? You want people think I weak, that okay to steal my mother and burn her house down?"

Lúpe gets up to leave. "Well, you're not getting my help if that's what you intend to do. I think the boy acted out of loyalty to his parents. You didn't give him any alternative."

"No, not true. If he turn himself in, I let his parents go."

"Yes, but that would have been offering himself up to your executioner. I think he did the wise thing; now he's still alive and his parents are off somewhere else."

Francisco scowls. "I give you nice place to stay, good food, new clothes...and you no thank me; you say no when I ask small favor."

Lúpe puts her hands on her hips. "I didn't ask to come here; you kidnapped me. Nice place to stay you say. Am I supposed to feel grateful? Maybe you've forgotten that I'm your prisoner?... (*pause*)...I don't think I owe you a thing. Besides, helping you to find a boy so you can have him killed is not what I would call a small favor."

As soon as he gets back to his tree house, Jesús calls Manny in Oaxaca. "Hey, Manny, I got some interestin' news for ya. But before I tell you, how my parents doin'? D'ya get 'em a place to stay?"

Silence.

"Manny, you there?"

"Yes, I'm here, Sús. I was just about to call you. I've got some real bad news. You sittin' down?"

"What news?", the boy cries, not bothering to answer the question. "Tell me."

Manny sighs. "Somebody fire-bombed your parents' apartment here in Oaxaca, you know, the one we got for them. Whoever did it, threw a bomb into their living room from the street. According to a neighbor who saw what happened, the whole apartment went up in flames. Both your parents were badly burned before they could be rushed to the hospital."

"How are they now?", Jesus cries. They gonna be alright?"

"I'm afraid not, Sús. Your mama was dead by the time they got her in the ambulance; your papa died soon after they got to the hospital."

Silence.

"I'm sorry, really sorry, Sús.

Silence.

"Sús, you still there?"

"Yeah, I'm here. There's only one person who coulda done somethin' like that."

"You mean El Gordo?"

"Yeah, he musta had one of his thugs follow my parents to Oaxaca…and then to their new apartment."

Silence.

"I can't believe it…after all we did to get 'em outta Culiacán. I thought we was doin' the right thing."

"Of course. Our mistake was in underestimating Gordo's need to get back at you for what you did to his mother's house."

"But Manny, I didn't kill his mother. I made sure she was safe before burnin' her house down."

"Maybe Gordo didn't intend to kill your parents…just scare them by setting a fire in their apartment."

"Yeah, but you throw a fire-bomb into a small place like that and somebody's goin' to get hurt, maybe real bad."

"I agree. He must have known that he was putting your parents' lives at risk."

"I know why he did it. Yeah, he was gettin' back at me for burnin' down his mother's house…but the real thing is he couldn't take a young punk standin' up to 'im. Now that he's killed my parents, he figures he's on top again."

"I think you're right. He's got to have the last word. First, he forces your parents off their land; you respond by taking down his right-hand man, Fernando. Next, he retaliates by kidnapping your parents and holding them in his compound. You respond by kidnapping his mother and burning down her house. Next, he sends a henchman to Oaxaca to fire-bomb your parents' apartment. End of story…El Gordo restores order…gets the last word."

"Maybe, maybe not."

"Sús, what do you mean?"

Silence.

"Manny, you gonna have my parents' bodies sent back here to Culiacán?"

"Of course. I'll take care of that right away. You know how to set up a funeral?"

"I'll figure it out. I got a friend who's gonna help me."

"Before you hang up, Sús, you said you had some news for me. We don't have to talk about it now…I can wait if you prefer."

"No. that's okay. I jis' wanted to tell you that the woman helpin' the fat boy to hand out free food is the woman we call Peaches."

"Really."

"I'm sure of it. I tried what you told me to do…you know, sayin' her name and waitin' to see what happens. Well, she acted like…real upset. She wanted me to repeat what I said…and then she asked me who I was…all the while lookin' scared. I figured it's not the way she woulda behaved if that wasn't her name."

"Wow, I'll have to call Eduardo up in Juárez and pass this info on. I don't know if we can do anything about it, but it's worth a try. I'll give you a ring if he thinks we can get her out of there."

"Okay…and thanks for helpin' out with my parents."

"I wish I could have done more, Sús. But there's always a reason for these thing, however painful they might be at the moment."

"Whatcha mean, Manny?"

"Don't you think God knows what happened? He's got a plan, Sús. We're not smart enough to know what it is, but in the end it's all going to be for the best." Silence. "Well, goodbye for now kiddo. I'll call you if anything comes from my talk with Eduardo."

"Okay."

As soon as they're together, Jesús tells Raffi about his conversation with Manny. "Gordo did it; he killed my Mama and Papa."

"So, whatcha gonna do about it?"

"Like Manny said, fat boy thinks that now my parents are gone, everything's been squared. I don't feel that way. I ain't gonna feel right until somebody gets 'im."

"And who's that gonna be?"

"I dunno…haven't figured that out yet."

"If you want to get 'im on yir own, how you gonna get past all them guards and AK-47's?"

"I dunno. We figured out somethin' with Fernando…and it worked. Maybe we can do it again."

Chapter 26

A New Partnership

As soon as Francisco sets up a charitable account with an initial deposit of U.S. $1,000,000, Lúpe makes plans to travel. They agree that Oaxaca, a southern, middle-size city with no apparent drug problems, is the best place to start. Francisco demands that she take two well-armed bodyguards with her. When he insists on being kept informed, she agrees to call every night to let him know how things are going. At the airport, Francisco hugs her so hard she nearly faints. Upon arriving in Oaxaca, Lúpe heads immediately for the zocolo, the big plaza in the middle of town surrounded by six outdoor restaurants. Hoping to duplicate the experience of previous trips, she takes a seat in La Primavera and waits for the children to come by. When a few appear just beyond the restaurant, she waves, but no one comes to her table. In time, she realizes that it's the bodyguards with their guns who are frightening the kids away. As soon as the guards move to another part of the restaurant, the children come closer. Her strategy is to invite the children to her table, find out which ones need shoes, then take them to the nearby zapateria to buy new ones. Those who need shirts or pants instead get taken to Milano, the clothing store. The mothers, who are circling the plaza hawking their home-made fabrics, soon appear to inspect the gifts. After introductions and gracias, Lúpe is invited to their homes where she gets to see how they live.

What she finds is depressing. The typical home has a single room with dirt floor, no running water and little or no furniture. Family members, of which there are typically between five and ten (a mother, sometimes a father, and three

206

to eight children) sleep not on beds but on cardboard cartons spread out on the dirt floor; in the morning the cartons are folded up and stacked against the wall. Cooking is done over a wood fire just outside the front door. In the absence of tables and chairs, meals are eaten inside, with everyone kneeling on the dirt floor, holding plastic plates in their hands. There are no refrigerators for storing perishables, no stoves for baking, no washers or dryers, no showers, and no indoor bathrooms. Televisions are rare; trips to the doctor even rarer. Rents run from 500 to 700 pesos (U.S. $40 to $60) a month.

Once she has made contact with the parents, Lúpe identifies what they need the most and goes about buying it. The most popular items are beds and gas stoves. For others it's a table and chairs. For those with electricity, small items like blenders are coveted. For sheer excitement, however, it is hard to beat a trip to the supermarket where carts are quickly filled to overflowing with milk, cereal, fruit, pasta, tortillas, rice, soup, bread, eggs, meat, cooking oil, toothpaste, and soap. Lúpe smiles through it all, even when an occasional mother gets greedy and starts loading a second cart. If asked, she would say that she has never felt this kind of exhilaration before. Up to now, her life has been devoid of any real purpose other than being a good wife or good friend. For the first time in her life, she feels a sense of mission. When she calls Francisco at night to share her experiences, she bubbles over with joy. To anyone listening to their conversation, it is clear that there is a new warmth in her voice. For her part, there is no more thought of escaping. El Paso seems light years away. Even Ned enters her mind less often now.

Despite her new contentment, Lúpe struggles to make sense of the conflict between Francisco's generosity and his brutality. As the relationship evolves, she is alternately drawn and repelled by what she sees. Confusing the issue further are signs of a growing attachment on his part. Keeping him at bay physically while encouraging his generosity represents a tight-rope act that demands her constant attention.

In one of their nightly conversations, Francisco brings up the possibility of a 'partnership'. Before Lúpe can react, he spells out what he means. "You use power to get rid of rival gangs... and I give you money for poor people in Mexico."

She quickly demurs. "But I would be helping you to do something criminal."

"Is same what you did before...like with Mata...only now you work for me. Tell me where rivals hide out...and I do to them what your people do to Mata."

"But I don't want to help you kill people," she replies.

"But you do that before, no?"

"I guess you're right. But it feels different. Before I was helping to eliminate drug dealers. You want me to help you sell drugs...to make you top dog."

"Si...only dog left (*laughing*). You say me criminal and you no like, but there is other way to think. Americans spend 65 billion U.S. dollars a year to buy drugs...I read this in magazine. That money help people in Mexico."

"But most of it goes toward fancy cars, clothes, yachts, and alcohol...even garish tombs for dealers who have died, yes?"

"Some, yes, but most get down to little people. I hire 40 guards and hundreds of dealers to get drugs over border...also pay good money to informants...city police, state police, army, and agencies like PGR. Without me, people who work there not have money to buy food and clothes and cars. So, most money not wasted."

"And you think that justifies your criminal behavior?" Francisco pauses. "Better to think this way. U.S. government not willing to give money to help poor in Mexico...but Americans who buy cocaine or marijuana for parties do same thing. They help us."

"I don't think that's their intention."

"Si, just want to have fun or relax...but money come here anyway and help poor Mexicans."

"So, you're saying that this whole drug business is really a good thing; Americans get high and Mexicans get to eat better."

Francisco laughs. "Good way to say. When you help me sell drugs to Americans, you help people in my country."

"And I can help you by what...locating your rivals so you can have them whacked?"

"Maybe whacked, maybe just scare away. For your help I give lots of dollars so you help poor families in Mexico. Is good deal, yes?"

"I don't know. It still sounds warped. I need to think about it. Right now I have to get to bed so I can get up early tomorrow. I promised to take the Bautista family to the Mercado so they can buy food. They're down to their last tortilla."

"Okay, goodnight my cariño."

"Darling? I thought we were just friends."

"Friends now...cariños later, yes?"

"Goodnight, Francisco."

While Lúpe is off in Oaxaca, Gordo learns that another gringo is in Culiacán asking questions. Alarmed, he sends José to investigate. A quick survey of motels in the area reveals a credit card with the name Ned Kinsman on it. When informed, Gordo erupts. "What the hell? I told you to put 'im on a plane back to Texas."

"I did, boss, but he turn around and come right back."

Francisco shakes his head. "He's gotta be her lover. No wonder she don't want me to get rid of 'im…(*pause*)…Okay, here's what we gonna do. You take him into woods and make sure he never come back. You got it? That way Lúpe never know he return to Culiàcan…so can't blame me for havin' 'im whacked."

On Tuesday morning Jesús is traipsing through the woods to check on the Infiniti he and Raffi hid in the bushes when he hears a strange sound. Creeping closer, he is startled to see a man digging a hole with a shovel. He is about to reveal himself when he catches sight of another man standing ten yards away. The second man has a machine gun and is pointing it at the man with the shovel.

"Keep diggin'. You ain't deep enough yet," the man with the gun says.

The man who is digging, a gringo with beach hat, beard, and horn-rimmed glasses, wipes his forehead. He is breathing quickly.

"But it's rocky here," he gasps.

Jesús looks more closely, curious about the shoveler's identity. It's only when the man removes his hat that something clicks. *He's gotta be the gringo who was goin' around town askin' people about an American woman. The guy with the AK-47 is one of Gordo's men…I seen 'im before…so this has gotta be an execution. They're gettin' rid of the gringo because he was askin' too many questions.*

At that moment, it isn't important to Jesús that he understand why questions about an American woman should bother Gordo. It's enough that the man who ordered his parents killed is about to have somebody else whacked. Once his mind is made up, he reaches into his backpack and pulls out the bow…then places an arrow against the string. Still hidden behind the bushes, he takes aim at the man with the gun and draws the bow string. As he does so, the thug takes several steps closer to inspect the hole. By now it is about a foot deep, clearly not enough for a burial. The executioner is getting frustrated.

"Hurry up, for Christ's sake. I ain't got all day."

The gringo studies the thug's face carefully…as if he were planning some kind of move, a move, in Jesús's judgment, that is likely to get him killed. It is clear to the boy that if he is to act, he must act now. Just as he's ready to let an arrow fly, a butterfly lands on the target sight, obscuring his aim. In brushing it away, he accidentally moves his foot. A twig snaps, drawing a frightened glance from the gunman.

"Who's there?", he shouts, stepping closer. He cocks his head, listening carefully. There is nothing to be heard…not even birds overhead. He leans forward, straining for another sound. The air is breathless as time stops, yielding to the moment. Then, from the bushes a taut string is plucked and a whir of feathers splits the air. A scream fills the woods as the arrow finds its target, toppling him to the ground. Before Jesús can reveal himself, the gringo leaps out of the hole and races to the gunman who is writhing on his back with an arrow protruding from his stomach. Without looking around to see who shot it, the gringo picks up the AK-47…fumbles momentarily for the trigger…then fires a volley into the gunman's chest. He stares at the trembling body, waiting until the eyes have closed.

Satisfied that his would-be executioner is dead, he turns to Jesús who has come up behind him. "Wow. You came just in time. The guy was getting antsy…(*pause*)…Who are you, anyway?"

Jesús shakes his head. "We don't have no time for introductions. We gotta get outta here before somebody finds us. We can talk in the woods." Once they are safely in the woods and know each other's names, Jesús asks, "You the guy who was askin' people in town about a woman you was lookin' for?"

"Yeah, she was kidnapped up in Juárez; I came here looking for her."

"I guess somebody don't want you to find her. You lucky I was walkin' through the woods."

"You saved my life; no question about it. Thank you."

"Can I ask you a question?"

"Sure…go ahead."

"What d'ya wanta find this woman for? She your wife?"

"Not exactly. She's going to be my wife as soon as I can get her back to El Paso. Gordo saw me waving to her last Saturday at the food giveaway…and put me on a plane back to El Paso. But I couldn't leave her here, knowing she's a prisoner."

"I think I saw her too. Is she the woman who was helpin' Gordo hand out free food?"

"Yes. That's her."

"She looks a lot like you said. I thought she could be the person I worked with up in Juárez. Gordo is always lookin' over at her so I had to be careful, but I got close enough to whisper the name we called her in Juárez."

"What name was that?"

"Peaches."

"Peaches? Pretty crazy name for a grown woman."

"Well, I didn't know her real name, but that's what she called herself when she was workin' for a guy in D.E.A."

"You say she was working for someone at D.E.A. Can I ask what kind of work she was doing?"

Jesús pauses to assess the situation. "Let's jis' say she passed on info for us to hunt down drug dealers."

Ned leans forward. "Was the guy at D.E.A. named Bob Dunwoody?" "Yeah, how'd you know that?"

Ned smiles. "And was the info she passed on to your group something she saw in a trance?"

"Somethin' like that. I never know how she did it, but she saw buildings and things miles away. That's how we caught this guy Mata...(*pause*)...I probly shouldn'ta told ya this much."

"It's really okay, Jesús. I'm on your side. I'm the guy who suggested she go to Dunwoody in the first place and offer her psychic gifts."

"You mean you know all about this stuff...Mata and the rest?"

"I do. One thing I didn't know was that the woman we're talking about called herself 'Peaches' when she was helping you. Her real name is Jessica Branson. I guess she was afraid of being identified by the wrong people, that is, people working for the drug capos. And she had good reason to be afraid. The wrong people eventually kidnapped her..."

"...and brung her back here to Culiacán."

"Exactly. Now she's caught in El Gordo's web and can't get out. The reason they tried to kill me is that they think I'm trying to take her back to Texas."

"Well, are you?"

"I want to…yes…more than anything. Like I said, her divorce is final now so we can get married as soon as we're back in El Paso."

"But how you gonna get her outta here? You ain't even tried yet and Gordo sent somebody to whack you. He must know who you are or he wouldn'ta bothered."

"Yes, he saw me taking pictures of Jessica at the food giveaway last week…that's when he put me on a plane back to Texas."

"But you come back?"

"Yes. I had no choice."

"You one brave man, Señor Ned."

"Maybe foolish, I don't know. But this woman means the world to me. I can't imagine living without her."

"You got a plan for gettin' her outta here?"

"Not really. I figured something would come up. I'm new to this 'Mission Impossible' stuff."

"Mission Impossible?"

"You know, sneaking behind enemy lines, planting bombs, helping prisoners escape… that kind of thing."

"Gettin' Peaches away from Gordo is not goin' to be easy. People say she never alone."

"I don't understand why he's keeping her here. I hate to speak of it, but why doesn't he have her killed? The whole idea behind kidnapping her was to get rid of her, wasn't it?"

"I think he likes her."

Ned reddens. "What makes you say that?"

"Well, she beautiful…and he sent his wife away right after Peaches get here."

Ned's heart begins to race. "You think he's in love with her?"

"I dunno. Maybe. Maybe he wants to make his wife jealous… or maybe he gonna use Peaches to catch people. No say. But when they together, she don't act like a prisoner."

"Hmm. When you saw her, did she seem at all depressed or frightened?"

"No, she was smilin' at everybody; she liked givin' away the food, I could tell."

"How about physically? Could you tell if she had been beaten?"

"She looked good to me…maybe most beautiful woman in Culiacán. You lucky man, Señor Ned."

Ned clears his throat. "Well, I'm glad of that. Thank you."

Jesús stops and points to the open land just ahead. "But you gotta be careful now. When they find the man with the machine gun and see no body in the grave, they're gonna come lookin' for you. If I know El Gordo, they gonna look in every hotel in Culiacán. The safest thing is for you to leave here…go to Durango…and wait to hear from me."

"By bus, you mean?"

"Yeah, but don't go to the bus station here. That's first place they gonna look. Take a taxi to the next village and get bus to Durango from there."

"Okay, but I want to help. I can't leave the area while Jessica is still in danger."

"Comprendo, Señor Ned, but you stay here, Gordo kill you. Best thing is stay outta the way until we have a plan for gettin' her out."

"Okay, but who's going to do that?"

"Right now, nobody, but I've got friends who might help us…you know, the guys I worked with up in Juárez; they know all about stuff like this. Besides, they have the right equipment."

"Are they coming down here?"

"Maybe. I gonna call 'em today."

"Okay Jesús. Here's my cell number (*writes on a piece of paper*)…call me as soon as you hear something."

"Yeah…and watch out in Durango. The fat man has spies everywhere."

An hour later, Jesús calls Manny and tells him he's positive the woman handing out food on Saturdays is Peaches. Manny says he'll call his brother in Juárez to see if they can get a rescue team together. At Jesús's prompting, he promises to call back as soon as he knows something.

Chapter 27

Clash in the Desert

In her call to Francisco that night, Lúpe is especially excited. She has rented an office near the zocolo and put an ad in the Oaxaca papers announcing a new program for adults who dropped out of school early and want to go back and finish up. "There have been no takers yet," she adds, "but the ad will continue to run for a whole week." Francisco barely responds. When she asks what's wrong, he says that Rodrigo, one of his most trusted lieutenants is missing.

"Missing?'

"Si, gone."

"Maybe he's been hurt and needs help."

"No," Francisco says, "he took wife and kids with 'im...even furniture. And he no answer his phone."

"What do you think happened?"

"I think he go over to La Familia."

"What's that?"

"Drug gang in Guadalajara...worse than Zapas. You know how they get rid of people they no like?"

"No."

"They use barrel of acid."

"But why would Rodrigo leave you for another group?"

"He from that area…grow up there…maybe make more money…not know."

"Can you replace him?"

"Yes…but he know too much. We have big shipment come in Friday from Columbia. Rodrigo know all about it…even help plan operation."

"You think he might try to stop you."

"Not jis' stop me…take cocaine…cost me millions. He know where submarine docks…and…"

"Submarine? You use submarines to ship cocaine from Columbia."

Francisco chuckles. "Not big submarines…just little ones… two men and cargo. Only half underwater…other half above but painted blue so pilot no see from air."

"That's amazing."

"Si…invisible…can sail right under helicopter."

"And Rodrigo knows about this?"

"Si…also where we take drugs next."

"And where's that?"

"We use small plane to move drugs from submarine into secret place in desert."

"The desert? Why the desert?"

"No people see us there…best place to load drugs into trucks and take to U.S. border."

Lúpe pauses to take a sip of tea. "So, what are you afraid Rodrigo might do?"

"He know place in desert where plane land…can hide there and steal drugs from us."

"Can't you change the place where the plane is going to land?"

"Too late now…everybody have instructions."

Silence.

"So, what are you going to do, Francisco?"

He pauses long enough to savor the sound of his name. "I need your help. I need you find Rodrigo for us. If he in desert waiting, I send men to wipe him out before plane arrive. Just have to know where in desert."

"You want me to see if I can find Rodrigo for you."

"Si. You do for me, I send photos so you know how he look."

Lúpe hesitates. "I guess it's alright…after all he is a criminal."

"Thank you Lúpe. I never forget you help. If you need more money for Oaxaca, tell me and I send to bank."

"Okay. You said you have some photos of Rodrigo you can e-mail me?"

"I send right now. When can you try see him?"

"You say the shipment is arriving on Friday. That doesn't give us much time. I'll start as soon as I get back to my hotel room."

"You call me as soon as you see him, yes?"

"Yes, I will."

"Thank you Lúpe. I miss you."

"Goodnight for now, Francisco."

•••••••———————•———————•••••

"Hey Sús. I hear you've found Peaches."

"Yeah, well I think so, Sebastián."

"Manny said she comes into town on Saturdays to hand out free food to the locals. True?"

"Yeah, but she ain't there every Saturday. She didn't come last week. I dunno why."

"Did El Gordo come?"

"He was there, passin' out freebies and smilin' at everybody like he was Christ himself."

"You don't sound too impressed."

"Didn't Manny tell you what he done to my parents?"

"Well, yes he told Eduardo. I'm real sorry to hear that, Sús. I can understand why you're sore."

"So, Sebastián, you comin' down here to take Peaches back?"

"Yes, I can come, but Eduardo is too busy in his new job as director of PGR. And Carmelo has a new job coaching high school basketball."

"Basketball? I thought he was a football player."

"He was, but he also knows a lot about basketball. So, he can't come. It will be just me and Manny…plus some equipment. Is there a hotel there where we can hang out until it's time to make a move?"

"Yeah, I'd try Las Golondrinas up on San Luis Ropo. It's sort of outta the way."

"Okay. I'll call you before I start out. Manny's a little closer so he'll probably get there before I do."

"Okay."

••●▬━━●━━●▬●••

"Thanks for the photos, Francisco. They helped. I'm not positive, but I think I've located Rodrigo."

"Bueno…where?"

"I'm getting impressions of a van, in fact three vans…like a caravan or safari."

"Where are vans…in city or no?"

"There are houses all around…more like a city or suburbs."

"Is road dirt or tar?"

"They're not on the road; it looks more like a garage or warehouse…like they're still loading."

"Okay…good Lúpe. Means that Rodrigo is getting ready for desert. Like I thought, he wants steal my drugs."

"So, what are you going to do?"

"Plane come tomorrow. It take him eight hours to reach Coahuila where plane land. We much closer…just on other side of Sierra Madre mountains…so have plenty time to get there first and catch him in ambush."

"Hmmm."

"What's the matter. You no like idea?"

"Just thinking…you said he was very smart. So, won't he figure that you'll do exactly what you just said he will do?"

"Si…he cunning, like fox."

"Well, he knows you're going to be angry at his leaving you…and that you are aware that he knows all about the delivery on Friday."

"Si."

"He also knows how much that shipment is worth. And he's aware of how you think."

"Si, we work together many years; he know how I do things."

"So, if he knows how your mind works, won't he assume you're going to get there first and ambush him before he can get to the plane. In other words, won't he try to one-up you?"

"No comprendo."

"What I mean is, won't he try to do to you what you intend to do to him?"

Francisco buries his face in his hands. "You right, Lúpe. Why I no think of that?"

"The answer, I should think, is to leave very early Friday morning…get there before he arrives…and take up a position near the landing site."

"Si, exactamente. But one problem…all around the landing site no trees…just creosote bushes and yucca. No can hide there. Only trees on hill to north of landing area. Rodrigo come in from south…so we if we hide on hill, we too far away to attack him."

Silence.

Lúpe pauses. "I'm trying to picture the area in my mind. If I'm Rodrigo, I'm looking for a spot where I can attack you before you get to where the plane is going to land. Now, wouldn't that hill you're talking about be perfect for him and his men. You'll be coming in from the north, so you have to pass through the trees on the hill on your way to the landing area. He could fire on you from behind the trees and you'd have no place to hide. So, wouldn't his best bet be to get to the hill before you do and wait until you arrive?"

Francisco gasps. "Si, like Gettysburg where Union army get to Cemetery Hill first. Poor Pickett, he out in open with no cover. Very foolish for him to charge."

"So, you know a little American history."

"Enough to know you right, Lúpe. We leave very early so we get to hill first…hide there until Rodrigo come…then whack him."

Lúpe shudders. "Okay. Call me tomorrow when you get to the hill. I'll be thinking of you."

"Thank you, Lúpe. Before you go, I have question…ok?"

"Of course."

"Where you learn to think like that? Your daddy a general or somethin'?"

"No army brat here…just an ordinary housewife. To tell you the truth, I'm surprised to hear myself talking this way. Maybe the ability has always been there, but no one ever asked to see it. My husband, who is much smarter than I am, would never consider asking for my opinion about a military problem. In eighteen years of marriage we never once discussed anything to do with the army. So, it's nice to be appreciated."

"I more than appreciate you, Lúpe. I …"

(*Interrupting*) "Goodnight, Francisco. Call me tomorrow."

In the middle of the night, with street lights still on, a caravan of pickup trucks, sedans and commercial-sized vans can be seen heading into the Sierra Madres. Inside the vehicles is a contingent of forty heavily-armed men. As Francisco predicted, it will take about five hours to climb over the mountains and down into the Chihuahuan Desert. By the time the sun peaks over the mountain tops, the caravan is within three hundred yards of the hill, north of where the plane is scheduled to land. Francisco, who is in the lead vehicle, scans the hill with his binoculars, looking for signs that Rodrigo might have gotten there first. When he sees nothing suspicious, he signals the driver to move closer. Still nothing. When they are within 25 yards, Francisco gets out and walks up to the first row of mesquites, peers into the woods, then waves for everyone to follow. There are whoops of joy as men pile out and run toward the trees. Juan, Francisco's, second in command, orders the vehicles to be hidden on the north side of the hill. "Cut some mesquite branches and cover up the hoods," he shouts. Francisco looks at his watch; it is now 8:45 A.M…and still no sign of Rodrigo. He breathes a sigh of relief, then orders his men to fan out and take up a position behind a tree. "When Rodrigo comes, he be comin' from down there (*pointing toward the landing site*). Make sure you got plenty of ammo."

At 10:05, Juan shouts, "There he is. It's Rodrigo's gang, headin' for where the plane is goin' to land." Francisco immediately joins him, binoculars dangling from his neck. "Okay," he says, "are they gonna stay there until the plane comes or are they gonna come up here to the hill like Lúpe said?"

He doesn't have long to wait for an answer. Rodrigo, pressing now for time, doesn't even stop at the landing site. All three vans keep moving north until they reach a spot about fifty yards below the trees where Francisco's men are hiding. Rodrigo gets out and scans the hill carefully. His plan is to park the vans on the south side of the hill where Gordo won't see them as he approaches. He looks again, then turns to his second in command, "You see anything, Jaime?"

"Not a thing," comes the answer. "Shall we go in?"

Rodrigo is about to nod his approval when someone in the woods lights a cigarette.

"Wait, I think I just saw something…a light…there may be somebody in there."

"A couple of campers?", Jaime offers

"Out here?", Rodrigo barks. "Who the hell would want to camp out here? Let's wait." He pauses. "Jaime, take two of your guys and get a little closer." As Jaime inches toward the woods, Rodrigo turns around. "The rest of you guys, back up. We're too close."

Inside the woods, the man who lit the cigarette receives a blow from the barrel of Juan's machine gun. "Asshole," the lieutenant sputters.

Francisco, oblivious to what happened, crouches behind a tree, his eyes fixed on the thirty men arrayed in front of him. Like a leopard eyeing his prey, he tenses his muscles, ready to spring. When he sees Rodrigo wave his men back, he leaps to his feet, shouting, "Oh oh…they smell a rat. Let's get 'em."

Out from the tree, he aims his AK-47 and fires a round at Jaime; when Jaime falls, he fires at the other two men. As all three lay dying, Francisco runs out onto the sand, waving for everyone to follow. One by one Rodrigo's men drop to the ground and fire back. The exchange of gunfire reaches a crescendo as noise ripples across the desert floor. When it finally subsides, most of Rodrigo's men lie dead on the ground. Aware that he has been out-smarted, Rodrigo flees to the vans parked a few yards below. Without turning to look, he jumps into the closest one, waits for several of his men to follow suit, then starts the motor. A hail of bullets rips into the van as he races down toward the landing site. Thirty yards later, both back tires are hit with machine gun fire and explode. The van slows. Before it stops altogether, Rodrigo leaps out and begins racing toward a patch of creosote bushes on the other side of the landing site.

Francisco gives pursuit. As he lumbers downhill, El Gordo's overweight body heaves with each step, his brow soaking wet in the desert heat. His quarry may be a few years younger, but Rodrigo's betrayal is taking its toll. He turns once to look, cringes, then races on across the landing site. The sand is firmer here, making it easier to run. Francisco, thirsting for revenge, is now only ten feet behind and gaining. As he struggles to catch up, he reaches into the sheath on his hip and pulls out a hunting knife. One more burst of energy and he has Rodrigo by the collar. Wrestling him to the ground, he turns him on his back and raises his arm. When Rodrigo sees the blade glistening in the sun, he reaches for the pen knife strapped to his ankle. Before Francisco can act, he plunges the knife into his assailant's side. El Gordo's scream can be heard all the way up the hill where his men wait to celebrate their victory. As they watch with horror, Francisco shouts, "You piss dog"… then plunges the hunting knife into his victim's chest. There is a second scream as the blade slips between two ribs into Rodrigo's heart, splashing both men with fresh blood. Francisco struggles to his feet, then staggers back toward the woods, holding a kerchief to his side.

A cheer goes up as Juan orders everyone down the hill to help. Suddenly there's a shout. It's Paco, the man who lit the cigarette and is desperate to redeem himself. He's pointing to the sky: "The plane is coming; look, there, it's the plane." Everyone stops to look…then a second cheer goes up as the plane begins to circle the landing site. Juan orders the drivers to round up the three vans on the north side of the hill. The other men, unwilling to wait for a ride, begin racing down the hill toward the plane.

Minutes later, the pilot brings the aircraft to a bumpy landing and gets out. Francisco, still holding onto his side, watches from a distance as his men begin transferring packets of cocaine from the plane into the three vans. Each of the packets is about the size of a fat dictionary. When the transfer is complete, two vans are full. Juan uses the occasion to come where Francisco is sitting. "How's your side, boss? You gonna make it alright?"

"Si," comes the unemotional reply. "The doc can sew me up once we back at compound." He looks at his wrist watch. "But we gotta go…now 2:00." Juan looks around. "But what about dead bodies?" he asks, pointing to Rodrigo's men. Francisco bites his lip. "Leave 'em for vultures. But get their guns first."

As rain-soaked clouds drift teasingly across the desert, the men pile into their vehicles and head for home. Half-way back to Culiacán, Francisco dials Lúpe's number. "Hey, Lúpe, where are you?"

"Oh, Francisco, I'm in the car with my two protectors, on our way to the compound. And you? How did things go in the desert?"

"You right about everything, Lúpe. We get there and hide in woods before Rodrigo come. He no see us until too late. No problem anymore. I chase him with knife and…"

(*Interrupting*)…"please, spare me the details. I'm glad it went well." "Yes, very good. The shipment safe. Tomorrow we send it north to U.S. border."

"I'll be at the compound by 7:00…see you then."

"Okay, Lúpe. I see you tonight. Maybe we celebrate. Eat lots of squid." "Ugh. A slice or two of pizza sounds better."

"Oh yeah, I forget. You no like squid. Maybe on top of pizza?"

"I'll take pepperoni and mushrooms if that's okay with you."

"Sure okay…anything you want, my cariño. Oh, I forget to ask how everything go in Oaxaca. You do lots of good things?"

"Yes, Francisco, but let's leave it for tonight. I'll tell you everything then." "Okay, see you at home."

"Home? I thought the compound was my prison."

"No more. You free woman now."

"How come I have two bodyguards watching me all the time?"

"They for your protection, Lúpe. If enemies find out you part of my group, they come after you."

Lúpe blinks. "I'm part of your group? When did that happen?"

"We talk about it when you get back, yes?"

"Alright, Francisco. See you then."

Chapter 28

A Different Perspective

In the car, Lúpe's thoughts turn to a previous discussion in which Francisco suggested a different way of looking at the drug business. She leans back and closes her eyes. *He's saying that when Americans spend money on marijuana, cocaine and other recreational drugs, much of it ends up in Mexico where it trickles down to poor families. I'm not so sure about that trickling down…but he does have a point. Mexicans aren't doing too well these days selling corn or computers, but they are making a bundle selling drugs. If the drug business dries up, a lot of poor families will suffer. But there's a downside to all this. People who use these drugs, meth and heroin in particular, can end up getting addicted. There's a lot of suffering there…not to mention the cost of treatment.*

But what about tobacco and alcohol, she continues, millions of Americans are already addicted to those things…and we seem to take it in stride. And if marijuana were all that bad, would some experts be talking about decriminalizing it or even making it legal? Cocaine of course is more dangerous but who knows, even that may someday be sold in shops under government supervision. Heroin is the most deadly. We'd have to rule that out altogether. She pauses. What am I thinking? Am I losing my mind? I've always considered the drug business a blight on civilization, but here I am trying to look at it through Francisco's eyes…or at least from a different perspective. Is being cooped up in that compound getting to me…robbing me of my commonsense? Or maybe it's what I just saw in Oaxaca…that all this drug money from the U.S. can do wonderful things for the poor people of Mexico. Just think of what happened these last few days.

The money I brought with me, Francisco's money, changed the lives of everyone I met. People who used to sleep on dirt floors are now sleeping on beds; mothers who spent half the day washing clothes by hand are now using washing machines. And some twenty-year olds who dropped out of school in 9th grade are now back in the classroom, preparing for careers in business or administration. She shakes her head. *But what about the violence? Isn't it all the killing that makes this such a problem? Gangs killing each other, gangs killing policemen and innocent bystanders...even gangs challenging the government itself. What if there were no violence, or say a limited amount of it? Would we look at the drug trade differently? Perhaps it would still be a problem...but no longer one interesting enough to make the daily headlines. Is it realistically possible to eliminate the violence...what with all these thugs competing for a limited amount of business? To ask the capos to cooperate...join forces and divide up the business... sounds idealistic. I know they've tried ceasefires before, but they never last. It would be like asking stags during rutting season to share their harems...you know, take turns breeding the does. Crazy. So, does that mean warfare among drug dealers is inevitable? Do people in places like Juárez or Tijuana have to go on living in terror?*

She opens her eyes and looks out at the passing scenery. The sight of children playing outsdie a wooden shack reminds her of Vicente's family back in Oaxaca. *It really can't be called anything other than a cave,* she mumbles, referring to the home the 12-year-old boy invited her to. *So dark and airless, a single bulb hanging overhead, and both rooms filled with smoke from the cooking fire just inside the front door. The only piece of furniture I could see was a single bed over in the corner. When I asked the mother where they ate their meals, she put a piece of cardboard on the dirt floor, then knelt down, plastic plate in hand, to show me. And to think that ten people live there, two adults (mother and elder daughter) and eight children. When I asked her what she needed most of all, she said money for rent. It turns out that she was almost a whole year behind in her payments and had been notified that the police would soon come to eject them.*

She looks out the window again. *I know what I would like to do...not just for Vicente's family but for others like them. I want to move them out of those wretched homes they're living in now and into a place with a kitchen, stove, indoor bathroom, hot running water, beds, dining room furniture, and refrigerator. Think of what a difference that would make in their lives. With Francisco's money, I could help fifty or even a hundred families like that...every year. Of course, there will be those who say that I'm making them dependent on me when I should be helping them to help themselves...you know, teaching them how to fish instead of giving them fish. There's some truth in that. But I think there's a way to handle it. What if I offer to move a family and pay their rent for three years only, after which they have to come up with the payment themselves? Once they've moved, I could hire an occupational counselor to teach them new ways of making money...or get them placed in an educational program... perhaps going back to school to get their high school diploma. Those who finished high school might be interested in getting advanced training in a special field...like journalism, accounting, cooking or carpentry. For those with an entrepreneurial itch, we could even lend them money for starting a small business...a fruit stand perhaps or clothing outlet or even a jewelry store.*

As her breathing accelerates, she leans back and closes her eyes. *There's so much to be done. Thank goodness I have Francisco's money. He's generous with his own people, but doesn't seem to identify with other Mexicans. I feel fortunate that he likes me enough to let me do what I want in Oaxaca. But at the same time, I don't want to lead him on. There's Ned to think about too.* As Ned's image arises, she breathes a sigh of relief. *At least he's safe by now back in El Paso. That was foolish of him to come down here, right in the heart of Francisco's territory, and think he could rescue me.* The next thought takes her by surprise. *Do I really want to be rescued? Do I want to go back to the life of a professor's wife...with my tidy little suburban house, my flower bed and carefully mowed lawn? My God, the most serious problem we ever had was deciding whether or not we could afford a backyard swimming pool.* An image of Vicente's cave-like home returns, bringing tears to her eyes. *What exactly was the purpose of my life back in El Paso? Did I have any purpose at all, other than being a good wife and homemaker? I wasn't even good at that... after all, the marriage ended in divorce. Ned clearly loves me...more passionately than Lloyd ever did. But will becoming his wife make my life any more meaningful than it used to be?* She sits up and rubs her cheeks. *I really don't know. Maybe I don't want to know.*

As the car passes through Mazatlán, she calls out to her driver, "What do you think, Miguel, another hour or so until we get there?"

"Maybe hour and half, Señora."

Chapter 29

Ambush

As Lúpe nears Culiacán, Manny and Sebastián enter the hotel room Jesús reserved for them. They are soon joined by a disguised Ned who has taken a room in the same hotel. Jesús has promised to join them later. By 9:00 that evening the whole group has assembled and snacks have been ordered from room service. Sebastián is the first to speak. "So, what do we know about Gordo's whereabouts…and Peaches as well… anyone?" All eyes turn to Jesús.

"On most Saturdays, she and Gordo drive down from their compound and go straight to the park where the food is handed out. I seen 'em do it three times now."

Manny asks, "You saw them coming down the road?"

"Yeah, they come down with three black Infiniti's…Gordo and Peaches in the middle one. I watched 'em from the woods as they went by; the car window was down so I got a real good look. But she wasn't there last week, so I dunno if she's gonna come tomorrow."

"How far apart were the cars?"

"Maybe twenty yards between each one."

"What's the road like?", asks Sebastian. "I assume it's dirt… but how wide? Room enough for two cars or just one?"

"Just one," replies Jesús. "It's gotta a ditch on each side."

"How deep? I mean, could we get around a parked car by driving through the ditch?"

"Maybe, if you was a good driver."

The reason I ask is…if we want to block their way, it looks like we'll need a vehicle parked sideways across the road. But I'd hate to use our van in case it gets rammed; we'll need it to get back to Juárez. Besides it's got a lot of our equipment in the rear. Maybe we should rent a car or pickup."

Jesús straightens up. "I got a car we can use…it's the one Fernando had when we whacked 'im. After we finished 'im off, we hid it in the woods somewhere. Probly still there."

"Great," replies Sebastián. "It looks like we've got everything we need."

As the discussion continues, a strategy slowly emerges. The plan is similar to the one used to get Mata up in Juárez…grenade launchers fired from the trees next to the road…followed up with rifle fire if anyone tries to get away.

Ned is the last to speak before the group breaks up. "Hey, let's be sure that we don't do anything to hurt Jessica. This whole operation sounds pretty dangerous to me."

Sebastián smiles. "Hang on, old man. I didn't come all the way down here to preside over your fiancée's funeral. This ain't gonna be a walk in the park, but we'll be careful."

Saturday morning is overcast with a light wind, cool for Culiacán in the fall. As arranged, the group meets in the hotel lobby for breakfast, then drives to Badiraguato where they drop Jesús off near the hidden Infiniti before continuing on to the dirt road leading to Gordo's compound. A half a mile up the road, Sebastián nestles the van into a small open area in the trees. Satisfied that it is hidden, the group proceeds to unload. Each takes a weapon and ammunition; Manny and Sebastián take grenade launchers, Ned a rifle.

"What about Jesus?", Ned asks.

"He's got his bow and arrow," replies Manny. "He says that's all he needs."

It is now 8:30. According to Jesús, the three-car caravan from the compound usually arrives at this point on the road at about 9:30. With an hour to go, there's no need to rush. As planned, the three men set themselves up at the edge of the woods. Sebastián is given responsibility for taking out the lead car with his launcher; Manny takes a position about fifty yards up the road toward the compound where he will target the third car. Ned is told to set up somewhere in between where he'll have a clear view of the middle car, his assignment being to blow out the car's tires. In the group's haste to get ready, no one has bothered to ask whether Ned has ever fired a rifle before. That omission will prove costly later in the day.

About fifteen minutes later, a black Infiniti can be seen coming up the road from below. Sebastián stands to look. It's Jesús. The boy stops fifty yards from where Sebastián is standing, waves, then backs the Infiniti into the bushes. From there, it will take only seconds to move the car out onto the road where it can be used to block anyone trying to get past.

In the silence that follows, all eyes are on the curve a hundred yards up the road. As the minutes tick by slowly, each man rehearses his assignment and checks his equipment. Both grenade launchers are set with one grenade loaded and a second in the magazine. Ned has a full ammunition clip and Jesús a full quiver of arrows. And then comes a whistle unlike any bird call.

It's Manny, pointing to the place above where the first Infiniti can be seen coming around the curve. Sebastián checks his magazine, then grips his grenade launcher. When he waves his readiness, Manny waves back, indicating he's all set. From his place further down in the trees, Jesús sees the Infiniti coming and turns on the ignition. He waits until the first car is within fifty yards, then moves out onto the road. Satisfied that no one can get past him, he rolls down the window and places the bow in his lap.

When the driver of the first Infiniti sees Jesús's car, he slams on the brakes and raises his arms in alarm. Twenty yards back, Francisco leans forward, straining to identify the car straddling the road. Unbeknownst to either men who are looking ahead rather than to the side, Sebastián remains hidden in the trees, just a few yards from the lead car. He scans the road to make sure the three Infiniti's have kept their original spacing. Reassured that they have, he swings his launcher into place and aims at the passenger door of the first car. At the last second, Valentino, who is sitting in the passenger's seat, sees something move in the trees and reaches for his pistol. Sebastián returns his stare, tenses his trigger finger…and fires. The grenade hits the car broadside, igniting a giant fireball and hurtling glass, doors, seats and body parts into the air. Small fires start as debris falls among the dry grasses.

Within seconds, a similar explosion is heard as a grenade screams into the third car. Auto parts and body parts are once again thrown into the air as flames engulf the target. In the middle car, Francisco is thrown forward by the explosion behind him; the ensuing heat quickly becomes intolerable. "We gotta get outta here," he shouts as he opens the door behind the driver. Grabbing Lúpe by the wrist, he leaps from the car and pulls her across the ditch and into the woods.

With the middle car right in front of him, Ned aims his rifle at the tires and pulls the trigger…or at least tries to. Unaware that the safety catch is still on, he pulls harder. When nothing happens, he steps out onto the road, shielding himself from the falling debris. In vain, he looks for Jessica. By now, Francisco, Lúpe and their driver are already in the woods and heading up a deer trail. When Ned spots them, he races around the burning vehicle, still carrying the rifle, and gives pursuit. Ten yards into the woods, he stops, slips off the safety, and lifts the rifle. Before pulling the trigger, he yells. "Jessica!" She immediately wheels around and faces him.

What she sees confuses her…a man with a beard, wearing a floppy beach hat and horn-rimmed glasses. She murmurs, *Who is this man who calls me by my real name?* Seeing the rifle, Francisco grabs her by the wrist and yanks hard. This time she refuses to budge. In response, Francisco nods to his driver who turns and aims his AK-47 at the intruder. As Jessica looks on in horror, a hail of bullets rips into Ned's body, dropping him to his knees. She screams, then pulls free from Francisco and rushes to his side. "Oh my God, Ned…it's you. What…what are you doing here?" He hears her but cannot respond. With blood oozing from his chest, he stares at her, eyes distant and clouding, lips poised as if to kiss…then drops to the ground. Huddling over him, she cries, "Oh no."

Above on the trail, Francisco nods to his driver, then resumes his flight, leaving Lúpe to her own fate. When he hears a strange thud, followed by a gasp, he turns to look again. It's the driver stumbling toward him. "What's wrong?", he yells. There is no answer. It is only when the driver falls to the ground that Francisco sees the arrow stuck in his back. Frantically, he looks around, his eyes sweeping the forest below.

At first, he sees nothing…then, from behind a tree, a young boy steps out and lifts his bow. Francisco freezes, then wheels and races up the trail. Jesús follows, gradually closing the gap. For the boy, there is no need to hurry. He can see that his target is unarmed except for a hunting knife. Besides, El Gordo's breath is coming faster now as the trail steepens along a narrow ridge. When his quarry stops to catch his breath, Jesús strings an arrow and lets it fly. Gordo hears the twang of the bow string but has no time to duck. The arrow strikes him just behind the shoulder, sending him to his knees. Unable to pull the arrow out, he stares at the archer, then shouts, "You can't kill me, you piss-dog. I kill your mama and papa...but you too scared to kill me."

Jesús says nothing, but continues to move closer. Still struggling for air, the capo heaves his corpulent frame further up the trail. The pain in his shoulder is excruciating, his steps faltering, his awareness blurred. He stops where the trail makes a sharp turn to the left...and bends over. Unable to go further, he turns to face his assailant. Rising defiantly, he stretches out his arms and shouts, "Okay, Tarzán...I make it easy for you... (*gasping*)...or you afraid?"

Jesús watches as his victim struggles to breathe. Superimposed on the target before him is an image of his parents being fire-bombed in Oaxaca. His lips curl with the memory. With an imperceptible nod to his quarry, he grasps the leather holder, pulls the string taut, pauses one more time to aim...then lets fly his messenger of death. As if guided by invisible hands, it finds the capo's chest and penetrates his lungs. Francisco stumbles. The pain is unbearable, but he will not let the boy hear him cry. As Jesús stares, the kingpin of the drug world steps to the trail's edge, teeters for a moment, then falls headlong into the woods below. He twitches once, then stops.

High in a tree overhead, a raven cries "Aaawk!", unfolds its massive wings, then flies away.

Chapter 30

Succession

The day after the capo's funeral, members of the cartel's inner circle meet to discuss strategy in the board room. Maria, Francisco's wife, and her three adult children are invited and asked to sit in one of the chairs along the wall. Juan makes sure that Lúpe also attends. Symbolizing the business at hand is the empty chair at the head of the table, the chair typically reserved for Francisco. At the other end of the table is Gilberto, a tall and slender man with graying hair who rarely talks about business, but whose judgment in assessing the character of new recruits has proven invaluable over the years. According to Francisco, he has an uncanny ability to ferret out potential traitors…and to identify those who are likely to remain loyal. It is no surprise, then, that when no one rises to speak, all eyes turn to Gilberto. He is aware of their respect, but says nothing. Five minutes pass and still no one dares to break the silence. Finally, having made his decision, Gilberto shifts his feet, places his hands on the table, and rises. He looks at each of the men in turn, then turns to the people along the wall. His jaw is square, his eyes fixed. When he senses that all eyes are on him, he raises his right hand. Like a trumpet echoing in the halls of a medieval castle, he cries out, "The king is dead; long live the queen." He says nothing more and sits down.

In the ensuing silence, all eyes shift to the woman and children sitting along the wall. Still, no one moves. Then, convinced she is being summoned, Maria rises from her chair and walks toward the empty seat at the head of the table. Before she can get there, Juan, acting solely on instinct, leaps from his chair to intercept her. Gently, he turns her around and points to the wall. Several of the men around the table nod approvingly, but no one speaks. Again, it is Gilberto who breaks the silence. Rising again, he calls out, "Señora," pointing to Lúpe. When Lúpe fails to respond, he walks over to her and takes her by the hand. Slowly, he leads her to the empty seat at the head of the table and waits until she sits down. To others at the table, the solemnity of the act, brief and simple though it may be, has all the earmarks of a formal coronation. In keeping with the spirit of the occasion, everyone at the table rises and bows to Lúpe. Maria, making no attempt to conceal her disgust, calls to her children and stomps out of the room, never to return.

Once seated, Lupé looks around the table. She studies the men's faces, carefully examining their eyes. Nothing is said, but all eyes are on her, studying her in return. She looks at each one, man by man, hunting for signs of resentment or suspicion. What she sees in their faces is quite different…a feeling that can only have originated with El Gordo himself. It is a feeling of respect. She nods humbly. As she does so, a series of images rises before her. She sees Lloyd back in his study, preparing the next day's lectures. She sees her house, the huge kitchen with its island oven and maplewood cabinetry. She sees Ned, the man she promised to marry, whispering goodbye while clutching his bloody chest. Images of friends, the university, the city, her love for America… all rise in turn…beckoning her home, testing her resolve.

Then, as if from behind her, she hears the children of Oaxaca, calling to her from their dark caves…begging for something to eat, a new pair of shoes, a bed to sleep on. Silently, she answers them now, her promise to come carried on the wind. Around the table, grown men stare as they attempt to read her mind. Juan, sitting next to her as he did when Francisco was alive, whispers, "Señora?" Just a single word, but it is enough to wipe the cloud from her eyes. She looks up, and clears her throat.

"What do you want of me?", she asks.

All eyes turn to Gilberto. He looks directly at her. "We want you to take Francisco's place."

Lupé shakes her head. "But why me?"

Still standing, Gilberto answers, "Francisco say to us if anything happen to him, we ask you to take seat at head of table. He say that right after you help take down Rodrigo's gang. Francisco have much respect for you, Señora."

"But I don't know anything about running a drug business. What makes you think I can help?"

Ramon, second in age to Gilberto and the only one to wear glasses, takes a deep breath. "Francisco say you very smart woman...and have many new ideas for our business."

"True, I do have many new ideas, but they are very different from what you are used to hearing." When no one speaks up, she continues. "I really don't want to be part of an organization that is only interested in making you rich...and that relies on violence to achieve that end."

Silence.

Gilberto asks, "What you interested in, Señora?" Without hesitation, she answers, "Helping people...helping the poor people of Mexico."

Around the table, jaws drop at the unfamiliar words. Men stare at each other, unable to make sense of what they just heard. Gilberto is the first to respond. "Why you want to help poor people, Señora? In our business, we no worry about other people; we look out for ourselves. You forget about yourself and you get whacked."

"Well yes," she responds, "that's why I don't think I belong here. Our interests are too different."

Silence.

Ramon looks around the room before responding. "So why Francisco say you be our leader?"

"I don't know for sure but my guess is that he thought the Sinaloa organization was ready to change direction...at least that's what I got from my recent talks with him."

Ramon bristles. "What kind of change you talking about, Señora?"

"Well, what I was talking about before...becoming an organization that uses its profits to help the poor people of Mexico."

"But we all hafta live, Señora...have families to support." Lúpe smiles. "I don't see why we can't do both...there's plenty of money coming in every day. In fact, we're already doing both. I'm sure you've all heard that I've been spending time in places like Oaxaca where cartel money is being used to lift families out of poverty. We even have a fund for that purpose now; we call it the Francisco Fund, since he's the one who provided the money."

Ramon leans forward on his elbows. "But you say you no like violence. Impossible in drug business to succeed without violence. Like a jungle...everybody out to get you and they get you if you no get them first."

Lúpe sits up straight. "Yes, Ramon, I'm sure that's the way it is now...but I don't think it has to be that way." She stops to let the idea sink in. "What if we stopped trying to take away other gang's territory and just concentrated on what we already have?"

"But in this business," Juan replies quickly, "if you don't keep expandin' your territory, you gonna get swallowed up. People gonna think you weak, that you gettin' old or somethin'." Ramon is quick to add, "If we don't keep expandin', gangs like the Zapas and La Familia are gonna come after us. They're gonna think that now Francisco gone, we're scared and can't defend ourselves…and we don't want that to happen." Lupe watches nervously as the men nod their heads in approval. Sensing resistance, she decides to play her ace card. "Do you recall how Mata, the Zapas leader, was brought down? If not, let me remind you. I seem to have the psychic ability to locate targets even when I can't see them with my eyes. I used that ability to notify the narcotics team in Juárez of Mata's whereabouts. A hit team was waiting for him when he came out of the restaurant. He made it as far as the highway where he was gunned down by one of our sharpshooters."

"Yeah," says Ramon, "that's why Francisco kidnap you. He afraid you get him next."

"Exactly. Francisco was on our radar, but he got to me before we could zero in on him."

"So, what you sayin', Señora? You can use power to help us?"

"I hope I can, Ramon."

"But how does it work?"

"I'm not exactly sure, but let's assume that one of the other cartels sees that we're no longer trying to expand our territory. They figure we've been weakened by Francisco's death and decide to move in on us. In that case, our strategy is straightforward. We take down their leaders like we took down Mata in Juárez."

"You can do that for us?", asks Juan, scratching his head.

"I can't guarantee anything, but it's worked before."

"But how you do it?"

"I get familiar with a man's photo, then sit down, relax and go into a trance. Usually within a few minutes, I get an image of where the person is…a restaurant perhaps, or a car, or a familiar building in town. I concentrate on that image until it becomes very clear. The next step is to identify the location, you know, the restaurant or building that I saw in the trance. Once I'm pretty sure of the target location, I let somebody know and they take it from there."

Juan smiles. "You mean, they go to the location and whack the guy."

Lupé (*squirmng*): "Something like that, yes."

Ramon shakes his head. "But if we take down boss, won't somebody rise up and take his place?"

Gilberto leans forward to speak. "Sure, but with Señora on our side, we take him down too…and next guy…until they give up. Is that the idea, Señora?"

"Pretty much. If it works, other groups will see what's happening and think twice before coming after us. Of course, there will always be some young turks who are hungry for power and want to give it a try, but overall things should begin to settle down. With less violence to deal with, we can concentrate on our real mission which is to use profits from the drug business to help communities prosper…(pause)… Anyway, that's how I see it. If you want me to continue sitting in Francisco's place, this is the way we're going to do things. If you don't feel comfortable with this strategy, I'll leave and you can get somebody else to sit here."

Before the meeting breaks up, Juan asks, "What about all the money Francisco had stashed away in Swiss banks? Who's gonna get it?" All eyes turn to Gilberto.

"I've seen the will and all of us will get some money, but the lion's share goes to his wife and kids. That means we gonna hafta start from scratch…(*pause*)…But I think we can do it."

As Lúpe rises to leave, all seven men stare at her. A few nod; others look puzzled, only one is shaking his head. When she is no longer within hearing distance, Florio, the head shaker, leans forward, fists clenched. "What the hell is a woman doin' here anyway? She don't know shit about drugs. Is she gonna tell me how to run the meth plant?" He shakes his head again, more vigorously this time. "And you guys not only wanna let her in but make her our boss? You crazy or somethin'?" Silence. "So, she don't like violence. Just like a woman. Maybe we should ask a padre to lead us…or maybe the Pope himself. If we gonna succeed, we need a man in that chair, somebody who knows the business, somebody who don't mind a little whackin'."

"True," replies Juan, "but Francisco said he wants Lúpe to take charge. He musta knowd somethin'about …"

(*Interrupting*) "C'mon. Francisco was in love with her…he couldn't see straight. It's easy to lose yir head over a woman, especially if she's a looker. We all know that, don't we (*laughing*)?" Only Amérigo, the leader of the sicarios hit squad, nods his approval. "Florio speak truth," he says. "The drug business ain't no place for a woman, specially one who's afraid of a little whackin'."

When no one else raises his hand to speak, Gilberto says, "Let's think it over and meet again here on Friday."

Back in her room, Lúpe sits down on the edge of the bed, her face in her hands. Softly, so nobody can hear, she murmurs, *I can't believe I said those things. This isn't me. What am I doing with these men? In many ways, I despise what they stand for…lawlessness, violence, greed. Yet, here they are, asking me to be their leader, despite our difference in values.* As she lowers her head, thoughts of Ned return, followed by an image of his body being loaded onto a van for the trip back to El Paso. *It would be so easy to follow him there now. With Francisco's death, I'm free to go wherever I want to… (pause)…But do I want to return to the life of a suburban housewife?*

Her reverie is broken by the sound of loud voices just outside her bedroom. Juan can be heard telling the others that two of the men from Francisco's gang have been killed in Mazatlán and a third badly injured. "Miguel is gonna be okay but he say it start when guys from Tijuana try to take over one of our protection accounts. That ain't all. Now they want a piece of our coke business too. They let Miguel get away so he could deliver the news."

Florio's deep voice comes through the door. "So, what are we gonna do about it?"

Juan answers quickly. "First thing is to tell Lúpe…see what she says."

Florio snickers. "You think she's tough enough to handle somethin' like this?"

Juan immediately heads for Lúpe's room. "Let's find out." When told of the killings, Lúpe responds with a question. "Who is the leader of the Tijuana gang?" "Really two men," says Juan. "Emiliano Rodriguez is brains of the operation. He goes by the name, El Cerébro,' cuz he's so smart. He handles their operations… you know, all the stuff to do with planes, subs, transports, and trucks. Then he runs a distribution network up through San Diego, LA, San Francisco and Seattle. They say he keeps most info in his head…don't need to write anything down."

Lúpe takes a seat. "You say there were two men."

"Yeah, the other guy is his brother, Florentino. They call him El Papa (*the Pope*) 'cuz he's so religious. He's their main hit man; anybody gets in the way of the gang, he takes 'em down.

Once their dead, he stands over them and does a little prayer, then arranges the body in a cross...you know, the feet together and arms outstretched." Juan smiles. "They don't call him El Papa for nothin'."

Lúpe grimaces, then asks, "Do we have any photos...of either man?"

"Yeah," says Juan. "I got a couple we took from the newspapers." "Okay. Let's start with El Cerébro. Bring the photo to my room."

Later that day, Lúpe sits down on her bed, crosses her legs and holds the photo of El Cerébro in front of her. Slowly she slips into a trance. Minutes go by without any images appearing. Frustrated, she opens her eyes and looks around. On the table to her right, she spots the other photo, the one of Florentino, the one known as El Papa. She picks up the brother's photo and tries with him. Once her eyes are closed, an image of a church suddenly appears before her. Inside the church, there is a huge stained-glass image of St. Francis holding a lamb. She looks for other details. The nave of the church is decorated with long rows of white flowers, possibly lilies. She uncrosses her legs, rises and goes out into the conference room looking for Juan. He is sitting in a large upholstered chair waiting for her.

"Any luck, Señora?"

"Perhaps. Florentino is in a church...or at least, was in one... but I can't tell which one."

"What kind of church, Señora?"

"Well, for one thing, it has a large stained-glass picture of a monk, presumably St. Francis, holding a lamb."

"Where is picture...on right as you come in, or to left?"

"To the right...and there were lots of white flowers strung in a line across the front of the church."

"Easter flowers, yes, tomorrow Easter Sunday...big day in Mexico."

"Do you know the church?", Lúpe asks.

"Yes, but maybe we call in the others and ask them."

When Juan is joined by the others, Ramon is the first to speak. "That sounds like St. Francis Basilica up in Tijuana. I been inside a coupla times...most beautiful church I ever been in." Juan adds, "It's Florentino's favorite. Newspapers say he give church million pesos every year."

Lúpe gets up. "So, he's probably there right now. There's not much we can do from here...but like you say, if he gives a lot of money to the church, he probably goes there often."

"In the article I read," says Juan, "it said he prays there every morning. They open the church up early jis' for him." Ramon adds, "Makes sense...if he gives 'em that much money." "Yeah", responds Juan, "that means we know jis' where to find 'im."

Lúpe starts back toward her room. Turning at the door, she says, "I'll leave the details up to you people. The only thing I might add is that if you're looking for a sharpshooter, you won't find anyone more qualified than a boy named Jesús. He worked for the team that got Mata up in Juárez."

"But ain't he the kid who got Francisco with a bow and arrow?", asks Amérigo, clearly upset. A low rumble of discontent fills the conference room.

Yes," answers Lúpe from her bedroom door, "but he had reason to be angry. He wanted revenge for Francisco's killing his parents." Silence. "I think we can persuade him to be on our side now."

"You sayin' to give this kid a job, Señora?", asks Gilberto.

"Yes, let's find him and make him an offer. Don't tell him about the Rodriguez brothers yet. Save that for later."

"Okay. So, where do we find 'im?", asks Juan.

As she shuts her bedroom door, Lúpe answers, "I've seen him several times at the Saturday food giveaway. Let's start there."

Before the group can disband, Amérigo, the cartel's official hit man, rises to speak, his face red, his eyes glowering. "Why do we need some punk outsider to do our whackin' for us? Don't she know we got our own people?...*(pause)*...Like Florio said, she don't know shit how this organization works. If you wanna whack the Rodriquez brothers, let us sicarios do it. We never let you down before."

All heads turn to Gilberto. "Lúpe has her own ideas about who should do it. If we want her to be our boss, we gotta let her make the decisions. She's already proved that she knows what she's doin'."

Chapter 31

Rendezvous in Tijuana

On Saturday morning, Lúpe is quick to spot Jesús at the back of the crowd. She waits until he looks at her, then waves him closer. "You called me Peaches two weeks ago…remember?"

"Yeah," he answers warily.

"And you must be Jesús."

"So?"

"Apparently we worked together on the Mata thing up in Juárez. I guess we made a good team."

"What d'ya mean?"

"Well, we got him, didn't we?"

"Oh yeah, we got 'im real good."

When Jesús appears restless, Lúpe comes down from the platform. Whispering, she says, "Do you have a job, Jesús?"

"Yeah, at a sports good store, but we're shut down right now. Somebody tried to torch the place."

"How would you like to come and work for me?"

"Doin' what?"

"Same thing you did for the team up in Juárez."

"You mean takin' down drug dealers?"

"Yes. We have some people trying to move into the Sinaloa territory and we need to remove the threat."

"You mean kill 'em?"

Lúpe turns her head. "That's one way to put it."

Jesús squints. "Who's side you on, anyway?"

"I'm working for the Sinaloa organization now; we've changed our mission. Most of our profits from now on will go toward helping poor people throughout Mexico."

"Whew. I never heard of gangsters worryin' about poor people. Sounds weird."

"I agree that it's different, but the members of the gang—at least most of them---seem ok with it. So, from now on, we're going to use some of the profits to help people improve their housing and get more education. We're already helping some people start new businesses. In the future, we want to go further…perhaps pay cities to renovate their old buildings and plant more trees and flowers. That'll attract more tourists who in turn will spend money and create more jobs."

Jesús wrinkles his nose. "How can you do all that Salvation Army stuff and still go around killin' people?"

"When the men asked me to take over Francisco's place, I insisted that we use violence only to defend our territory, but not to expand our operations."

Jesús shakes his head. "Pardon me, Señora, but this don't make sense." "I understand, so we'll have to do more talking. In the meantime, is there a possibility that you will come to work for us?"

"Maybe. I dunno."

"Alright, let's meet again next Saturday. That will give you time to think it over."

On the following Saturday morning Jesús shows up at the food giveaway with his friend, Raffi, at his side. Once Lúpe sees them in the crowd, she calls them over to the platform.

"This here's my friend, Raffi," Jesús says. "If you wanna hire me, you gotta hire him too."

"How do you do, Raffi. If Jesús vouches for you, that's enough for me. By the way, I'm...let's see...who am I these days? Jesús knows me as Peaches; the men here know me as Lúpe, but my real name is Jessica, although nobody here calls me that."

"So, what we call you?", asks Jesús, smiling.

"For the time being, why don't we make it Lúpe. Anything else will sound strange to the people in our group."

"Okay, Señora Lúpe."

"Now, as soon as we finish handing out food, I want to take the two of you up to the compound where we can talk in private."

"Okay."

Later, up in the compound, Jesús and Raffi are introduced to members of the inner circle, including Gilberto, Ramon, Florio, Amérigo, Paco, and Juan. The discussion quickly turns to strategy. Sitting at the head of the table, Lúpe summarizes what is known about the situation so far. "While we don't have all the details, it's clear that the Tijuana cartel is trying to move into Sinaloa. It is imperative that we stop them before they obtain a foothold. As much as I dislike the idea, I am resigned to the fact that the best way to stop them is to eliminate their leaders. In other words, both Emiliano and Florentino Rodriguez must go. I haven't had any success so far locating Emiliano, but I have seen Florentino at the St. Francis Basilica in Tijuana."

Jesús raises his hand to speak. "What dya mean you saw 'im in the church? You mean like you "saw" Mata at the restaurant?"

"Yes, something like that. I "saw" Florentino in a church… and the men here identified the church as the St Francis Basilica in Tijuana. The huge stained-glass picture of St. Francis holding a lamb was a dead giveaway; the display of flowers across the nave was another clue."

Juan signals that he wants to say something. "We know from the newspapers that Florentino goes to the Basilica every morning to pray."

"What time?", asks Gilberto.

"Not sure," answers Juan.

"So, our first step is to monitor his whereabouts until we are sure when he goes to the Basilica," says Lúpe. "For that, we need someone unknown to the Tijuana group, someone like Jesús and his friend Raffi." Turning to the boys, she asks, "Is that something you could do without attracting attention?"

"Maybe," says Jesús. "Depends on what we hafta do." "Just stick around the Basilica," says Juan. "Check out when he gets there, how long he stays and who's with him." Gilberto adds,

"And keep an eye open for a place where you can set up a snipin' rifle without bein' seen."

"Where we gonna get a snipin' rifle?", asks Raffi.

"Don't worry about it; we gonna get you a good one."

"Do we get a vehicle?", says Jesús. "Tijuana is a pretty long walk."

"We'll get you a nice, black Toyota…somethin' that won't stand out. You got a valid driver's license?"

"I do", says Raffi, reaching for his wallet.

Jesús and Raffi set out for Tijuana the next day. On reaching the Basilica, they take up a position in a doorway, kitty-corner from the church. From that spot they have a clear view of whatever happens across the street. Precisely at 7:15 two black Cadillacs pull up in front of the church and park. First out is a burly, long-haired bodyguard carrying an AK-47. Next is Florentino, followed by another guard. Both men in the second car get out and stand by the curb. The path from the curb to the church entrance is about 30 yards, a distance Jesús figures should take Florentino about a minute to traverse. Turning to Raffi, he whispers, "This is a lousy angle. One of his goons is gonna be right behind 'im all the way to the church.

"Yeah," says Raffi. "We need to be up there somewhere (*pointing to a mid-rise apartment building to their right*). Maybe we can get an apartment near the top…that's the best angle." Jesús nods his approval. "Let's wait until El Papa finishes his prayers and leaves. Then we can check out the apartment building."

Once Florentino and his entourage have left, the boys walk over to the apartment building and approach the manager who tells them that there are two units available on the side facing the square. Because of their desirability, units on that side are more expensive.

"Which floor?", asks Jesús.

"One on the second floor, the other on the fourth," says the manager in a tone less than welcoming.

"We wanna see the one on the fourth floor," says Jesús.

"Okay, but we don't take checks here," the manager answers, sizing up the two youths. "Cash or credit card only…in advance. And one week minimum."

"No problem," Jesus says quickly.

When the apartment on the fourth floor turns out to be ideal for the mission at hand, the boys indicate their approval and leave with a promise to return in the morning with money for one week. Back in the compound, the group endorses the idea of the apartment and gives Jesús 4,200 pesos ($350) for rent. "When can you go back up there?", asks Gilberto.

"Tomorrow," answers Jesús. "Florentino comes every day, so it don't matter which day we pick. Maybe we'll jis' check 'im out the first day…then, if everything's okay, we'll get 'im on the second."

"Better give us time to get you a snipin' rifle," says Gilberto. "They don't grow on trees, you know."

"I think I know where to find one today," says Juan. "My cousin Antonio up in Mazatlan sells all kinds of guns. He was tellin' me the other day about this new Orsis model. I think it's called the T-5000. He says it's accurate from 2.4 kilometers. They even use it in Afghanistan, so it should be good enough to pick off El Papa at 150 yards."

Early the next day the boys drive up to Tijuana and settle into their new apartment. The first job is to arrange the furniture so they have a clear visual path to the front of the Basilica which is about 150 yards away. "Trouble is," says Jesús as he pushes the couch to one side, "from this angle I can't get a clean shot. Florentino's bodyguard is still gonna be in the way."

"Yir right," says Raffi. "Let's try the roof. Should be a lotta space up there." Jesús agrees. Together they head for the stairs. Once they find their way to the roof, both break into broad smiles. "Wow," shouts Raffi, pointing to the far-left corner of the building. "From over there, we can get 'im from the side, so the goon behind 'im won't block your view."

Jesús follows him to the corner, kneels, and takes imaginary aim. "Perfecto," he says, pointing to the church entrance. "I could get a mouse from here."

"Great," answers Raffi. "That leaves one big, fat question. How we gonna get outta here after you shoot 'im?"

"No problem," says Jesus, standing up. "Park the car in the alley behind the apartment buildin' and keep the engine runnin' while I finish off El Papa. Once I get 'im, I gonna run down the stairs and jump in the car before somebody figures out where the shot came from."

"Sounds good."

Satisfied with their plans, the boys head back to the compound. By dinner time, Juan has the promised Orsis T-5000 sniper rifle. It's broken down into separate parts, each packed snugly inside a black plastic case. Amidst oohs and aahs, Jesús puts the pieces together, then strokes it like a Stradivarius. "So, where can I practice?", he says, beaming.

"There's a place out back of the compound where we practice shootin'", says Juan. Not waiting for further instructions, the boys head for the range and set up the rifle. Raffi insists on being given a turn, even though the plans call for Jesús to do the shooting. Together they practice until it's too dark to see, then resume early in the morning. By the end of a few days practice, Jesús declares their readiness for a trip to Tijuana. By then, the promised Toyota has arrived and given a thorough checkup. Shortly after lunch, they head for the rented apartment and prepare themselves for Florentino's visit the next morning.

At the apartment their sleep is fitful, punctuated by dreams of gunfire, sirens, and flashing cruiser lights. Upon wakening, they dress quickly, eschew breakfast and climb the stairs to the roof. Jesús scans the roof tops of adjoining buildings before setting up the Orsis. No one is watching. On the street below, precisely at 6:45, two black limos arrive and park outside the church. First to get out is the bodyguard known to the boys as goon #1. Florentino is right behind him. As expected, a second goon follows several feet behind. With eyes fixed on his intended target, Jesús drops into a prone position and aims the rifle.

"You got a clear shot?", asks Raffi. "Yeah," comes the answer.

"Okay, I'm goin' down to the car and start the engine. Still favoring his knee, he heads down the stairs. Just as he hits the second floor landing, a single shot breaks the morning silence. He smiles, rubs the knee, then rushes down to the bottom floor rear entrance. Assured that no one is watching, he slips into the car and starts the motor. Minutes later, Jesús pulls open the door and jumps in. "Let's go," he shouts, cradling the still warm rifle.

In the square, traffic has come to a stop as drivers and pedestrians alike turn their gaze toward the fallen man outside the church entrance. "I guess you got 'im," says Raffi as he grips the wheel and guns the motor. "Not too fast," cautions Jesús. "We're jis' a coupla guys gointa work, right?"

"Okay, got it," says Raffi, extending his right hand for a 'gimme five.'

The next morning's television is filled with news of Florentino Rodriguez's assassination. Speculation focuses on rival groups; some point to the Juárez cartel, others to the Sinaloa organization. As concern in the Tijuana gang rises, Florentino's brother, Emiliano, strengthens security around headquarters.

Back in the compound, Jesús and Raffi join the inner circle in a discussion of what steps to take next. Soon after the meeting opens, Lúpe is called in from her reading room where she is practicing Spanish with a tutor. At her suggestion, Emiliano's photo is passed around and information about his habits shared. By the time she leaves the meeting she has a good idea of that he looks like and how he spends his days. Back in her room, her first effort produces nothing. Later the same day, she tries again. This time her trance narrows the focus to an outdoor scene with acres of cut grass. In the distance is a metal pole with a flag fluttering in the breeze. Never having played golf, she is stymied until she meets again with the advisory group.

"Sure sounds like golf course, Señora," says Gilberto who is an avid player himself.

"But do we know which one Emiliano plays?", asks Juan.

"Two outside Tijuana," Gilberto answers. "One is nine-hole course, good for beginners. Everybody know Emiliano Rodriquez is low handicap golfer; he even win prizes. He never play course meant for beginners. When he play, he play at Tijuana Country Club, one of hardest courses in Mexico."

Armed with this new information, Jesús and Raffi announce their eagerness to check the course out. Gilberto has a better solution. "We need to go to course and figure out which holes give best chance of takin' Emiliano down. Two boys who don't know shit about golf not gonna work."

Juan sighs: "So?"

"So, better I play a round of golf and Jesús caddy for me. That way we scout out course and nobody pay attention. You come too Raffi, but stay in clubhouse." Raffi opens his eyes wide, "And do what?" "Keep eye out for Emiliano's men and call me on cell phone."

The plan is quickly agreed upon by the group.

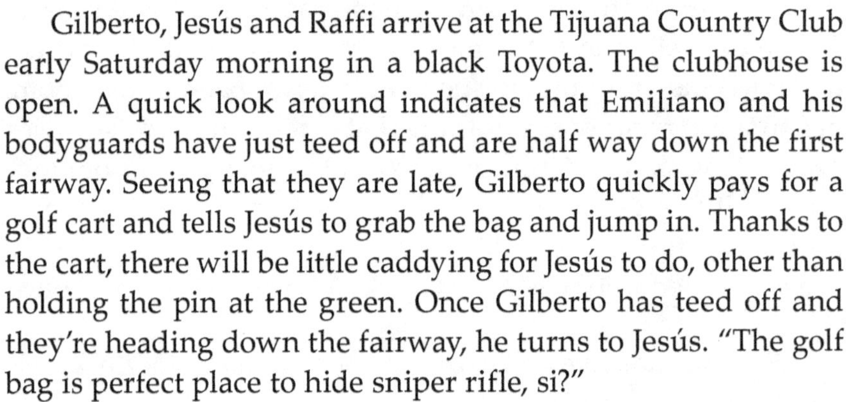

Gilberto, Jesús and Raffi arrive at the Tijuana Country Club early Saturday morning in a black Toyota. The clubhouse is open. A quick look around indicates that Emiliano and his bodyguards have just teed off and are half way down the first fairway. Seeing that they are late, Gilberto quickly pays for a golf cart and tells Jesús to grab the bag and jump in. Thanks to the cart, there will be little caddying for Jesús to do, other than holding the pin at the green. Once Gilberto has teed off and they're heading down the fairway, he turns to Jesús. "The golf bag is perfect place to hide sniper rifle, si?"

"Yeah, can't see any of it."

Gilberto flashes a toothy smile. "All we do now is find a spot where you pick 'im off and nobody see you."

His prayers are answered when they reach the fourth hole. While the first three holes hug the perimeter road, the fourth dips down into a recessed area 30 yards from traffic. From the tee, players face a steep ravine directly in front of them; the hole itself is on the opposite side of the drop-off. Because the green is surrounded by woods, people playing the hole cannot be seen either from the road or by golfers playing other holes. As Gilberto and Jesús approach the tee, they can see Emiliano and three other men getting ready to putt over on the green. Gilberto takes out his binoculars and looks. He smiles. "It's Emiliano, his cousin Estafan…you know, the one he's groomin' to replace him, and Jorge, his nephew; he's takin' over Florentino's job as head hit man. All three in one place…plus bodyguard, the one on right not playin'." He smiles. "Ducks are on pond, Jesus, just hope they come again next Saturday."

The plan is agreed upon back at the compound and put into effect the following week. Gilberto, Jesús and Raffi arrive at the golf course a few minutes after 7:00. To their great relief, Emiliano, his cousin and nephew are all on the practice tee hitting shots. The bodyguard watches from a distance. At a signal from Gilberto, Raffi disappears into the clubhouse restaurant which is just opening. His agreed upon mission is to keep an eye out for trouble and inform Gilberto by cell phone if he senses anything wrong. Later, once Gilberto and Jesús have reached the first green, he's to take the car to a spot on the road closest to the fourth hole and park it. Having scouted the area the week before, he knows exactly where to go.

As Jesús heads for a cart, Gilberto goes into the clubhouse to pay for the round. Having made sure he and Jesús are next in line to play, Gilberto feels no pressure to hurry. With a casual eye on Emiliano, he goes over to the practice tee, hits several drives, then switches to his irons. Out of the corner of his eye, he watches as Emiliano moves to the first tee and gets ready to hit his drive. Once El Cerébro and the rest of his troupe have finished driving, Gilberto picks up his bag and joins Jesús who is sitting in a cart just behind the first tee. By the time Gilberto readies his ball to play, Emiliano is half way down the fairway…a good 250 yards from the tee. Because it is still early in the morning, no other parties are lined up to play. Gilberto pulls out his binoculars to get a better look at his quarry. Satisfied that he has his man, he takes the driver from his bag, being careful to keep the rifle fully covered. His drive sails 225 yards down the fairway, slightly to the right but in a spot that allows him to keep an eye on the group ahead. By design, a similar distance between the two groups is kept for the remainder of the hole… and then again on the second and third holes as well.

As they approach the fourth hole, Gilberto turns to Jesús, "Raffi's gonna park over there (*pointing*). Should take two minutes to reach car once we finish our job." Jesús nods his agreement as he maneuvers the cart down to the tee. Both men take a seat on the bench. With a finger to his lips, Gilberto points to the figures on the green on the other side of the ravine…a distance of perhaps 150 yards. Emiliano, sporting white pants and a purple silk shirt, can be seen approaching his ball on the green, about 15 feet from the pin. The cousin, in pink and white striped camiso, is in the sand trap in front of the green, while the nephew, the only one wearing shorts, is even with the pin but on the apron to the right of the green. The bodyguard, machine gun in hand, is standing on the path leading up to the next hole.

Jesús drops the golf bag behind a tree to the right of the tee and pulls out the rifle. Gilberto watches with his binoculars as Emiliano's nephew swings his club from deep in the sand trap; the ball lands no more than five feet past the pin, getting him a tap on the shoulder from his impressed uncle. The cousin is next to hit from the apron over on the right. The ball trickles up to a spot just three feet from the cup. While Gilberto is too far away to hear their conversation, it is clear that the mood on the green is light and gay. He looks over at Jesús and nods. Nodding back, Jesús sets the rifle on the ground and spreads the support legs, then gets down on the ground himself. Carefully he takes aim.

"Be sure to get Emiliano first," whispers Gilberto. "But don't let any of the others get away."

Jesús nods. He checks again to see if he has enough bullets in the magazine. Confident that he does, he stretches out on the turf and places his finger on the trigger. Sweeping from one side of the green to the other, he brings the telescopic sight to rest on Emiliano. Meanwhile, Gilberto moves the cart into the trees to the left of the tee. Once he is satisfied that neither he, Jesús or the cart can be seen, he steps behind a tree and waits.

As Gilberto watches from his hiding place, a shot rings out, piercing the summer air. A second later the man in the purple shirt staggers, then falls to the ground. The nephew, on his way from the trap to the green, stops and turns abruptly. As he scans the tee behind him, searching the area, a second shot rends the air. The nephew falls, then rolls back into the sand trap, clutching his neck. By now the cousin on the apron has dropped his club and is racing up the path into the trees. Just yards before he disappears into the pines, his feet slip as a third bullet buries itself in his back. Flat now on his stomach, he claws his way toward the safety of the trees, only to collapse when he loses consciousness. Sensing that his turn is next, the bodyguard chooses life over loyalty and races into the woods before Jesús can pick him off.

Smiling, Gilberto comes out from behind the tree to view the carnage. Jesús asks, "The bodyguard…let's follow him." Gilberto pauses to consider their options. "No", he says finally. "Let him report back to the others in Tijuana. The message should be clear. Stay the hell out of Sinaloa."

Jesús struggles with his disappointment, then smiles as he returns the rifle to the golf bag. Together, the assassins hurry back up to the fairway and out onto the road where Raffi is waiting with the car, engine running. Grinning all the way, Gilberto and Jesús climb into the Toyota and breathe a collective sigh of relief.

"Went okay?", Raffi asks, already convinced that it did. "We got three outta four", answers Gilberto. "Three big ones."

"Wow, so all the leaders is gone," shouts Raffi. "Yeah," says Gilberto, "I don't think they gonna bother us again anytime soon."

The next day's newspapers feature photos of three bodies lying prone on or near the green at the fourth hole of the Tijuana Country Club. As expected, the article beneath the photos speculates that the assassinations were the work of a rival gang seeking to expand into the Tijuana territory. The mayor, police, and local military all promise to bring the culprits to justice but no one who knows Tijuana takes them seriously.

"I think Lúpe is gonna be pleased," says Jesus, safely back in the compound and enjoying a cold Mexican beer.

"Yir right," says Gilberto, slapping his shoulder, "Without her we never know where to find these guys. She's really great. I can see why Francisco gave her the name Guadalúpe. Maybe she's got funny ideas about how to run a drug organization, but she can do things that nobody else can do. She's a miracle worker, that's what she is."

Gilberto is not alone in his thoughts. Although no one ever says it openly, it is tacitly agreed that Lúpe is too familiar a name for such an unusual woman. From now on, she will be known by the name of her famous and much-loved ancestor, Guadalúpe.

Chapter 32

Oaxaca

Relieved that that the threat from the north has been blunted, Guadalúpe begins making plans for another trip south to Oaxaca and San Cristóbal. Before leaving she sits down with the inner circle and maps out a strategy. The meeting begins with a report from Gilberto about the assassinations in Tijuana. This is followed by news from Juan that the Tijuana gang has withdrawn from the protection business in Sinaloa. When voices fall silent, Guadalúpe takes the opportunity to broach a troublesome issue. "Now that violence has subsided, I think it's appropriate to take a closer look at what we are doing."

"What dya mean, Señora?", asks Gilberto.

Guadalúpe looks around the table. "I'm referring to the kinds of drugs we're selling...crystal meth and heroin in particular. I don't like the idea of helping our customers become addicted to such powerful and life-threatening drugs." Silence. She looks over at Florio, the manager of the meth plant, who has his shoulders hunched, with hands outstretched, palms up. Undaunted, she continues. "Juan, what percentage of our overall sales comes from meth and heroin combined?"

Juan hesitates, closes his eyes to think...then says, "Around 15-20%, Señora." Guadalúpe nods. "So, if we stopped producing and selling those two drugs, we'd still have 80% of our business." A slight rumbling can be heard in the room as the men whisper to each other. Guadalúpe stands up to leave. "Well then, it's agreed. From now on we sell only marijuana and cocaine. Florio, see to it that your meth plant over in Montero is shut down immediately and that all orders for opium are canceled."

Florio's lips curl in silent protest. He murmurs, "Is crazy idea. We shut down, somebody else take over…just as many Americanos gonna die." Unspoken is his decision, previously tentative but now finalized, to leave the Sinaloa organization and join the Zapas in Juárez. Almost imperceptively, he nods across the table to Amérigo who shares his doubts about their new leader and is considering a similar move. Nothng is spoken openly.

With the threat from Tijuana behind her, Guadalúpe is free to concentrate on what she wants to do. The prospect of having millions of dollars to spend every year stokes her fertile imagination. *Charity is fine,* she murmurs back in her room, *but it's time to go further.* Before giving in to her fantasies, she reviews what she has already done or what is now in the works. In Oaxaca City, a back-to-school program for adults who dropped out early is in progress. Ten adults, mostly women who left school after seven or eight years to help their mothers make clothing have returned to school with all expenses paid by the Francisco Fund. She smiles as she recalls the case of Maura, a poor woman of 36 who makes a marginal living by selling home-made clothes to tourists. Left with the sole responsibility of raising four children when her husband abandoned her, she can't make enough money to pay for rent, food, and clothing. After years of delay, she has come to the realization that the only way out is to get more education. Apparently, in the pueblo where she grew up, there was no local school, so she never received any formal education. Now in Oaxaca where there are plenty of schools, the opportunity to better herself exists. So, what does she do? She enrolls in first grade.

Guadalúpe recalls the woman's smile as she describes what it is like to be seated in a classroom with a group of seven-year-olds (Maura is 5'4" and at least 50 pounds overweight…and needs a special chair. "The first day" she says, "was kinda tough. When the recess bell sounded, I followed my classmates out into the hall where we watched as the third-grade children filed past on their way to the playground. My nine-year old daughter was among them. What could I do but smile and wave?"

Guadalúpe stops to shake her head. *Can you imagine,* she murmurs, *what it is like to know that your own child is two grades ahead of you in school? What courage that must take…what grit. This is a woman who is desperate to become educated. We've got to do everything we can to make things easier for her.*

Before Guadalúpe sets out on her trip through southern Mexico, the inner circle meets to go over security issues. When Amérigo offers to come with her, she politely declines, asking for Jesús instead. Jesús agrees to accompany her, hesitating only long enough to ask if Raffi can come too. Guadaúpe says yes. Away from the others, Amérigo approaches Florio. "D'ya hear what she said; she wants those two punks to go with her. What's the matter with us sicarios? We're good at this stuff. We been protectin' Francisco for years…why the fuck can't she see that." Florio nods approvingly. "I guess she don't like the way you go about it. She don't like to see anybody get whacked."

"So, what if a guy is comin' at ya with a knife? What are ya s'posed to do…talk gentle-like? Hey Señor…would you mind puttin' that knife down. It's makin' me nervous." Florio laughs. "The way I see it, Amérigo…we don't belong in this group no more. It's time to get out. The guys up in Juárez already tole me they want us to come join 'em."

"Okay, but I still don't like the idea of this punk kid takin' my job."

"So, what d'ya wanna do about it?"

"What do I wanna do? I wanna have him whacked."

They agree that the best time to get Jesús is during his trip to southern Mexico while he's guarding Guadalúpe. "Maybe we should get rid of her too," Amérigo adds, "make it look like somethin' La Familia done."

Florio smiles. "You think big, Amérigo. But why not? She don't belong here either."

In Oaxaca, Guadalúpe and the boys check into the Marques de Valle, an upscale hotel right next to the zocolo. As arranged, they are given two adjoining suites on the second floor. After settling in, they go for a walk around town, ending with a visit to Monte Alban, the sprawling area up on a hill where Jesús's ancestors, the Zapotecs, lived and thrived from the 9th to the 16th Century. Jesús, of course, is familiar with the city from his stay with Padre Garcia. But all is new for Raffi who has spent little time outside Culiacán.

At lunch, the three talk about Guadalúpe's plans for helping the poor people of Southern Mexico. Later. the discussion turns to Amérigo and his discomfort upon hearing that Guadalúpe preferred Jesús as her protector. Raffi grits his teeth and wrinkles his brow in an attempt to imitate the pained look on Amérigo's face. Guadalúpe says she saw it too…and is worried.

When they get back to the hotel, Guadalúpe sits down in a chair to relax, but is bothered by the face she keeps seeing. Unable to shake the image, she moves to the bed, crosses her legs and slips into a trance. *Where are you Amérigo? I need to know.* At first, her thoughts get in the way; she pictures him back at the compound, sitting across the table, staring at her, his face contorted by scorn. She knows from experience that any image brought on by deliberate thought is unlikely to reveal anything interesting. She shakes her head and tries again, this time leaving herself open to whatever comes. Moments later, a muffled scream pierces the wall separating the two suites. Raffi yanks open the partition door and rushes in, expecting to see an intruder standing over Guadalúpe's bed. Instead, it's only his boss, sitting up in her bed, head in her hands, sobbing.

"What is it, Senora?", Raffi asks.

"He's here," comes the unexpected answer. "Amérigo is here in Oaxaca, perhaps in the hotel."

"Right here in this hotel?", asks Jesús who follows Raffi into the room, stopping long enough to pick up his revolver.

"Well, maybe not in the hotel itself," she continues, "but the fountain. You know the fountain in front of the hotel? That's what I saw in the trance…a fountain just like the one outside the hotel."

"Yir sayin' he's out there (*pointing*)?", Raffi gasps.

Let me go down and take a look," says Jesús, heading for the door. Guadalúpe shakes her head. "Don't go down there, Jesús. You can look from our window. The fountain should be just below our room." "Yeah," adds Raffi. "If he's there, we don't want him to know we seen 'im."

Jesús goes to the window and positions himself behind the drapes. He focuses on the area around the fountain. "There ain't nobody there except for a guy on a bench, readin' a newspaper." When Raffi comes over to look, Jesús points to the bench. "See the guy there (*pointing*); it's hard to make out his face 'cuz he's in the shade."

"Yeah," replies Raffi, "and the sunglasses and beard don't make it any easier." "Beard?", asks Guadalúpe from the bed. "Amérigo doesn't have a beard, does he?" "No", answers Jesús, "but maybe a disguise. The guy down there looks about the same size as Amérigo…short…kinda muscular…a real sicarios type." All three agree that if they do have an assassin in their midst, Jesús is the likely target…jealousy being the obvious motive. "So, what do we do?", asks Raffi. When no one comes up with a good plan, they agree to meet again at dinner and talk about it some more.

By dinner time, Jesús has a plan to offer. "If I'm his target, let 'im follow me around town for a while. Once I'm sure he's onto me, I'll duck into the church, you know, the big one over there (*pointing*) where Padre Garcia preaches."

"You mean the Catedral?", asks Guadalúpe who knows the church well.

"Yeah, that one," Jesús answers. "I been there many times when I was livin' here. Eduardo's brother, Manny, is a good friend of mine. Maybe he can help." "So, whatcha gonna do in the church, Sús?", asks Raffi, "hide behind the altar? Ain't Amérigo gonna come in after ya?"

"Well, yeah, that's what I'm hopin'. I jis' need to work out somethin' with Manny first…in private."

"How you gonna arrange that?"

Jesús smiles. "In the confessional."

"I don't get it. How's the confessional gonna help you get Amérigo off yir back?"

As Jesús leans forward to answer his friend's question, there is a knock on the door. It's room service with the chicken molé they ordered for dinner…a Oaxacan specialty. Jesús presses his finger to his lips. "I tell you later."

Early the next morning, Raffi raps on Guadalúpe's door. "Señora, are you up?"

"I am now," she says, straightening her skirt. "Come in."

"The bearded guy is still there," he says as he and Jesús enter the room. "We jis' seen him down by the fountain."

"Oh, oh," she says, "that's not good news."

"Jesús wants to go over to the Catedral now. We can watch from here to see if the guy follows 'im."

"Don't you think we should have some breakfast first?", Guadalúpe offers. "Besides, the padre at the church might not be ready for confession this early in the day. But tell me, Jesús, what do you plan to do when you get to the church? I don't want you to do anything rash."

"I dunno. It jis' feels right. If I can get to see Manny, I know he'll help me. He helped me before when I come to Oaxaca…gave me food and a place to stay. Later we worked together on the Mata job. I know he's on our side."

Raffi turns to face Jesús. "Yeah, but that was when you was fightin' the drug dealers. Now we're workin' for one. Anyhow… the Señora is right. Maybe you should wait before you let that bearded guy see you. Besides, it's too early in the morning for confession."

By noon Jesús has Guadalúpe's permission to put his plan into action. He leaves the hotel by the front door as Guadalúpe and Raffi watch from the window above. Within seconds, the bearded man drops his newspaper and rises from the bench. When Jesús begins walking toward the Catedral, he follows. Once he gets to the church, Jesús turns to see his pursuer, then hurries inside to the confessional. It's empty. He quickly enters and pulls the request cord. Back in his chambers, Manny, who is busy working on Sunday's sermon, hears the ring and dons his collar and robe. By the time he enters the main part of the church, all the pews are empty…except for one man seated near the middle. As he passes, Manny nods to the man, then heads for the confessional door. Once he is seated, he turns toward his hidden parishioner and says, "What do you wish to say, my child?"

"Manny," comes the whisper. "It's me, Jesús."

"What?", comes the startled response. "What are you doing here? I thought you were back in Culiacán."

"I got a new job…protectin' the Señora…ya know, the one called Peaches. She's here in Oaxaca. But right now I need some protectin' myself. That's why I come here."

"Who's after you?"

"Did you see anybody as you come in?"

"Just one man…didn't recognize him."

"Did he have a black beard?"

"Yes, he did…*(pause)*…Who is he?"

"He's the guy who usta do dirty work for El Gordo…you know, one of the sicarios. His name is Amérigo. But Guadalúpe… the name Gordo give to Señora…doesn't like violence, so she's easin' him out of a job. She tole everybody she wanted me and my pal Raffi to do the work now."

"You mean, you're the new hit man?"

"Not really. I'm jis' s'posed to protect her, that's all. If somebody attacks her, I'm like her bodyguard. If I have to whack somebody, I will, but only in an emergency."

"Is she in danger now?"

"Maybe. We don't know for sure. The Señora thinks that if it's this guy Amérigo, he's probly after me, not her."

"And what makes her think that?"

"Cuz he's mad at me for takin' his job."

"Is that Amérigo seated in one of the pews?"

"Well, somebody followed me here, so it's gotta be him."

"So, what do you want me to do?"

All talking stops when they hear someone walking past the confessional booth. Manny nods, puts his finger to his lips, waits, then slips out of the booth and heads back to his office. A minute later, just as Jesús is getting ready to leave, an alarm goes off. Manny comes running, "Fire, fire," he shouts, pointing to the front door. Not hesitating, the bearded man jumps up and runs to the door. Assured that he is gone, Manny grabs Jesús by the arm and drags him to his office in back of the church. "There," he says, "he'll never find you here. Now, what hotel you staying at?"

"The Marques de Valle."

"Well, you can't go back there. Try El Nido...it's up on Espàna Villas...about ten blocks northwest of the Marques."

"Yeah, I seen it before."

"As soon as you get there, call Guadalúpe and Raffi and tell them to leave the Marques immediately and go to El Nido where you'll meet them."

"Yeah, good idea Manny. But I may have to do more than that if this guy keeps followin' us."

"What do you mean?"

"Well, what would you do if a guy whose job is killin' people puts on a fake beard and follows ya to another city?"

"I'd pray."

Jesús smiles. "Yeah, well, you better start prayin' for this guy 'cuz he's gonna need it." The two shake hands, then go their separate ways. As soon as he signs in at El Nido, Jesús calls Guadalúpe to tell her what happened. Within minutes, Guadalúpe and Raffi are on their way to the new hotel where they take a room down the hall from Jesús's. After everyone is settled in, Jesús leaves without saying where he's going. Suspecting that it has something to do with Amérigo, Raffi says nothing but follows at a safe distance. Suspecting as much, Jesús slips around a corner and waits to ambush his friend. When Raffi appears, Jesús pounces like a cat and wrestles him to the ground. "What the hell you doin' Sus?", Raffi sputters, wriggling free. "This ain't no time for foolin' around. For all we know, Amérigo is watchin' us right now."

"Okay…let's see if he's still at the fountain."

"If he is, whatcha goin' to do?"

"Let's make 'im think we still got our room at the Marques. We can go in the front door and out the back door. He'll never see us leave." Amérigo proves to be more clever than that. He not only sees the boys leave through the back door but is right behind them as they head for the Catedral. Smiles give way to shock when Raffi looks back and sees the bearded man no more than thirty yards behind them. "What do we do now?", he cries.

Jesús sucks in his breath. "We can still shake 'im if we go into the church through the front door and out the back door. I know how to do it."

"What do we do then?"

Jesús pauses. "We need to get outta town. I have a friend out in Teotitlán who could put us up for a night or two…long enough to make Amérigo think we skip town."

"O.K. so, how do we get to Teotitlan?"

"There's a bus that leaves every hour from the Central. To be sure we get a seat, go there now and buy us some tickets." Raffi throws his hands up. "With what? I got three pesos on me." Jesús reaches into his pocket. "I think it's ten pesos a person. Take this fifty…might as well get a roundtrip. Okay, now I gotta go."

"Be careful, Sús. Remember, this guy would whack his own mother if he thought she crossed 'im." Jesús giggles. "He had a Mama?"

At this time of day, the plaza is full of people on their way to work. Some stop briefly to cross themselves as they pass the Catedral. Others turn and bow before moving on. Jesús walks quickly to the church and opens the door. Once inside, he looks back to make sure Amérigo is still following, then hurries down the aisle past the confessional to the door to the right of the altar, the door that leads to the private exit in the rear. Amérigo enters and takes a seat in one of the middle pews, not far from the booth, and watches. When Jesús disappears through the door to the right of the altar, the hit man rises and walks over to the confesssional booth. After a quick look around to make sure no one is watching, he slips inside. Convinced that it is only a matter of minutes before Jesús returns, he pulls out his hunting knife and waits.

When Manny hears footsteps outside his study door, he puts down his pen and goes to look. There's no one there. Still concerned about Jesús, he enters the main part of the church and looks around. Seeing no one, he heads for the front door to make sure it's not locked. *It's a bit strange*, he mutters, *that no one has come in to pray.*

Inside the confessional, Amérigo prepares to strike. *I'm gonna get the little punk now for sure*, he mutters, convinced that it is Jesús walking up the aisle. Reassured that the front door is unlocked, Manny turns around and heads back to his office. As he passes the confessional, Amérigo suddenly leaps from the booth and grabs him around the neck. As Manny twists to get free, Amérigo drives the knife into his shoulder, knocking him to the floor. The assailant gets up, rubs his eyes…then recoils in horror when he realizes that the man he just stabbed is not Jesús but a robed priest. Quickly he sheathes his knife and races outside. Bleeding but still conscious, the padre struggles to hs feet and stumbles toward the front door. At that moment, a visitor opens the door, hoping to take pictures of the art work along the wall. He shouts to his wife who is right behind him when he sees a man stumbling toward him, clutching his arm. Before the visitors can turn and run, the morning sunlight shines through the open door, illuminating the interior of the church.

Oblivious to what happened, Jesús walks out the back door, relieved that he has shaken his pursuer. Moving quickly, he makes his way past street vendors selling tomatoes, peaches, and fried grasshoppers. When he reaches the Central, Raffi is waiting with two tickets in hand. They only have to stand there for ten minutes before boarding the bus to Teotitlán. Once seated, Jesús tells of his easy escape from the would-be assassin. He concludes, "I don't think the guy's as smart as people say he is."

"How long d'ya think we hafta stay in Teotitlan?", Raffi asks.

"A few days I should think…long enough for Amérigo to think we left town."

"But aren't we s'posed to be guardin' Guadalúpe?"

"Yeah, I'll call her from my friend's house in Teotitlán. She'll understand. Besides, it's only for a few days, then we can get together and continue the trip. Amérigo should be back in Culiacán by then."

In Teotitlán, the boys receive a warm welcome from Jesús's old friend, Hector. Feeling flush with the money Guadalúpe gave him, Jesús takes Raffi and Hector out to lunch the next day. There is only one restaurant in Teotitlán…the Descanso, whose specialty is a Mexican-style pizza featuring ham, pork and a variety of local vegetables. When they go to sit down at a window table, Jesús notices a newspaper on one of the seats. "Oh my God," he shouts, staring at the headlines. 'Priest stabbed in Catedral de Oaxaca.' It's Manny," he cries. "Amérigo got Manny."

"How the hell?", cries Raffi.

Visibly trembling, Jesús reads further. "They say he was hidin' in the confessional booth and jumped Manny as he was walkin' past."

"Is he gonna live?", asks Hector, afraid to hear the answer.

"They says he's in hospital…intensive care…whatever the hell that is. But I guess he's gonna live."

"I don't get it," Raffi says. "Why would Amérigo wanna kill Manny? He don't even know 'im."

Jesús looks at his friend. "You stupid or somethin'? He thought it was me walkin' past that booth. It's dark inside the church, so he couldn't see my face. Get it?"

Raffi gulps. "Holy shit. What are we gonna do now?"

"I think it's time for a change."

"What d'ya mean?"

"I mean we gotta stop runnin' away from this guy…and go after 'im instead. Manny deserves as much."

"Yeah. And there's Guadalúpe to think about. Amérigo might decide to go after her too."

Chapter 33

The Trap

Back at Hector's house the two boys plan their next move. Jesús is the first to speak, "We gotta go back to the Marques and see if Amérigo is still there. If he is, we let 'im see us…and then draw 'im into a trap.

"And if he ain't there?"

"We go to what gringos call Plan B."

"Which is…?"

"I dunno. Don't rush me. I gonna think of somethin'."

As they approach the Marques, they make no attempt to conceal their presence. On the contrary, they walk right in front of the bench where the bearded man is sitting. Raffi whispers, "He's still here…jis' changed his beard from black to red…well, sorta orange-like."

"I figured he might do somethin' like that," Jesús says, "seein' that accordin' to the newspaper, somebody tole the police they saw a man with a black beard comin' outta the church right after Manny was stabbed."

"He coulda jis' shaved it off."

"That's probly his next move."

"So, what do we do now?"

"On the way back here from Hector's place, an idea come to me. There's a dead-end alley offa Palermo Calle...about five blocks from here. I used to eat at an Italian restaurant there when I lived in Oaxaca. Me and the owner's son, Alonso, were both into soccer and got to be good friends. I ain't seen 'im for a coupla years, but I'm sure he'll remember me." "What this got to do with Amérigo? I thought we was s'posed to trap 'im."

"Lemme finish. The restaurant is up on the second floor and has a big balcony where you can eat while lookin' down on the street. You could hide up there and wait for an enemy to come along below...then get 'im before he knows yir there."

"You think you could pick 'im off without arousin' the whole neighborhood...and the police?"

"Not with a pistol; too much noise. But with my friend here (*patting his knapsack*), no problema."

"Okay. But how do we get 'im into the alley if we're holed up in the restaurant? If he follows us around the corner, looks into the alley and don't see anybody, ain't he gonna back out?"

"Lemme think."

As they head for the alley, they steal occasional glimpses back at their pursuer. "Slow down a little," Jesús says. "We ain't tryin' to shake 'im this time."

They enter a men's clothing store and pretend to look around. As they check out the blue jeans, Raffi asks, "You come up with any ideas for gettin' Amérigo into the alley...you know, so you can pick 'im off?"

Jesús stifles a laugh. "Well, an idea did come to me... if you're willin'."

"I don't like the sound of that."

"It may sound a little risky but it really ain't. Once we inside the alley, you just hafta stay down on the street, rubbin' yir bad knee while I go up to the restaurant. Pretend that you tripped and need help; maybe call my name; but when you yell, be sure you look at houses across the street from the restaurant. By the time Amérigo gets here, I'll be on the restaurant balcony on the second floor. When he comes around the corner, he'll see you down on your knees and figure I've gone into one of those houses yir lookin' at." "So, what's he gonna do…come over to me, pull out his huntin' knife, and say he's gonna cut me up if I don't tell 'im which house you went inta?"

"Somethin' like that, yeah."

"So, what do I say…or do I refuse to talk and let 'im dice me up like a potato?"

"Jis' point to one of the houses…it don't matter. His back will be turned, makin' 'im an easy target from the balcony."

"And if you miss…?"

Jesús laughs. "I jis' hafta forgive myself."

As they enter the alley, Jesús points to the restaurant over on the left. "That's it…up on the second floor. See the balcony…all I gotta do is ask Alonso to let me hide out there until Amérigo comes."

"Well, it's a coupla hours before lunch time now so there ain't gonna be any customers."

"Yeah. Now, the best place for you to fall down and grab yir knee is right there (*pointing*). Make sure you stay in the middle of the street, just even with the restaurant. As soon as I tell Alonso a hit man from El Gordo's drug cartel is followin' me, he gonna let me use the balcony."

"Jis' make sure he don't let anybody else out onto the balcony. We don't want some waitress makin' noise and tippin' Amérigo off that yir up there."

When he hears that his old friend Jesús is in town, Alonso bursts from the kitchen and greets him with a bear hug. A quick explanation on Jesús's part establishes the purpose of his visit. Alonso hesitates, then agrees, with the proviso that he be allowed to stay on the balcony to watch. Jesús agrees, but warns him there may be some shooting.

Out on the balcony Jesús unpacks his bow and takes up a position next to one of the tables. A quick wave to Raffi down on the street draws a nod of confirmation. Minutes later, Amérigo can be seen turning the corner and entering the alley. He hears a voice and stops to listen. It's Raffi, yelling Jesús's name. From the way he is bent over, massaging his knee, it is apparent that he has fallen and is calling to Jesús for help. Jesús is nowhere to be seen, although the angle of Raffi's head suggests that his partner has entered a house on the side of the street opposite the restaurant.

Sensing that he has his quarry cornered, Amérigo approaches Raffi with knife drawn. When he is a few feet away, he yells, "Where is he? Which house he go into?" Raffi says nothing but continues to look at the house across from the restaurant. There is only one doorway there. To Amérigo, that means one thing: he must first kill Raffi, then hide outside the doorway until Jesús comes out. He smiles at the simplicity of his plan.

Up on the balcony, Jesús watches as the scene unfolds. He unpacks his bow and inserts an arrow; all that is needed now is for Amérigo to turn his back. When Amérigo reaches Raffi and stands over him with knife in hand, Jesús draws the bow string. Just as he gets ready to shoot, the balcony door opens and Clara, the bookkeeper comes in, saying Alonso has a phone call. When he hears voices on the balcony behind him, Amérigo turns and stares. Instead of strangers chatting, he sees Jesús with bowstring pulled taut. In desperation, he reaches into his jacket pocket and pulls out a pistol. Before he can fire, Raffi, still kneeling, grabs him by the ankle and yanks him to the ground. As the two men struggle for the gun, Jesús moves a step to the left, takes aim and sends an arrow directly into Amérigo's thigh. The hit man groans, then grabs the gun, and shoots wildly at the archer on the balcony.

Clutching his thigh, he shakes off Raffi's grip and heads back out of the alley, pistol in one hand, knife in the other. When he turns to see if Jesús is still on the balcony, he stumbles, dropping the gun. Jesús aims again…and lets a second arrow fly. It hits a telephone pole just inches to Amérigo's left. Jesús begins to panic. The target is now only yards from the main street intersection where he can easily disappear into traffic. Fully aware of the danger, he quickly inserts another arrow and draws the string all the way back. The thud can be heard throughout the alley when the arrowhead buries itself in the assailant's side. As Amérigo drops to his knees, writhing in pain, Raffi comes running up the alley. Oblivious to the soreness in his knee, he kicks the pistol away, then yanks the knife from Amérigo's hand and plunges it into his chest. Before his eyes close for the last time, the hit man looks up at his young foe. With blood gushing from his mouth, he clenches his teeth and whispers a curse. "You ain't gonna last long. Somebody gonna get ya." Raffi nods, then wipes his hand on the man's trousers. Seconds later, Jesús comes running to the scene, bow still in hand. "Is he dead?", he asks, searching the prone man's face for signs of life.

"He ain't gettin' up any time soon," replies Raffi. "That last arrow of yours got 'im real good."

Jesús looks down on Amérigo's chest. "Looks like you finished 'im off with his knife."

Raffi grins. "Jis' wanted to make sure…(*pause*)…What are we gonna do with the body? Jis' leave it here? Won't the bulls be able to trace it back to the compound…and to us."

Jesús smiles. "Hey, amigo, what d'ya think all that money is for…you know, the money the organization pays to the police for protection? Quit worryin'. Guadalúpe's the boss now. Let her handle it."

"Hey, if you say so."

With a final look back at Amérigo's body, they head out of the alley and down the street to El Nido where Guadalúpe is waiting.

Chapter 34

The Visit

Soon after their wedding, Lloyd and Dolores fly to Mexico to visit their old wife and friend. At the Culiacán airport, Jessica greets them warmly before introducing her two protectors. Later, on their way into town, she provides a condensed version of her kidnapping and an even shorter explanation of her elevation to a leadership role in the cartel. Questions about her life in Mexico come quickly, with Dolores leading the way. For his part, Lloyd is shocked. To this very proper man, it is incomprehensible that the woman he was married to for fourteen years, the same woman whose interest in the world rarely transcended the evening news and the well-being of her flower garden, is now running a drug organization in Mexico. He shakes his head in bewilderment. In private, he murmurs, *Is it possible that I never really knew her? Was she just pretending to be nothing more than a suburban housewife? Or has she really changed?*

At dinner that night, her guests do their best to persuade Jessica to return to El Paso. "Your house is still there," Dolores says. "Lloyd and I are happy living in the house Ned and I shared. So, you could move into your old house at any time." The mere mention of Ned's name brings Jessica to tears. "Where is he buried?", she asks. "In the old cemetery up on Wilson's Hill?"

"Yes," replies Dolores. "He's in a beautiful spot. There's even a bench there, so you can sit and be close while you're thinking of him. Lloyd and I go there often."

In turn, Jessica provides the details of Ned's death in the woods, the same woods where Francisco was killed. "He came to rescue me...and paid the price for his bravery. He didn't seem to realize how dangerous the situation was." "Or maybe he did", offers Dolores, "but came anyway. He was madly in love with you, Jessica. I hope you know that. You would have made a beautiful couple." Throughout the conversation, Jessica is struck by how different Dolores seems. *She's much happier and radiates more energy now. She looks a lot healthier too; her skin isn't that lifeless gray it used to be; her eyes have a new sparkle. That much is clear, but there's more to it than her looks. She talks a lot more now...as if she's come out of a shell. And Lloyd seems pleased to have it that way. He too seems more relaxed...not as authoritarian or combative as I remember. I wonder if I brought out that side of him. I hope not...but it's possible.*

Before the conversation ends, Jessica invites them to spend the next few days touring Oaxaca, Guadalajara, and San Cristóbal where she has used money from the Francisco Fund to start a variety of projects. Dolores agrees but with a noticeable lack of enthusiasm. Lloyd says okay, but points out that they have reservations for a week-long stay in Acapulco starting next Thursday.

Off by herself, Jessica questions their response to her invitation. *They don't sound all that interested, but this is the only way I can explain why I want to remain in Mexico. They probably think I'm crazy but if they see for themselves what we are doing here, they just might understand.* In Guadalajara, she escorts them to a restaurant she helped start with venture capital from the Francisco Fund. The owner, who also serves as manager, greets his guests with a welcome typically reserved for celebrities. Unprompted, he gushes over his good fortune and that of the 22 employees now working at the restaurant. "We never do it without your help, Señora. Everybody here thank you." Still smiling, he adds, "And lunch is on us...please."

As they immerse themselves in a lunch of garlic soup, salad, stuffed mushrooms, and carnes asadas (roasted meats), the conversation turns to Jessica's projects in other cities. "In San Cristóbal, we helped a cement manufacturer buy the trucks he needed to get started. In Durango, we provided the funds for a grocery chain to expand into towns where a local mercado was the only source of food. Up in San Luis Potosi, several clothing stores wanted to merge but lacked the necessary capital. At their invitation, we bought 40% of the shares in the new company; now they are not only thriving but are ready to expand next door into the state of Guanajuato. Last month, we worked with some recent college graduates in Michoacan who needed start-up capital for a series of stores offering TV's, computers, and DVD players; now, thanks to the new outlets, residents from small villages no longer have to travel two hours to buy a television. The Francisco Fund now owns shares in over 100 companies in Mexico…mostly in the southern part of country where poverty is greatest." "Very impressive, Jess," says Lloyd, struggling to believe that this is his ex-wife talking. "But how can you be sure that the profits will ever trickle down to the poor, the people you want to help?"

"Wherever possible, we insist that companies offer their workers a chance to buy shares in the company. Our ideal is to end up with companies that are owned at least in part by the people who work there. I know it's worked elsewhere…like in the U.S…so I don't see why it can't work here as well."

Lloyd scowls. "Where did you pickup this idea about employee ownership? You were never interested in things like that when we were married."

"True. But back then I never realized what a difference owning shares in a company could make. Before, it didn't seem very personal; it does now. I still don't know very much about the subject…it' rather complicated, but I don't have to know all the details. That's what we have experts for."

After two days of traveling, Jessica senses that her guests have seen enough and are anxious to move on to Acapulco. The signs are evident: more time spent eating, fewer questions about the projects, and more conversations from which Jessica is excluded. With nerves on the verge of fraying, the three return to Culiacán for a final dinner before Lloyd and Dolores leave in the morning.

At the airport, hugs are exchanged and promises to write made. Jessica is in tears as she stands behind a large window in the terminal, watching Lloyd and Dolores climb up the ramp. For Lloyd, who turns to wave a final goodbye, her tears are a clear sign of regret for the decision she has made. For Jessica, they speak not of regret but of the realization that she is entering a new phase of life and can never go back to the old. Of course, the memories will linger…memories of a quiet, untroubled existence, of a beautiful house, of financial security, of a position of respect in the community, of the peace that comes with knowing what tomorrow will bring. But all that is gone now…soon to be forgotten as something new takes its place. With a shake of her head, she wipes away the tears, waves a last goodbye and turns to leave.

Inside the airport a young girl of eight or nine is selling gum, candy and cigarettes to travelers. Before heading for the door, Jessica stops and beckons her closer. In Spanish she asks, "What's your name?"

"Chorita."

"That's a lovely name Chorita…as beautiful as the dress you're wearing…but why aren't you in school today?"

"I don't like school," comes the answer. Having seen many girls selling cigarettes and candy when they should be in school, Jessica is not fooled. She bends her knees to speak. "There are lots of things to learn in school…and other children to meet."

Chorita says nothing.

"Do you know how to write your name?", Jessica asks. taking the girl's hand. She shakes her head. Jessica reaches into her pocketbook for pen and paper. "Here, let me show you." Slowly she makes each of the letters, then asks the girl to copy them. Painstakingly, Chorita copies the letters one by one… C..H..O..R..I..T..A…"That's perfect," says Jessica. "In school you'd learn how to write all kinds of words…and to read books, beautiful books about animals and fairies and castles…even about children from other countries. Would you like that?"

Chorita nods shyly.

"So, how would you like it if I talked to your Mama and Papa…and persuaded them to let you go to school?" The girl beams. "I just need to know where you live so I can come to your house and meet them."

Chorita narrows her eyes, then lowers her head. "But Mama needs money to buy food for us."

Jessica smiles. "Don't worry. I'll take care of that."

As Lloyd and Dolores reach the plane door, they turn for a final look. What they see says more than words can convey. Behind the giant window, Jessica has her arm around the girl's shoulders. Both are smiling. When Jessica sees Lloyd waving, she waves back, then holds up Chorita's hand as well. In response, Lloyd bows his head…then steps into the plane. Just behind, Dolores lifts her hand as if to wave, then pulls it down. Resisting the urge to look again, she shakes her head, then follows her husband inside.